Classical Chinese Love S
中国古代爱情故事

The Peony Pavilion

牡 丹 亭

Tang Xianzu

汤显祖（明）

Adapted by Chen Meilin

陈美林　改编

New World Press
新世界出版社

First Edition 1999
Second Printing 2001

Translated by Kuang Peihua and Cao Shan
Edited by Zhang Minjie
Book Design by Li Hui

ISBN 7 − 80005 − 433 − 0

Published by
NEW WORLD PRESS
24 Baiwanzhuang Road, Beijing 100037, China

Distributed by
NEW WORLD PRESS
24 Baiwanzhuang Road, Beijing 100037, China
Tel: 0086 − 10 − 68994118
Fax: 0086 − 10 − 68326679
E − mail: nwpcn@public.bta.net.cn

Printed in the People's Republic of China

杜丽娘

柳梦梅

春香

杜宝

FOREWORD

Love is an eternal theme. Since ancient times the arts the world over have sung its praises and love stories make up a vast body of literature. Many of them are excellent, portraying spirited and worthy characters, lofty ideals, and the love shared by men and women. They allow readers to renew their souls, lift their spirits and appreciate the meaning and value of life. Readers are inspired to lead a more fulfiling life. At the same time a love story must be influenced by the author's life and environment, his economic circumstances, the existing political and social system, his philosophical and cultural background and moral concepts. Reading love stories acquaints readers with such external factors and helps them to realize their significance, thus promoting changes in society and progress. Hence reading and reviewing good love stories is most important.

Ms. Zhou Kuijie and Ms. Zhang Minjie of the New World Press asked me to adapt the traditional love dramas *The Peony Pavilion*, *The Palace of Eternal Youth* and *The Peach Blossom Fan*, whose English-Chinese editions are to be published. In the 1980s, Ms. Zhou Kuijie, who worked for the Foreign Languages Press, caught sight of my book *The Collection of Zaju Stories of the Yuan Dynasty* (*zaju* is a poetic drama set to music, a form that flourished in the Yuan Dynasty) written under my pen name. She liked it and thought that it should be introduced to readers overseas. She contacted me through Mr. Wang Yuanhong of the Jiangsu People's Publishing House. Thanks to the efforts of Ms. Zhou Kuijie, Mr. Chen Yousheng and Ms. Yang Chunyan, the English edition of this book was published at the end of 1997, and the French edition will be published soon. After this collaboration, though I was busy, I was determined to find time to adapt the books for New World Press.

In the 1950s when I taught ancient literature at a university I started writing ancient Chinese dramas as stories. With few teaching materials, I found it especially difficult to lecture on ancient stories and dramas. I had to briefly introduce each drama to students who knew nothing about them. The experience made me decide to rewrite the dramas as short stories or medium-length stories for my students. In the early 1980s Mr. Wang Yuanhong thought these stories should be published. The collections, *zaju* stories of the Yuan (1279-1368), Ming (1368-1644) and Qing (1644-1911) were published in 1983, 1987 and 1988, a total of 700,000 words. In the summer of 1995, Mr. Liu Yongjian, deputy editor-in-chief of the Jiangsu People's Publishing House suggested to Mr. Wang Yuanhong that the legends that I had put aside be published. After several discussions with the publishing house, the *Collection of the Chinese Opera Stories* which included some stories based on *zaju*, *The Story of the Lute*, *The Peony Pavilion*, *The Palace of Eternal Youth*, and *The Peach Blossom Fan*, was published.

When I write a story from an ancient drama I stick to the original plot and themes. The story is a different form of expression but I abide by the artistic rules and follow designated aesthetic standards. Re-writing dramas as stories is a creative process although it may appear simple.

The original versions that I adapted from the dramas *The Peony Pavilion*, *The Palace of Eternal Youth* and *The Peach Blossom Fan* range from 30,000 to 50,000 words. However the New World Press asked that each story be about 80,000 words, and include several chapters, each with a subtitle. After careful consideration I decided to rewrite the stories from the original drama rather than extend the adapted versions. I chose this method because the extra length meant that I had to reconsider the form of the stories and re-evaluate their plots and roles. I am not sure if this new version is satisfactory and sincerely welcome comments or suggestions from readers.

Written on August 9, 1998
at the foot of the Qingliang Mountain
by the Stone City

序

　　爱情是文学艺术的永恒主题,在古今中外的文艺创作中歌颂爱情的作品如恒河沙数,其中为人称道的优秀之作,大都能通过对爱情的描写,肯定和赞扬人的美好心灵和高尚品德。读者在阅读这些作品时,常能经受一次灵魂的洗礼和精神的升华,认识到生命的价值和人生的真谛,从而萌发对美好生活的憧憬和追求。同时,由于作者所描写的爱情故事,离不开他们所生活的时代和生存的环境,因而必然受着一定的经济基础、政治状况、社会制度、哲学思潮、文化背景以及道德观念等等因素有形无形的制约,读者在阅读这些作品时,还可以明白造成男女爱情悲欢离合的外部因素,认识到这些外部因素的实质,从而促进社会的变革和人类的进步。因此正确地阅读、评述优秀的爱情之作,也是一项极有意义之举。

　　新世界出版社周奎杰、张民捷先生约我为他们改写爱情剧《牡丹亭》、《长生殿》和《桃花扇》,出版英汉对照本。早在八十年代,当时在外文出版社工作的周奎杰先生,见到笔者用笔名出版的《元杂剧故事集》一书,认为可以介绍到海外,便通过江苏人民出版社王远鸿先生与笔者联系,在周奎杰以及陈有昇、杨春燕等先生努力下,此书英文版已于 1997 年年底出书,法文版不日亦将出书。有此渊源,尽管手边任务甚繁,也排除万难,接受新世界出版社的约稿。

　　笔者尝试改写工作,起初完全是出自工作需要。五十年代在高校讲授古代文学,并无现成教材可资凭借,需要自编自讲。尤其是讲授古代小说、戏曲时，很多作品不易寻觅，学生无法知其内容，教师便无法进行评述，只能在评述之前先介绍作品的故事情节。为此，当年曾将古代戏曲的名作，效法《落花乐府本事》，写成一类似短篇、中篇的小说，以应付教学之需。八十年代初期，王远鸿先生认为此可发表，便先后于 1983 年、1987 年、1988 年分别出版了元、明、清三本杂剧故事集，总计七十万字。1995 年夏，王远鸿先生告知该社副总编刘勇坚先生认为当年延搁的传奇部分也可出版。几经磋商，先行将部分杂剧以及《琵琶记》、《牡丹亭》、《长生殿》、《桃花扇》四部传奇合为一集《中国戏曲故事选》先行出版。

将戏曲改写成小说，虽然题材不变，故事情节相同，但体裁不同，表现手段各异，改写者必须遵循不同体裁的艺术规则和特定的审美要求从事。尽管如此，这其实是一项看似容易却实不易为的工作，因此有识之士认为这样的改写其实也是一种"创作"。

笔者对《牡丹亭》、《长生殿》、《桃花扇》三剧原有改写本，分别为三、五万字不等。此次新世界出版社约稿，要求每本在八万字左右，同时要考虑海外读者阅读习惯，需分章立节、出小标题。为此，笔者斟酌再三，只能放弃在原改写本上增加篇幅的打算，而是按照原剧重新改写。因为篇幅的增加并不意味着简单地增加一些文字，这牵涉到全书的结构布局、故事情节的演变、人物性格的发展，甚至人物活动的场所与时序的变化等等，都需重新做全盘的考虑与安排。因此，这次改写工作不是对原改写本的简单增删，而是对原剧的重新改写。当然，改写得是否尽如人意，笔者亦不敢自信，敬希广大读者有以指正。

1998 年 8 月 9 日，时届立秋，而暑热未退，
于石头城畔清凉山麓挥汗为序

ABOUT THE ORIGINAL PLAY
The Peony Pavilion

The Peony Pavilion was written by Tang Xianzu.

Tang Xianzu (1550-1616), a native of Linchuan in Jiangxi Province, was a famous writer and dramatist of the Ming Dynasty (1368-1644). He styled himself Yireng, Hairuo and Ruoshi. As there was a Qingyuan Tower in his house, he also called himself Qingyuan Taoist. In his later years, he styled himself Jianweng.

In his youth Tang Xianzu was a famous man of letters and in the fourth year of the Longqing reign (1570), when he was 21, he passed the imperial examination at the provincial level. In the fifth year of the Wanli reign (1577), he prepared to sit the highest imperial examination.

Senior Grand Secretary Zhang Juzheng tried to help his son Zhang Sixiu become a successful candidate in the imperial examination and recruited outstanding scholars from all over the country. His son, Zhang Sixiu, followed his instructions and tried in every way to make friends with Tang Xianzu and Shen Maoxue, two young scholars who enjoyed a high reputation all over the country. However Tang Xianzu, an upright young man, was not willing to curry favor with the powerful. Finally he failed in the examination. Shen Maoxue, a friend of both Zhang Juzheng and Zhang Sixiu, came first and Zhang Sixiu came third.

Tang Xianzu became a metropolitan graduate in the 11th year of Wanli reign (1583) when Zhang Juzheng died. Later he was appointed adviser of the Court of Imperial Sacrifices in Nanjing and five years later he served as administrative aide in the Ministry of Rites. In the 19th year of Wanli reign (1591) he submitted a petition to the emperor to impeach Shen Shixing, grand secretary of the Grand Secretariat, and exposed the court's failure in administration.

As a result he was demoted to a clerk in Xuwen County, Guangdong Province. Two years later, he was transferred to Zhejiang to be the magistrate of Suichang County. As an upright local official, Tang Xianzu did not attach himself to those in authority and was more concerned about ordinary people's lives. Other officials attacked him and he was so unhappy as a magistrate that he left his post for home in the 26th year of the Wanli reign (1598). Three years later, he was formally removed from office. Tang Xianzu then moved from the suburbs to the city proper and built Jade Tea Studio where he devoted himself to writing.

In his youth his teacher was Luo Rufang, a disciple of Wang Gen, a famous scholar belonging to the Taizhou School. He was also friendly with Li Zhi and Da Guan. Both Li Zhi and Da Guan were ideologists opposed to feudal ethics and exerted great influence on Tang Xianzu who thought highly of them and regarded them as "two heroes". In addition, Tang established good relationships with Yuan Hongdao, Yuan Zhongdao and Yuan Zongdao who were outstanding representatives of the Gong'an School which advocated new ideas and approaches and opposed simple imitation. Influenced by them, Tang Xianzu founded the Linchuan Theatrical School.

Traditional dramas written by Tang Xianzu include *The Purple Hairpin*, *The Peony Pavilion*, *The Story of Nanke*, and *The Story of Handan*, which are known as *The Four Dreams of the Jade Tea Studio*. Tang Xianzu also wrote many poems, some of which are included in *Collected Works Written at Jade Tea Studio*, which was published before his death. Five years after his death *Book of Jade Tea Studio* edited by Han Jing came out. Later *Collected Works by Tang Xianzu* edited by Qian Nanyang and Xu Shuo was published.

Of all the traditional dramas written by Tang Xianzu, *The Peony Pavilion* is the best and the most famous. Tang Xianzu once said, "I have had 'four dreams' in my life, and the dream of *The Peony Pavilion* is my favorite." As a matter of fact, the drama was warmly received as soon as it was performed and became "known to every household and almost made *The Western Chamber* appear inferior." At that time, many famous writers, such as Lu Yusheng, Shen Jing, Zang Maoxun and Feng Menglong, adapted *The Peony Pavilion*, for such works as *Two Dreams the Same* by Shen Jing and *A Love Dream* by Feng Menglong. The former has been lost, the latter still exists. There are various versions of *The Peony Pavilion*. Until now *The Peony Pavilion* has been performed on the *kunju* stage (a local opera style from Jiangsu Province). Some opera items, such as "Chunxiang Makes Trouble in Class," "Startling Dream of Wandering Through the Garden," and "Picking up the Portrait and Speaking to It," are all derived from *The Peony Pavilion*.

In the Song (960-1279) and Ming (1368-1644) dynasties, a Confucian school of learning, devoted to the study of classics, was in vogue. It stressed "preserving heavenly principles and getting rid of people's desires." During the Ming Dynasty people attached great importance to a women's virginity, and spared no effort in praising virgin girls and women who did not marry in widowhood. The number of eminent women included in *Biographies of Eminent Women of the History of the Ming Dynasty* is for greater than those who appear in *History of the Later Han Dynasty* and the history books of the following dynasties. The scholars of the Taizhou School opposed the feudal Confucian school of learning and Tang Xianzu created dramas criticizing feudal ethics. In the preface to *The Peony Pavilion*, he proposed: "a person could die for love and a dead person could revive after death. If a person does not die for love, or does not revive after death, it means he or she has not devoted themselves to love." In reality it was impossible for Du Liniang to revive after death, but Tang Xianzu believed that "it is impossible only according to your beliefs and it could happen if one was deeply in love." Tang Xianzu praised highly sincere love between men and women and through his description of Du Liniang's experience of romantic love, he criticized the inhuman society in which she lived. After Du Liniang returned to life and was married to Liu Mengmei, her father, Du Bao, who adhered to feudal ethics, still refused to approve of his daughter's marriage. This showed how stubborn the feudal forces were and how hard it was for young men and women to struggle for their own love and happiness.

The publication of *The Peony Pavilion* had a great influence on society and there were repercussions among women who had been ruled by feudal ethics. In one extreme case, Yu Erniang, a lady of Loujiang, cried so bitterly after she had read it that she died. Shang Xiaoling, an actress of Hangzhou, was so sad when performing the drama that she died on stage.

Some characters in the story are created by the author and should not be compared with figures in history.

原作简介

《牡丹亭》为汤显祖所作。

汤显祖(1550－1616)，江西临川人，明代著名的文学家、戏曲家。字义仍，号海若，又号若士，因家有清远楼，故又自署清远道人，晚年自号茧翁。

汤显祖年轻时即有文名，隆庆四年(1570)，二十一岁就考中举人。万历五年(1577)参加会试，当时首辅张居正欲使其子嗣修中第，招纳天下名士以抬高其子地位。张嗣修秉承其父旨意，结交汤显祖，沈懋学等人，汤、沈当时极负文名。汤显祖为人耿直，不愿趋附，也不受其延揽，以致落第而归；沈懋学则愿与首辅张居正及其子交好，乃得以高中状元，张嗣修则中榜眼。直到万历十一年(1583)张居正死后，汤显祖方得考取进士。但又因不愿趋附新的权贵，被派往南京冷衙门任太常寺博士，五年后改任南京礼部主事。万历十九年(1591)又因上《论辅臣科臣疏》惟，弹劾内阁大学士申时行，并评议朝廷失政，因而被贬为广东徐闻县典史。两年后改任浙江遂昌知县，但依然不肯依附权贵，又十分关心民瘼，因此遭到非议。他便于万历二十六年(1598)弃官回乡，三年后被正式免职。此后即由城郊迁入城内，在自己建筑的玉茗堂内潜心创作。

汤显祖在少年时代曾跟随泰州学派王艮的三传弟子罗汝芳读书，后又与李贽、达观等人交游，他们都是反对程朱理学的思想家，对汤显祖的思想影响颇大，汤显祖对他们二人十分倾倒，尊他们二人为"一雄一杰"。汤显祖又与袁宏道等公安派作家有交谊，文学思想颇受三袁(袁宏道、袁中道、袁宗道)影响，重视立意，倡导意趣，反对摹拟，不受格律束缚，从而在当时曲坛上形成以他为首的临川派。

汤显祖创作的戏曲作品《紫箫记》以及根据此剧改写的《紫钗记》、《牡丹亭》（又称《还魂记》）、《南柯记》、《邯郸记》，合称"玉茗堂四梦"或"临川四梦"。诗文创作有《红泉逸草》、《雍藻》（已佚）、《问棘邮草》以及生前已刊印的《玉茗堂文集》。在其卒后五年有韩敬编辑的《玉茗堂集》等。今人钱南扬、徐朔方合编有《汤显祖集》。

在汤显祖创作的戏曲中，以《牡丹亭》成就最高，它是作者思想和艺术趋于成熟时的作品，可谓其代表作。他曾"自谓一生'四梦'，得意处惟在《牡丹》"（见王思任《牡丹亭叙》），这并非作者自诩，因为此剧一出，的确受到当时观众的广泛喜爱，所谓"家传户诵，几令《西厢》减价"（沈德符《顾曲杂言》）。当时还有不少名家如吕玉绳、沈璟、臧懋循、冯梦龙等人为之改编，如沈璟的《同梦记》、冯梦龙的《风流梦》等。沈本已佚，冯本今存。《牡丹亭》刊本极多，尚有批评本，如吴吴山的"三妇合评本"。直到今日，这部传奇在昆剧舞台上还盛演不衰，如《春香闹学》、《游园惊梦》、《拾画叫画》等折子戏，即《牡丹亭》中《闺塾》、《游园》、《拾画》、《玩真》等出。

《牡丹亭》的故事是有所本的，作者自序说："传杜太守事者，仿佛晋武都守李仲文、广州守冯孝将儿女事。予稍为更而演之。至于杜守拷柳生，亦如汉睢阳王收拷谈生也。"所谓"传杜太守事者"，是指收辑于《燕居笔记》中的明代话本小说《杜丽娘慕色还魂》；李仲文事见《搜神后记》卷四（亦见《太平广记》卷二七六《幽明录》）；冯孝将事见刘敬叔所著《异苑》（亦见《太平广记》卷二七六《幽明录》）；睢阳王事见干宝《搜神记》卷十六（亦见《太平广记》卷三一六《列异传》）。但是，《牡丹亭》传奇并非这些故事的改编，而只是作者借用这些既有的故事生发出新的情节来。显然，它包涵了作者的个人生活经验和时代社会特色。例如《谒遇》一出，显然是根据他被贬徐闻时路经澳门的经历而创作的;《围释》一出,杜宝借贿封李全之妻为讨金娘娘从而招降李全的情节,不能不使人联想到王崇古、吴兑、方逢时、郑洛等守边将军在张居正支持下利用三娘子招降俺答之事。

宋明以来,理学盛行,强调"存天理、去人欲",对妇女贞操要求极为苛严,并竭力表彰贞女节妇,《明史·列女传》所收节烈妇女数目,比《后汉书》以下任何一代正史要多出许多倍。泰州学派从哲学思想上反对封建正统的理学,而汤显祖却以戏曲创作表彰情爱来批判理。在《牡丹亭》"题记"中,他倡导为了情,"生者可以死,死者可以生。生而不可与死,死而不可复生者,皆非情之至也。"杜丽娘为情而死,又为情而生,这在现实生活中是不可能有的,但汤显祖却认为"第云理之所必无,安知情之所必有邪?"不必以"以理相格"(《牡丹亭·题记》)。这正表明汤显祖对"情"的重视与颂扬,与之相对立的则是对"理"的否定与抨击。作者以浪漫主义的手法写出杜丽娘的遭遇,实际上也就是对她所生活着的扼杀人性的现实世界的有力批判。当她经过生生死死的磨难,终于和理想中的情人柳梦梅结合以后,封建礼教的体现者,身为乃父的杜宝依然不予承认,这不但反映了封建礼教势力的顽固,更显示了青年男女为维护自身的爱情幸福而抗争的艰巨。

《牡丹亭》问世后,对当时以及后世都产生了深远的影响,对生活在封建礼教统治下的广大妇女产生了极大的震撼力量,引发了她们对自身不幸生活的强烈共鸣,例如传说有娄江女子俞二娘因读此书,痛哭不已,断肠而亡;杭州有女演员商小玲,演出此剧时,自己首先被感动,伤心而亡,等等。

读者需要注意的是,传奇作品中出现的某些人物,只是作者所塑造的艺术形象,不必以历史人物的具体史实加以比附。

Contents
目次

CHAPTER ONE

Du Bao Employs a Tutor

Prefect Du Bao (styled Ziyun) of Nan'an Prefecture of Jiangxi Province in the Song Dynasty (960-1279) was a descendant of Du Fu, a famous poet of the Tang Dynasty (618-907). He started studying when young and became a successful candidate in the highest imperial examination at the age of 20. As an honest and upright official, who never encroached on the interests of others, Du Bao was held in high regard by the local people. Now that he was over 50 with grey hair he thought many times of resigning his post and returning to his hometown to live a quiet and peaceful life. However, he had not yet submitted his resignation. His wife Lady Zhen, a descendant of Empress Zhen of the Wei Dynasty (386-550), was a kind and virtuous woman. They had a daughter by the name of Du Liniang and the old couple regarded her as a pearl in the palm of the hand. Du Liniang was beautiful, dignified and unmarried. Whenever Du Bao thought of his daughter's marriage, he became anxious. One day, when he was not busy with official affairs, he asked his wife to come in and discuss it. The subject had also worried Madam Du. As a woman, she relied on her husband to decide on all family affairs. She had only taught her daughter how to do housework.

After his wife was seated, Du Bao said, "I agree that a girl must learn how to do housework. However our daughter is very intelligent and housework is easy to learn. She should be well educated and well brought up. When she is married to a scholar, she and her husband will need a common language. What do you think about it, Madam?"

"Master, I think you're right," Madam Du said.

Just then, their daughter Du Liniang arrived followed by her maid, Chunxiang, carrying dishes and wine. She greeted them saying, "Hello, Mum and Dad!"

"Daughter, why have you prepared these dishes and wine?" Du Bao asked.

第一章
延师教女

宋代江西南安太守杜宝,字子允,唐朝大诗人杜甫之后,自幼攻读诗书,二十岁就考取进士。杜宝为官清廉,不取民间分毫,颇著声名。如今已年过半百,头发花白,几度想辞官回乡隐居,但总迟疑未决。夫人甄氏,乃魏朝甄皇后的后裔,为人贤德。他们膝下只有一个女儿,名叫杜丽娘。夫妇二人百般宠爱,喜同掌上明珠。这女孩儿才貌端庄,但尚未婚配。每当念及女儿的婚姻大事,杜宝未免忧心忡忡。趁今日政务不多,难得清闲,特地请出夫人来商量。杜夫人也时常考虑这桩事情,但自身是妇道人家,一切须由丈夫做主。平日只教女儿丽娘学习女红。

杜宝见夫人上堂坐定后,便向她说道:"女儿习学女红,我也赞成。丽娘精巧过人,此非难事。但仅仅习学女红还不够,我看古今以来的淑女,无不知书识礼,今后嫁给一个读书人,才能谈吐相称。不知夫人意下如何?"

"相公,一切听凭尊裁。"杜夫人顺从地表示赞成。

正当杜老夫妇商议女儿终身大事时,杜丽娘带着丫环春香冉冉而至:"爹娘安好!"

"孩儿,你让春香捧着酒肴而来,有什么安排?"杜宝问道。

"今日春光明媚,难得爹娘有闲,女儿特备下一些酒菜,敬祝

3

"It is a fine spring day today. It is also unusual for you not to be busy. I wanted to see you happy and healthy and treat you to dishes and wine."

Du Bao and his wife were very pleased and both said, "It's very kind of you."

Du Liniang presented the first cup of wine to her parents, saying, "To your health!" She held the second cup of wine high and said, "Wishing Daddy smooth sailing in his official career." She then made a third toast to her mother, "I hope Mother will give birth to a younger brother for me!"

Du Liniang's words moved her parents. Du Bao allowed Chunxiang to pour a cup of wine for Du Liniang then he turned to his wife and said, "Madam, compared to my ancestor, Du Fu, I am unlucky. He has a son, but I have only a daughter." There were tears in his eyes.

Afraid that Du Liniang would be upset by this, Madam Du comforted her husband, "Don't worry, Master. If we get a good son-in-law, he will be like a son."

Du Bao laughed, "Like our son?"

Madam Du retorted, "A daughter can also bring glory to family. There is an old saying, 'Don't be happy to have a son, and don't be sad to have a daughter.' Sometimes a daughter is better than a son. Why are you talking about this?"

Du Bao had realized that he should not discuss these things in front of his daughter. He asked her daughter to clean the table and leave, and after she had gone, he stopped Chunxiang to ask what Du Liniang did each day in the embroidery room.

Chunxiang also thought that her master had said too much and answered, "What else can she do in the embroidery room? She does needle work."

"Does she do it all day long?" Du Bao asked curiously.

"She sometimes falls asleep," Chunxiang said.

Du Bao became very angry when he heard this and turned to his wife saying, "Madam, you are in charge of teaching our daughter to do a woman's tasks. How can you allow her to be idle and fall asleep during the daytime? Go and summon Liniang."

When Du Liniang arrived at the Rear Hall, she asked her father what the matter was.

Du Bao pulled a long face and said, "Chunxiang told me you fall

爹娘安康。"

老夫妇听得女儿如此孝顺,欢畅异常,异口同声地说道:"难为孩儿一片孝心。"

杜丽娘先献上一杯酒:"祝爹娘身体健康!"再献上一杯酒:"祝爹爹官禄永享。"第三杯酒:"祝娘晚来得一佳子,也让我逗着小弟弟在花间游赏!"

这第三杯酒的祝愿,说到老夫妇心坎深处。杜宝让春香酌酒一杯给杜丽娘,转过头来对夫人说道:"夫人,我比老祖宗杜甫公公更可怜,他还生有儿子,我只有一个女儿。"说罢,泫然泪下。

杜夫人见杜丽娘在面前,怕相公的这番话伤了女儿的心,连忙说道:"相公不要心焦,倘若招得个好女婿,不也与儿子一样!"

杜宝不禁失笑道:"好个一样!"

杜夫人倒有些不高兴,反驳道:"女儿不照样能光耀门庭,古语说的好'生男勿喜,生女勿悲,君今看女做门楣'——你还未老,就这样絮絮叨叨的!"

杜宝这才意识到不该在女儿面前说这些话,于是吩咐女儿收拾台盏自去。待杜丽娘退去后,他叫住春香:"春香,我问你,小姐终日在绣房中做些什么?"

春香也嫌老爷絮叨,答道:"绣房中的生活自然是绣。"

"绣些什么?"杜宝也感到意外。

"绣了纺棉!"春香更无好气地吊老爷胃口。

"什么棉?""睡眠。"

杜宝闻知,气不打一处来,转过身来对夫人发话:"好哩,好哩。夫人,你教女孩儿绣工,却纵容她闲眠,是何家教?——叫女孩儿。"

杜丽娘听见父亲呼唤,又回到后堂:"爹爹有何吩咐?"

杜宝收起刚才一副欢乐的笑容,板起一张脸孔说道:"刚才问

asleep during daytime. After finishing your needlework, you may use the time reading books on the bookshelves. We would be proud of you if you were well educated and a good match for a scholar. However you're so sluggish and it's because your mother does not discipline you strictly enough."

Madam Du agreed but was afraid that such stern words would upset her delicate daughter. She said gently, "Master, look at your daughter. She is a real pearl and she is beautiful. I am her mother and will be happy to see her well educated." She said to Du Liniang, "My daughter, you must consider your father's words carefully. Though you're a girl, you should also learn to read and write."

Du Liniang felt wronged and said, "Dad and Mum, you should not blame me. I have just finished drawing the embroidery manual. From now on, I'll find time to read the books on the shelves."

Madam Du was very pleased and encouraged her daughter saying, "You won't be able to read all the books on the shelves, but you must read *The Ritual of Zhou* (A book of ceremonies and proper conduct). You're from an official family. You must be skilled in needlework and know etiquette like Ban Zhao and Xie Daoyun* of ancient times." Then she turned to say to her husband, "Master, do you think we should find a tutor for our daughter?"

"Female teachers are not available. We may get an old male teacher but we must not neglect him. First, we should show our daughter how to pay him proper respect and second, we should take good care of his board and lodging. I learnt all of my skills from books too."

The news that Prefect Du would employ a teacher for his daughter quickly spread far and wide. All scholars were excited at the prospect and tried their best to win the position, except for one old scholar who did not take much notice.

He was Chen Zuiliang who started learning books by Confucius in his childhood and went to school at the age of 12. He later passed the imperial examination at the county level and the local government regularly supplied him with grain. In the following 45 years, he took part in the imperial examination at the provincial level 15 times. The exam was held

---

*Lady Ban Zhao was a historian during the Eastern Han Dynasty (25-220) and Lady Xie Daoyun was a poet during the Eastern Jin Dynasty (317-420).

了春香,你白昼睡眠,是何道理?刺绣之余若有闲瑕,可以阅读架上图书。日后嫁到人家,知书识礼,也是父母光辉。——这样疏散,都是你娘有失管教。"

杜夫人虽然觉得丈夫之言不无道理,但说得这般严厉,怕女儿受不起,便委婉地说道:"相公,你看看眼前的女儿,如同掌上明珠,的确是人中美玉。将她教养出来,我为娘的虽然辛苦,心中倒也着实高兴。"接着又转换话头:"呵,孩儿,你爹爹说的话,你也仔细斟酌。虽是女孩儿,也不能胸无点墨呀!"

杜丽娘见父母都如此要求,心中虽有委屈也不好辩白:"上告爹娘得知,这怎怪孩儿生性愚鲁——孩儿刚刚画完绣谱。从今以后,茶余饭后,当抽出时间细读架上之书。"

杜夫人见女儿应允,十分高兴,又劝勉了几句:"女儿呵,诗书太多,怎能念遍?但《周礼》不可不读,应该知道礼节。孩儿是大家闺秀,不能只会女红,应该像古代才子班昭、谢道韫那样——相公,要有个女先生为孩儿讲书才好。"

杜宝听见母女对话,也宽了心,说道:"女先生到哪里去请?要请只能请学堂里的老先生。不过,请来的先生却要好好招待,不可怠慢,一不可纵女失礼,二不可茶饭有缺。你看我治国齐家的本领,也全是从读书中得来。"

杜太守要请西席*的消息传到府学中来,顿时像刮起旋风一般,秀才们个个钻头觅缝地寻找门路,都想谋求这一职位。其中有个老秀才倒不把此事放在心上。这个老秀才姓陈,名最良。他的祖父原先行医过日,最良自幼学习儒业,十二岁进学,考取备取秀才,继而转为正取,又领得粮米补助,秀才也到顶了。此后就是参

* 西席:旧时对幕友或家中请的教师的称呼(古时主位在东,宾位在西)。

once every three years and he failed on every occasion. After the low scores in his last examination, the official in charge of the provincial examination decided that the local government should stop providing him with grain. From then on, no one employed him as a teacher and he had no source of income. Fortunately his grandfather was a doctor and ran a drug store. He had some medical knowledge and began practicing medicine to make a living. Some of his income came from the drug store left by his grandfather.

To everyone's surprise old and ugly Chen Zuiliang was the lucky one. More than 10 outstanding scholars had been recommended to Prefect Du by the professor of the local academy, but the prefect was not satisfied. He insisted that he would employ only an experienced and prudent scholar. The professor, who did not know what to do, discussed the matter with the academy's messenger who recommended Chen Zuiliang. When Chen Zuiliang's name was mentioned, the professor burst out laughing but he thought for a while and agreed. Chen Zuiliang was the oldest scholar in the county and, although talkative, he was good enough to be a girl's teacher. The professor recommended him to Prefect Du and the prefect agreed to employ him. The professor then asked the academy's messenger to send an invitation to Chen Zuiliang.

The messenger was overjoyed; his suggestion had been accepted. He felt light-hearted as he headed for Chen Zuiliang's home to tell him the good news. As soon as he entered the drug store, he shouted out in a loud voice, "Congratulations to Mr. Chen."

"What's the good news?" Chen Zuiliang asked. He was most surprised when the messenger told him everything.

When Chen Zuiliang realized that the appointment was a fact not a joke he frowned and said, "The evil of men is that they like to be other's teachers."

The messenger could not understand what he meant and said, "From now on, you'll have enough to eat."

Chen Zuiliang, who did not want to offend the messenger, said, "All right, I'll go with you."

"Mr. Chen, I found the job for you. You must show your gratitude to me," the messenger said, asking for some form of reward.

"You want me to thank you? I am not sure if the prefect will accept me or not!" Chen Zuiliang was not a generous man.

However the messenger urged him, "If you are accepted by the

加三年一次的乡试,争取考中举人;然后再参加三年一次的会试,以考进士。不过,陈最良参加乡试十五次,考了四十五年,不但没有考取举人,在最后一次乡试中,又由于成绩太差,被学政大人停发口粮,从此生活失去保障。幸亏他祖父开过药店,他也懂些医道,于是改行行医,靠着祖父遗下的药材店维持生计。

哪知道这个又穷又老又丑的陈最良,居然喜从天降。因为管理一府秀才的府学教授一连举荐了十几个秀才去杜府任西席,杜太守总是不满意,口口声声要请一个老成持重的秀才。教授没了主意,与学里门子商量。门子倒想起陈最良来。府学教授听了也不禁失笑。不过,学里的秀才再也没有老过他、酸过他的,教女孩儿倒也合适。教授就听从门子的建议,向杜府推荐。不想杜太守居然同意了。教授就叫门子拿着名帖去请陈最良。

门子见自己的建议居然实现,颇觉得有面子,便沾沾自喜地去找陈最良报喜信。前脚才踏进药店,口中即高呼:"恭喜陈先生。"

"何喜之有?"被人开惯玩笑的陈最良简直不相信自己的耳朵。门子一五一十地将杜太守如何请西席,教授如何推荐十余人均不中意,自己又如何推荐陈最良的经过,细细说了一遍。

陈最良这才相信,却又皱着眉头说:"人之患在好为人师。"

门子也听不懂陈最良此时是何等想法,反唇相讥道:"人之饭,有得你吃哩。"

"那么,我就去。"陈最良生怕恼了门子,立刻应允。

门子也不客气,对他说:"陈先生,我替你谋了这差事,你可不能过河拆桥?"

"你要我谢你?我还不知道那里要不要我哩!"陈最良平素为人就不大方。

门子可不管这些,继续开口索礼:"要是成了,逢年过节,太守

prefect, you should give me some gifts."

They talked as they walked and soon came to the prefect's residence.

Prefect Du Bao had been told that Chen Zuiliang would come that day. He decided not to handle any official affairs, asked the cooks to prepare a banquet, and told the janitor to give him good warning of the teacher's arrival.

For the meeting Chen Zuiliang put on a special blue robe which had not been used for a long time. The robe did not fit him, nor did it match his hat, but he looked like an old scholar. He thought to himself: "This is not the same as a meeting between a scholar and an official. As a tutor, I shall meet the host." With these thoughts in mind he raised his head which gave him an impressive bearing when he entered the prefect's residence.

A shout of "Scholar Chen Zuiliang is coming!" accompanied him as he made his way into the entrance hall. There he knelt down on the ground and said, "Humble scholar Chen Zuiliang pays his respects to Your Highness."

Prefect Du saluted him in return, and said to his runner, "I'll talk with Mr. Chen. Have servants from the Rear Hall attend to us."

Acting as the host Prefect Du said, "I have heard that Mr. Chen is a learned scholar. May I ask how old you are and whether your ancestors are also scholars?"

"I am 60 years old."

"How do you make your living?"

"I come from a long line of doctors. I am practicing medicine now."

"Oh, you come from a doctor's family. What else are you good at?"

"I also know something about divination and geography."

"You're really an erudite scholar. Although this is the first time we have met, I have long known about you. A large country is full of talented people."

"Thank you."

"I have a daughter who is fond of reading books and I invite you to be her tutor."

"It would be my duty to teach her, but I am afraid that I have too little learning and talent for the position."

Prefect Du ignored this and knew perfectly well that Chen Zuiliang feigned modesty. He said, "You are qualified. Today is a lucky day. Let

府里送你的礼物,你可得分点儿给我门子。"

两人边说边走,不一会儿就到了太守府。

杜宝太守早已从儒学教授那里得知陈最良将来府中任教,今日特别吩咐宅中厨房准备了酒食茶点,又通知门子及时通报。

陈最良为了今日初次拜见太守大人,将弃置多时的一件半新不旧的秀才蓝衫穿上身,尽管已不十分合身,衣与冠也不太般配,但穿戴起来,俨然也是一个老秀才模样了。他心想:今日会见不同往日秀才拜官府,而是西席与东主关系,可不能失掉这一身份。在门子导引下,他故作气宇轩昂地走进太守府。

随着一声"南安府学生员进",陈最良乃趋赴客厅,上前跪拜起揖,口称"生员陈最良禀拜"。

杜太守身为东主,先开口问道:"久闻先生饱读诗书,极富才学,敢问尊年多少,祖上可也习儒?"

"唉,儒冠误人,晚生年已六十。"

"近来做何生涯?"

"晚生世代悬壶,近日仍操此业。"

"原来是世医——先生还擅长何种学问?"

"除医外,星卜、地理之事,也略通。"

"呀,先生真是学问广博。虽然今日才识面,但闻名久矣,真是大地方出大人才。"杜宝不由赞叹道。

"不敢,不敢。"

"下官有一女,颇喜读书,特地恭请先生教导。"

"这是晚生应尽的责任——只怕晚生才疏学浅,不能胜任。"陈最良此话倒也不假。

杜宝太守不容他推让,也明知他故作谦逊,乃说道:"先生,你完全能胜任。今天就是选定的吉日良辰,叫孩儿出来行拜师之礼。"

my daughter meet her teacher."

When the servant heard this, he began to beat a clapper to inform Miss Du Liniang. Meanwhile the band started preparing.

Du Liniang had dressed herself for the occasion and was ready to come out. Her servant Chunxiang was uneasy and said, "Now that the tutor has arrived, what shall we do?"

Du Liniang, who knew that she would be meeting her teacher that day, looked relaxed. She comforted Chunxiang, "I have to go out to meet my teacher. Even the virtuous young ladies of ancient times knew how to read and write. A maid should also learn to read books." They came to the entrance hall while she was speaking.

"Miss is coming!" a family servant reported.

Du Liniang came to the hall where she bowed to her father who said, "Come here, my dear. There is an old saying, 'Jade must be cut and chiseled to make it a useful vessel and a person must be disciplined and educated to become a useful citizen.' I have found a teacher for you. It is an auspicious day. Come and meet him."

The band began playing and Miss Du Liniang bowed to Chen Zuiliang. She said, "I am an ignorant student. I hope that my teacher will often instruct me." Chen Zuiliang replied in a modest way and Prefect Du ordered Chunxiang to kowtow to the teacher and said that she could keep her company.

Chen Zuiliang turned to Prefect Du and asked which books Du Liniang had read.

"She has read *The Four Books* for both men and women. I think *The Book of Changes* and *The Spring and Autumn Annals* are very difficult and are of no use to women. I hope she will start with *The Book of Odes*. The first chapter of the book is about the virtue of consorts and it suits her well. What do you think of it?"

"It's a very good idea. I'll start with it." Chen Zuiliang nodded his head.

Prefect Du said, "Tomorrow will be an auspicious day. You'll start teaching and if my daughter and Chunxiang misbehave, you must not allow them to have their own way. Discipline them strictly." Chen Zuiliang agreed without hesitation.

Prefect Du gave permission for Du Liniang and Chunxiang go back to their room then banqueted and drank wine with Chen Zuiliang.

家人听得此言,连忙敲起云板,传呼小姐,同时吩咐家乐,准备鼓吹。

杜丽娘在闺房中稍稍整理一下服饰,准备出来拜师。春香倒有些惶恐:"小姐,先生来了怎好?"

杜丽娘早知今日要行拜师之礼,倒也胸有成竹,安慰春香说:"那是少不得要出去拜见的。古代的贤淑女子,也要知书识礼的。你稍稍读点儿书,也是做丫环该做的。"主仆二人边说边出了绣房,姗姗来至客堂。

先有门外伺候的家人报道:"小姐到。"

随即,杜太守传命杜丽娘上堂来。杜丽娘先缓缓向爹爹行了礼,杜宝开口道:"我儿上来。《学记》上说'玉不琢,不成器。人不学,不知道。'我已替你聘了先生,今天是吉日良辰,来拜了先生。"

说罢,传呼吹鼓手奏乐,杜丽娘乃转向陈最良行拜师之礼,口称:"学生愚鲁笨拙,盼老师多多教诲。"陈最良也谦逊了几句。太守又命春香也来向陈先生叩头,并让春香陪伴小姐读书。

听见太守谈到读书,陈最良询问道:"敢问小姐读过些什么书?"

"男《四书》、女《四书》,她都读过了。先生,我想《易经》、《春秋》义理深奥,与女子没什么相干,还是读读《诗经》,开卷第一首便讲后妃之德,最宜课读。不知尊意以为如何?"

"老大人高见,学生谨遵台命。"陈最良频频点头。

杜太守当即择定开馆之期,说道:"明日吉辰,就请陈先生开课吧!凡她们有不守规范之处,请先生严加管教,不可放纵。"陈最良毫不迟疑地领会了。

杜太守见拜师之礼已成,乃吩咐春香陪侍小姐回绣房,自己则陪陈最良坐席饮酒。

CHAPTER TWO

Chen Teaches *The Book of Odes*

When Chen Zuiliang became Du Liniang's tutor, he explained *The Book of Odes* to her in the study everyday. Du Liniang was intelligent and worked hard at her studies. She also conducted herself with decorum. Chen Zuiliang liked her very much. Chen also taught Chunxiang, but she was too fond of play and often made him angry.

Early one morning, Chen Zuiliang went to the study and found no one there. He murmured angrily to himself, "What a spoilt girl! She has not shown up." He was determined to discipline her and banged the table with a ruler shouting, "Chunxiang, let Miss Du Liniang come to the study."

Du Liniang had in fact already got up. She was putting on a simple and elegant dress in exchange for a colorful one. Hearing the teacher she and Chunxiang hurried to the study. Chunxiang seemed unhappy and grumbled, "Why does he make us go to school so early?"

Du Liniang ignored her. She quickened her steps and entered the study. "Good morning, Mr. Chen!" She saluted her teacher.

Chen Zuiliang said to her, "As a girl, you should get up when the cock crows. After dressing you pay your respects to your parents. You should start study as a student at sunrise."

"From today I won't be late," Du Liniang said.

Chunxiang was not happy and retorted, "All right, we will stay up all night. We'll sit until midnight listening to your instructions."

Chen Zuiliang knew that Chunxiang had a very sharp tongue and ignored her. He turned to Du Liniang and asked her if she had reviewed the poem that they had studied the day before.

"Yes, and now I am waiting for you to explain it to me," Du Liniang replied.

"Could you please recite it?" Chen Zuiliang asked.

Du Liniang said calmly:

第二章
塾师授经

陈最良成了杜太守西席后,每日到书馆为杜丽娘讲授《诗经》。杜丽娘又聪明又用功,陈最良对她非常喜爱。春香也算是陈最良的学生,但这孩子贪玩,不肯用心,常把陈最良气得无可奈何。

一天清晨,陈最良走进书馆,看看屋里没有人,有些不满,自言自语道:"真是千金小姐,这般时候还不来上学,也未免太娇养了。"他将云板敲击了三声,并大声呼唤:"春香,请小姐来读书。"

其实,杜丽娘早已起床,脱去常穿的艳服,换了一套淡雅衣裳。听得先生呼唤,乃招呼春香随在身后一同前去书房。春香满肚子不高兴,嘟嘟噜噜地埋怨:"这么大清早,就催人上学!"

杜丽娘也不答话,走进了书房,向先生行礼:"先生早安。"

陈最良拿出先生派头,对着小姐教训起来:"大凡作女孩儿的,听到鸡叫,就要起床;梳洗完毕,得去向父母问安;太阳升起,就要做各自该做的事。如今女学生既然以读书为事,需要早起!"

杜丽娘连忙表示:"以后不敢迟到了。"

春香心中老大不服,说:"今夜不睡,坐到三更天,请先生讲书。"

陈最良知道这个丫头厉害,不去理她,只管对杜丽娘说:"昨日学的《毛诗》,你可温习过?"杜丽娘答道:"温习过了。只等先生讲解。"

"那么,你先背出来。"陈最良倒也认真。

"The sound of turtledoves cooing
Rises over the islets in a river.
The modest, retiring, virtuous young lady
Makes an ideal mate for our prince."

"Good," the teacher nodded his head. "Now let me explain the poem to you. The first sentence describes the cooing of turtledoves."

"Could you show me how a bird coos?" Chunxiang interrupted. She was trying to cause trouble and, although irritated, Chen Zuiliang showed them how a bird cooed. Chunxiang followed his example and cooed at the class which made Du Liniang laugh. Embarrassed, Chen Zuiliang stopped her and went on to explain the second sentence. "Turtledoves like a quiet environment and live on the islets in a river."

"I remember it was yesterday, or the day before, this year or the last year. There was a turtledove in our residence. Then Miss Du Liniang set it free, and it flew to the home of Magistrate He (*he* in Chinese means river)," Chunxiang cut in.

"Stop that nonsense! We are in the middle of a lesson," the teacher said. Then he explained that the last two sentences meant that a gentleman would seek a quiet and virtuous lady.

"Why does a gentleman need to seek a girl?" Chunxiang asked.

Chen Zuiliang had no answer to the question and was embarrassed and angry. He said, "Keep your mouth shut!"

Du Liniang came from a literary family. Though she had spent much time learning needlework, she knew some poems, and was very unsatisfied with her teacher's explanation. She said, "Teacher, it is not difficult to explain the poem according to the notes. I can do that by myself. Could you please tell me the meaning and purpose of *The Book of Odes*?"

Chen Zuiliang did not know this himself and attempted to divert her with a vague answer. "Of the six most important ancient books, namely *The Book of Changes*, *The Book of Odes*, *The Book of History*, *The Book of Rites*, *The Book of Music*, and *The Spring and Autumn Annals*, *The Book of Odes* is the best." He had to think of something. "The Cooing of Turtledoves" in *The Book of Odes* is a song of love but Chen Zuiliang said it sang the praises of elegant girls and virtuous consorts. Du Liniang could not agree and when Chen Zuiliang realized that his student would not accept his explanation, he tried to end the discussion. He said, "Confucius once said, to sum up, his 300 poems contain no sinister thoughts. In short,

　　杜丽娘立刻从容不迫地背诵了一遍:"关关雎鸠,在河之洲;窈窕淑女,君子好逑。"

　　陈最良点头道:"看来你确也温习过了——且听我讲解:'关关雎鸠',雎鸠是一种鸟,'关关'是鸟叫的声音。"

　　才解释得这一句,春香却调皮捣蛋地问道:"这雎鸠鸟儿叫声到底怎样?先生叫一声给我们听听。"陈最良讲得高兴,一时忘形,脱口而出地学了几声鸟叫,春香也跟着叫。杜丽娘忍不住掩口而笑。陈最良看见杜丽娘笑了,才觉得自己失态,连忙咳嗽一声,接着讲下一句:"'雎鸠'这种鸟性喜幽静,一般栖息在河之洲……"

　　春香又打岔道:"对了,对了。不是昨日就是前日,不是今年就是去年,我们府内关着个斑鸠,被小姐放去,一放就飞到那个做官的何知州家去了。"

　　"胡说!"陈最良不得不喝住。"你懂什么?这是作诗的方法。下文两句说的,'窈窕淑女',是指性格幽闲的女子;'君子好逑',是说有个男子好好地去求她。"陈最良耐住性子解释着。

　　春香兀自兴不可遏,仍不放松地问道:"为什么要好好地求她?"

　　陈最良被问得说不出更多的话来,恼羞成怒地喝道:"多嘴!"

　　杜丽娘原就家学渊源,平日虽以刺绣为主,但也并非全不知诗书,如今听得陈最良这般授课,虽然不好像春香那么胡闹,但不满足之情也油然而生,未免有些唐突地说道:"师父,依注讲书,学生也会——请老师把《诗经》的主旨讲授给学生听。"

　　陈最良哪里懂得什么诗的大旨,见女学生提出这样的问题来,怦然一惊,不得不依照注解敷衍一番,说道:"说起《易》、《诗》、《书》、《礼》、《乐》、《春秋》六经来,要算《诗》最有文采。"他人云亦云地胡诌,把《诗经》中类似《关雎》一类的情歌,说成是什么闺门风雅,后妃贤达,有风有化,宜室宜家的作品。这些陈词,杜丽娘也

the connotations of the 305 poems in the book are innocent. You must learn this by heart."

Then Chen Zuiliang asked Chunxiang to fetch paper, brush and an inkstone so that Du Liniang could practice calligraphy. Chunxiang went and came back a moment later saying that she had collected all the materials. She deliberately put them down in front of Mr. Chen.

Chen Zuiliang had never seen the elegant things placed before him. He was surprised and asked, "What ink is this?"

Du Liniang smiled and said that Chunxiang had made a mistake. "It is a black pigment used by women to paint their eyebrows."

Chen Zuiliang pointed a pen and asked, "What pen is this?"

"It is a pen used for painting eyebrows."

Chen Zuiliang frowned and said, "I have never seen them. Take them away! What is this paper? What inkstone is this? Why is there a double inkstone?"

"This is Xue Tao Paper and that is Mandarin-Duck Inkstone." Du Liniang replied.

Chen Zuiliang was interested and moved closer, "Why are there so many holes on the inkstone?"

"They are called tear holes," Du Liniang said.

"Why does it weep? Hurry up, take it away." Chen Zuiliang waved his hand.

"These things are not for Miss. I brought them for you to enjoy." Chunxiang smiled and took them all away. Mr. Chen cursed and said that she was a naughty girl. Chunxiang brought back the real pen, ink, paper and inkstone for writing a moment later. Du Liniang began to write.

Chen Zuiliang was surprised that Du Liniang's handwriting was so beautiful, but he did not know what style of calligraphy it was. He asked her.

"It is Beauty's Hairpin Style handed down by Madam Wei," Du Liniang replied earnestly.

Chen Zuiliang nodded and Du Liniang noticed that Chunxiang wasn't in the room. When she called her, Chunxiang came in and said excitedly, "I've been to the Back Garden. It is so big with colorful flowers and green willow trees."

Chen Zuiliang flew into a rage. "How dare you go to play in the garden rather than stay here to attend to Miss. I'll get a twig and give you a lesson."

听腻了。陈最良从杜丽娘的表情上看出自己的讲解并不能让她接受，赶紧收束道："孔夫子说过'诗三百，一言以蔽之，曰思无邪'。总之，这三百零五篇诗的内涵只'无邪'二字，你须好好地记住。"

讲过《诗经》，陈最良吩咐春香取笔墨纸砚，让小姐练字。春香不一会儿工夫便取了来，故意放到陈最良面前。

陈最良从来没有看见过这些精致的东西，诧异地问道："这是什么墨？"

"丫头拿错了，这是螺子黛，画眉用的。"杜丽娘含笑回答。

"这又是什么笔呢？"陈最良又指着一枝笔问杜丽娘。

"这便是画眉细笔。"杜丽娘说。

陈最良皱着眉道："这又是什么纸？什么砚？怎么是两个砚？"

"这是薛涛笺，这是鸳鸯砚。"杜丽娘一一解答了。

陈最良好奇地凑近，看着砚台问道："为何有许多眼？"

"叫作泪眼。"杜丽娘说。

"哭什么子？快快都拿去换了！"陈最良连连挥手。

"我原不是拿来给小姐写字的，是特地拿来给先生开开眼，长长见识的。"说罢春香笑着拿起走了。陈最良骂了一声："淘气的丫头！"随后春香把真的文房四宝取来。杜丽娘便开始伏案写字。

陈最良站在一旁，见杜丽娘写的字十分娟秀，却又认不得临的何种字体，便问道："我从来不曾见过这样好字。这是什么格？"

"这是卫夫人传下来的美女簪花格。"杜丽娘老老实实地回答。

陈最良频频点头。杜丽娘这时发现春香不在，正要呼唤，春香已笑盈盈地走了进来，兴高彩烈地说："小姐，我到后花园玩耍，那里有一座好大的花园，花红柳绿，才好呢！"

陈最良一听，不觉发怒："哎呀，你不在此陪小姐读书，却去花园玩耍！待我取荆条来教训教训你。"

Chunxiang was not frightened and replied, "What do you want to do with the twig? Beat me? We are women. We won't take the imperial examination. We only want to learn some of the characters. There is no need to be so serious."

Chen Zuiliang began telling them stories about some ancient scholars who studied very hard. However Chunxiang was not listening and heard a flower girl crying her wares. Du Liniang began listening too. Chen Zuiliang was so angry that he raised the twig to beat Chunxiang but she was very nimble and the old teacher missed her. She seized the twig and threw it to the ground.

As they were arguing fiercely, Du Liniang stood up to intervene. "Chunxiang, you've offended the teacher. Kneel on the ground!" Chunxiang dared not disobey Miss Liniang and fell on her knees. Du Liniang pleaded for her, "Master, please forgive her. I'll punish her for you." Chen Zuiliang was pleased and nodded.

"From now on, you are not allowed to go to the Back Garden," Du Liniang said sternly.

Chunxiang got on well with Miss Liniang. To show respect, she knelt on the ground, but when she realized that Miss Liniang was scolding her in earnest, she could not stand for it and began arguing.

The old teacher, who had never handled a dispute between women, tried to stop them as quickly as possible. He waved his hand and said, "Stand up, Chunxiang. I forgive you this time. It is true women do not take part in the imperial examination. However women should study as hard as men." He turned to Du Liniang and said, "You may return to your chamber after you finish your homework. I'll have a chat with your father." Then he walked out of the study.

Seeing Chen Zuiliang walking away, Chunxiang pointed at his back and cursed him saying, "You are an old idiot, an old bookworm. You're stupid."

Du Liniang scolded her, "Stop this nonsense! An old saying goes, 'One who serves as my teacher one day will be like my father all of my life.' He has the right to beat you, but you should not curse him!" Chunxiang didn't dare argue with her. She was sulky and stood there silently. Suddenly Du Liniang asked Chunxiang excitedly, "Where is the garden?"

Chunxiang deliberately ignored her. Du Liniang had to ask her again and smile. Angrily, Chunxiang pushed open the back window and pointed

春香满不在乎地与陈最良顶起嘴来："你拿荆条做什么？要打我么？我们女流之辈，也不要应试做官，只不过认几个字罢了，你又何须这般认真！"

陈最良又讲了许多古人如何苦读的故事，春香一概不听，倒听见墙外卖花的叫声，并转身告诉小姐仔细听。陈最良真的动了怒，举起荆条就向她挥去。春香身段灵活，老秀才怎能打着她？反被她闪身躲过，并夺过他手中的荆条投掷于地。

杜丽娘眼看这一老一小闹得不可开交，丫环春香的行为也太越轨，她一面扶陈最良坐下，一面指着春香斥责道："死丫头，得罪了师父，还不快跪下！"春香见小姐发了话，只得跪下。杜丽娘又向陈最良恳求道："师父，恕她初次犯过，由学生责治她罢。"陈最良乐得由她处理，点头应允。

"今后再不许去花园玩耍！"杜丽娘故作严厉地说。

春香与小姐平素相处十分和睦，也悉知小姐心性，向陈最良下跪认错，是给小姐面子；小姐真的数落她，她却不肯认输，主仆二人居然你一句我一句地拌起嘴来。

老秀才哪曾处置过这种纠纷，急急想脱出身来，踌躇了一会儿，把手一挥，对春香说道："起来，起来，饶过你这一次。唉，女孩儿是不要应试做官，只有这一点儿与男孩儿不同，但说起教书来，不论男女都是相同的。"说着，又对杜丽娘和春香说："你们做完功课，方可回到后衙去。我和相公闲话去了。"说完，踱出书房。

春香见陈最良已走，便指着他的脊背低声骂道："老书呆，老白痴，真不知趣。"

杜丽娘半是生气，半是好笑，说道："死丫头，俗语说：'一日为师，终身为父'，他打你是应该的，你怎能骂他！"春香不敢强辩，鼓着小嘴默默地伫立一边。杜丽娘突然兴致地向春香问道："你说的

with her hand. "It is over there!"

"Is the scenery in the garden beautiful?"

"Scenery?" Chunxiang wanted to tease Miss Liniang and hesitated. Du Liniang asked her several times and she said, "There are six to seven pavilions, a swing, a winding stream, a rockery, and many rare flowers and grasses. I don't know their names, but they are very beautiful. The whole garden is very beautiful!"

Du Liniang was taken by Chunxiang's description and said to herself, "There is such a beautiful garden over there!"

那座花园在哪里？"

　　春香故意不答，杜丽娘不得不再次笑着问她。春香气嘟嘟地用手推开后窗，指向不远处："不是在那里！"

　　"有什么好看的景致？"

　　"景致么，"春香故意一停三顿地逗杜丽娘，在小姐性急地追问下，方不紧不慢地说："有亭台六七座，对了，还有一架秋千。一条流送酒杯的曲水，太湖石堆砌的假山，啊呀呀，还有许许多多名花异草，我也叫不出名目来，委实好看，整座园子，绝色美丽。"

　　听了春香的描述，杜丽娘心有所动，自言自语地说："原来有这样一个所在！"

CHAPTER THREE

Miss Liniang Begins to Think of Love

When she returned to her room, Du Liniang did not want to do needlework. She held a copy of *The Book of Odes* and kept reading: "The modest, retiring, virtuous young lady / Makes an ideal mate for our prince." Soon she threw the book away, stood by the window, sighed deeply and said, "These two sentences display fully the sage's love in ancient times. It is also true of people today."

Chunxiang did not understand what the sage's love was, but she knew Miss Liniang well. She said, "You've studied for quite a long time. Why don't you take a break and enjoy yourself?"

Du Liniang thought for a while then went up to her and said, "Chunxiang, how can we enjoy ourselves?"

Chunxiang knew what was on her mind, and replied without hesitation, "Shall we go to the Back Garden and enjoy the scenery?"

Chunxiang's suggestion struck the right note, but Du Liniang was worried, "My father will be angry if he gets to hear of it."

"Your father has gone to the countryside for a few days. You don't need to worry," Chunxiang said.

Du Liniang walked up and down the room slowly, thinking. Suddenly she came to a bookshelf, took out an almanac and said to Chunxiang, "This will be the first time that I have been to the Back Garden. I must pick an auspicious day. Tomorrow and the day after tomorrow are not suitable. Three days from now will be auspicious. Please go to tell the gardener that I'll make a visit in three days."

The next morning Du Liniang told Chunxiang to ask Mr. Chen if they could be excused from classes for several days. Chunxiang was pleased with the idea and left straight away. As soon as she entered the winding corridor, she saw Chen Zuiliang in the distance. Chen was short-sighted. He did not see Chunxiang until the maid was very close. "Hello, Chunxiang. Do you know where the master has gone? Where is Madam

第三章
游园思春

　　杜丽娘回到书房后,无心刺绣,只是手持一本《诗经》,不断地吟诵:"窈窕淑女,君子好逑",继而又抛开手中之书,伫立窗前,深深叹道:"圣人讲的情理,充分表现在这两句诗中了。这种情致,古人今人都是一般的呵!"

　　春香却不知什么"圣人之情",估猜着小姐此时的心情,建议说:"小姐,读书久了,难免困倦,又生烦闷,咱们想个法儿,消遣消遣。"

　　杜丽娘沉吟半晌,轻步来到春香面前问道:"春香,你说有什么办法可以消遣?"

　　春香这个精灵的丫头早就胸有成竹,只待小姐来问,小姐一问,她便毫不思索地说道:"小姐,还是到后花园去走走,散散心罢。"

　　杜丽娘内心十分同意,口头却不得不说:"死丫头,老爷知道了,可不好办!"

　　"这几天老爷下乡去了。"春香早已摸清情况。

　　杜丽娘听说后也不搭话,走到书案前取出历书来看,看来看去,指着历书对春香说:"从未去过后花园,如今初次去,需要择个吉日良辰。你看,明天不佳,后天也欠好,只有大后天才宜——也罢,明日你去告诉花郎,让他清扫清扫花园,我们同去游玩。"

　　第二天一早,杜丽娘叫春香去向陈最良请假。春香才走到回

Du? Why hasn't Miss Liniang come to class?"

"Hi, Mr. Chen. Miss Liniang doesn't have time to study."

"Why?" Chen Zuiliang did not understand.

Chunxiang tried to tease him, "Mr. Chen, you're too clever to understand. You've stirred up trouble and the master blames you."

"What for?"

"You gave such an earnest explanation of *The Book of Odes* that Miss Liniang begins to think of love!"

Chen Zuiliang was surprised. "I only explained to her about the cooing of the turtledoves."

"After the class, she felt quite emotional. She sighed deeply and said that even turtledoves loved to stay on islets then asked why she was not as free as a bird. Now she has asked me to tell the gardener that she will visit the garden in three days."

"She wants to visit the garden?" Mr. Chen could not understand.

"It all comes from your explanations of *The Book of Odes*. Spring comes and leaves in such haste that it makes Miss Liniang sad. She decided that a visit to the garden would make her feel less melancholy." Chunxiang's explanation made Mr. Chen appear responsible for Miss Liniang's condition.

"She should not do that. A girl should cover her face when she goes out. How can Miss Liniang go anywhere she wishes? I'm 60 years old and have never gone sightseeing in spring." Teacher Chen used hackneyed and stereotyped expressions and Chunxiang ignored him. When he realized that Miss Liniang would not attend classes for a few days he said to Chunxiang that he would ask for a few days' leave. He told her to clean the classroom and books everyday. He then left.

Chunxiang was so pleased that she sent the old teacher on his way with a few words of her own. Afterwards she headed for the garden and on entering it shouted, "Gardener!"

The gardener was drunk and answered, "Sister Chunxiang, I'm here!"

As he was tipsy, Chunxiang made fun of him. "You sneaked out of the house to drink wine and neglected your own work. Have you sent the vegetables to the kitchen?"

"The vegetable grower did."

"Have you watered the fields?"

"The water keeper did."

廊上,远远就看见陈最良站在走廊转弯处。那老眼昏花的陈最良,直到春香走近方认出来:"呀,是春香。我问你相公何处去了?夫人在哪里安息?小姐怎不来上学读书?"

"唉呀呀,原来是陈先生——小姐这几天可没工夫读书!"

陈最良摸不着头脑地问道:"为什么?"

"先生,你还不知道,老爷怪你哩!"春香故意要耍耍老秀才。

"怪我何事?"陈最良倒有些慌张,把握不住了。

"说你讲《诗经》,讲的太精了!居然讲动了小姐的怀春之情!"这顶大帽子,陈最良真有些顶戴不起。

"我不过只讲了个'关关雎鸠'罢了!"

"对呀。小姐听了你的讲授,不禁感慨再三,说关起来的雎鸠,还想那洲渚。为何人反而不如鸟呢?如今吩咐我,后天要去游那花园。"

"这更不该!女孩儿们出门都要遮起头脸来,怎能到处闲游!我靠天度日也六十岁的人了,从来不晓得伤个什么春,游什么园!"老秀才仍用这些陈词滥调教诲春香,春香自是不理不睬。陈最良无可奈何,心想既然小姐这几天不上学,不如也请假回去几天。临别之际,仍不忘交代春香:"小姐既不念书,我暂且回去几天。你呵,要常常去书房看看,窗前案上堆的圣人之书,不要被燕泥污染,时时拂拭拂拭。"

春香见自己一番能言巧语打发掉陈最良,高兴不已,便赶紧去找看园子的小花郎。刚刚走进园门,春香便兴奋地叫道:"花郎!"

吃得醉醺醺的花郎应声而至:"春香姐,我在这里。"

春香见他醉成这模样,便半真半假地斥责道:"好呀,私出府门骗酒吃,正务都忘了。连菜也不送。"

"有菜夫。"

"水也不接!"

"有水夫。"

"Have you sent flowers?"

"I send flowers to Madam and Miss every morning."

"Why don't you send some flowers to me?"

"Oh, that's my fault. I'd forgotten." The younger gardener loved to make fun of young girls. However Chunxiang, who was very sharp, stopped him from going too far. Then she told him that Miss Liniang would come to the garden in three days.

On the day Chunxiang got up early to attend to Du Liniang who said, "Chunxiang, have the servants cleaned the path to the garden?"

"Yes." Chunxiang replied.

Then Du Liniang asked Chunxiang to fetch the rhombus mirror before she sat in front of the dressing table. Chunxiang helped her comb her hair, opened the jewel case, picked out the most beautiful ornaments and helped Miss Liniang put them on. After she had dressed herself up, Du Liniang looked in the mirror and saw a beauty who would cause the moon to hide or put blossoms to shame. She could not help feeling sorry for herself.

Finding her still in front of the mirror Chunxiang said, "Miss, it's time for early tea already. Let's go!"

Du Liniang stood up slowly and looked at the mirror once more before walking out to head for the Back Garden with Chunxiang. After they had passed the courtyard, the winding corridor, and the moon-shaped gate, they arrived at the garden where colorful flowers were in full bloom, birds chirped and the trees grew thickly. Goldfish swam in the pool and Du Liniang sighed and said, "What beautiful spring scenery! Without coming to the garden, I would never have seen it."

She went into the Peony Pavilion, sat down, looked at the flowers and thought, "If there were no green leaves to contrast with the red flowers, the colors would be dreary." She turned to look at the goldfish in the pool. They all swam in pairs happily but after seeing them she was sad and said to Chunxiang, "Chunxiang, let's go back to our room!"

"Why? It is such a large garden. You haven't seen it all. Why do you want to return?" Chunxiang could not understand why she wanted to go back.

"Don't mention the garden any more! It will be useless even if we visited all of the pavilions, terraces, towers and buildings here. We'd better go back!" Du Liniang turned and walked towards her room followed by Chunxiang.

"花也不送！"

"每早送花，夫人一份，小姐一份。"

"还有咱一份呢？"

"啊，这该打！我忘了。"小花郎见到女孩儿难免嬉谑一番，两人说笑过，春香便交代花郎务必清扫花园，后天一早小姐就要来游赏。

到了游园这天，春香早早服侍小姐起床，杜丽娘第一句问话就是："春香，可曾叫人清扫花径？"

春香答道："吩咐过了。"

杜丽娘又叫春香取过菱花镜来，坐在梳妆台边，春香帮她梳发理鬓，打开首饰盒，精心挑选首饰，一一戴好。杜丽娘试过翠色艳丽的衣服，对着菱花镜察看自己的妆扮，突然发现镜中的自己是这样美丽姣好，真有闭月羞花、沉鱼落雁的姿容。

春香眼见小姐久久地对镜忘怀，忍不住提醒她："小姐，已是早茶时候了。咱们走吧！"

杜丽娘闻言，缓缓立起身来，与春香步出香闺，向后花园碎步走去。经过庭院，穿过回廊，踱过月洞门，满园景色呈现在眼前。园内百花争艳，幽香扑鼻，莺歌燕语，婉转悦耳。假山上松柏参差，池塘内清水如镜，金鱼在水里游来游去。杜丽娘感叹道："唉，不到花园，怎知道春色如此美好！"

杜丽娘走入牡丹亭坐下，默默地看着那些红花绿叶，心想：红花虽好，没有绿叶扶持，也会黯淡无光！再回头眺望那池塘中的金鱼，成双成对，逍遥快活。不禁触景生感，顿时万种烦扰，涌上心头。她对春香说道："春香，我们回去吧！"

"怎么这么早就回去？"春香哪里能理解杜丽娘此刻的心情。

"就是游遍了园中的亭台楼阁也是枉然，还是回房去吧！"说着，也不等春香回答，径自回房去了，春香只得尾随而归。

After Chunxiang had attended to Du Liniang she told her to take a rest while she went to see Madam.

Alone, Du Liniang sat lost in thought. She remembered the love poems that she had read and thought that although she was a girl of 16, she had not found a lover. What a waste of youth! It made her very sad. Soon she felt drowsy; she leant on the table, closed her eyes and fell asleep.

She dreamt that she had returned to the garden. Suddenly she saw a handsome young scholar enter with a willow twig in his hand. He stood there looking around then caught sight of her. Overjoyed, he shouted, "Hello, Miss!" and stepped forward to bow to her. "Miss, I have followed you all the way here. I was very disappointed when I lost sight of you. I'm so happy to find you."

Du Liniang thought the scholar looked appealing but she was so shy that she did not know what to say. The scholar raised the willow twig high and said, "You know much about poetry. I have just broken off a willow twig. Could you please compose a poem about it?"

The request pleased Du Liniang. She raised her head and looked at him closely. He was young and handsome. She thought, "I have never seen him before, why has he come to the garden?" She said nothing and as she did not seem to be offended, the young man said boldly, "Miss, I love you with all of my heart."

Du Liniang did not respond, but the expression on her face showed that she was pleased. The young man became bolder. "Miss, you're so young and pretty. I have looked for you everywhere and finally I find you. However you hide and feel sad. It is a waste of youth." He took a step forward and suggested that they go somewhere else to talk.

Du Liniang stood there and blushed. The scholar reached out to hold her sleeve. "Where shall we go?" Du Liniang asked.

The young scholar pointed and said, "Behind the Chinese herbaceous peony garden and on the other side of the Taihu rockery there is a very quiet place." Du Liniang found the invitation irresistible. She stood up and began to walk.

The scholar whispered to her: "Miss, we are a natural pair. Let's be engaged right now. The opportunity is too good to miss."

Du Liniang blushed a deeper red and was too shy to say anything. The scholar lifted her up and carried her to the luxuriant flowers and trees.

　　春香照顾杜丽娘休息后,说道:"小姐,我去看看老夫人。"

　　春香走后,只剩下杜丽娘独自闷坐出神,想到自己常读的诗词中,有多少才子佳人相亲相爱。如今自己年已二八,尚未遇到一个可心的人,岂不是浪费青春、虚度光阴么?想到这里不由得不自怨自艾起来。闷坐无聊,不觉困乏起来,便靠着书案休歇,渐渐双眼合拢,竟然沉沉睡去。

　　杜丽娘又独自到了花园,忽然看见一个年青风流的书生,手持一枝柳条闯了进来。只见他四处观望,蓦然回头,见杜丽娘风姿绰约地立在那里,好不高兴,赶紧走前几步,深深一揖,说道:"小姐,小生一直跟着你回来,一时不见,哪知你却在这里!"

　　杜丽娘虽然觉得这个书生十分可爱,但毕竟陌生,于是任他诉说,只是不应。这书生将手中的柳枝半举,又对杜丽娘说:"小姐,小生刚刚在园中折得垂柳一枝,请为它题诗一首,可不可以?"

　　杜丽娘听见他恭维自己能诗善文,也颇为受用,再仔细盯了他一眼,长相倒也可人,心想与这书生素昧平生,他又因何到这花园中来呢。书生见杜丽娘不语,便大胆地说道:"小姐,我爱煞你了。"

　　杜丽娘仍不答话,书生于是更大胆起来:"小姐,你这般美貌,倒孤孤单单地躲在深闺中自怜自哀,这岂不是太辜负自己青春年华了!"说着,又上前一步:"小姐,我和你到那边说话去。"

　　杜丽娘虽然未曾动步,但已笑容可掬,书生便牵着她的衣袖拽她上前,此时她方开口问道:"到哪边去?"

　　书生用手一指:"转过这芍药栏前,到湖山石边去,那儿十分幽静。"杜丽娘抵挡不住书生的软软温语,身不由已地随着他挪动脚步。

　　书生伏在她耳边,喃喃低语道:"小姐,你我是天作之合,快快订了终身,莫失良机。"

All of a sudden, the flowers and trees shook and the leaves and petals fell. Du Liniang and the young man could not be seen. It happened that the Goddess of Flowers had come down to protect them. The god knew that Miss Liniang was fated to marry the young man, but they had no chance of meeting each other for some time. The god arranged a meeting by allowing the scholar to enter Miss Liniang's dream so that they could enjoy themselves.

The Goddess of Flowers knew well that the young man was not just an ordinary person. Du Liniang was a descendant of Du Fu, a famous poet of the Tang Dynasty and the young man's ancestor was also a famous poet of the Tang — Liu Zongyuan.

Liu Zongyuan, styled Zihou, was a native of Yuncheng in Shanxi Province. He once served as governor of Liuzhou Prefecture. The Liu family's fortunes declined later and his descendants lived south of the Nanling Mountains. One of them was the young man, now in his 20s, a brilliant scholar and a man of learning. However after he had passed the imperial examination at county level, he found no opening for an official career. Without an income he lived a hard life. Fortunately his ancestor Liu Zongyuan once had a faithful servant, Hunchback Guo, who was good at planting trees and growing flowers. He handed on his horticultural skills to his grandson who supported the young man by growing trees and flowers. Though they had adequate simple food all the year round, it was no life for a learned scholar. Low in spirits the young man often past time by sleeping in the daytime.

In his dream he entered a beautiful garden where he found a slim beauty beneath a plum tree. The young man fell in love with her at first sight. He went over and held her in his arms. The beauty said, "Master, you will have a happy marriage and a bright future only if we meet." After he woke up he changed his name to Liu Mengmei (Mengmei means: Dreaming Plum-Like Beauty).

Let's return to the dream of Du Liniang and Liu Mengmei. In the flowering shrubs the two young people stuck to each other like glue and finally fell asleep. The Goddess of Flowers, who had guarded for them for quite a while, decided to wake them by dropping a shower of flower petals.

Liu Mengmei woke first. He shook Du Liniang lightly and said, "The weather's been fine and we took a nap on the lawn." Du Liniang, both timid and shy, lowered her head without uttering a word. Liu Mengmei bent down to help her tidy herself, asked her never to forget the day, then

　　杜丽娘听了这话语,脸儿挣得通红,羞得说不出话来。书生趁势将她抱住,躲到花荫树丛中去了。

　　刹时,花木摇晃,落红缤纷,不见了这对青年男女。原来是花神下降,上天知道杜小姐与书生有姻缘,在人世间一时还不能相遇,便安排书生闯入小姐梦境,让他们无拘无碍地亲热欢会。

　　花神当然知道,这书生也非常人。同杜丽娘是唐代大诗人杜甫的后裔一样,他的先人是唐代大文人柳宗元。

　　柳宗元,字子厚,山西运城人。曾在柳州做刺史。他的后代就留在岭南居住。到了这个年青后生,家世衰颓,虽然年已二十出头,为人聪慧,又饱读诗书,经过三场考试,也成为一个秀才。只是一时没有仕进机会,生涯难免困难。幸亏先人柳宗元有个驼背的仆人叫郭橐驼,颇擅园艺,是栽种花果的能手。他有一个驼孙,跟着这个书生生活。书生就靠这个驼孙从乃祖学来的手艺,种树谋生,两人相依过活。尽管粗茶淡饭不愁,但一个饱读诗文的年青男子哪能就此混过一生!不免心事重重,白昼无事时也呆呆睡觉,打发岁月。

　　岂知他却在梦中进入一个花园,园中梅花树下,有一美人,身材修长,对人如迎如送,两人亲热之后,美人开口说道:"柳生,柳生,你遇到我才有姻缘,也才能发迹。"从此,他就改名柳梦梅——当然,这自然是梦醒以后的事了。

　　且说这两个人此刻正在花丛中你恩我爱。那花神为他们守护多时,不便让他们长久留连忘返,便散落片片花瓣惊破他们的好梦。

　　柳梦梅先醒了过来,轻轻摇醒了杜丽娘,悄悄说道:"这一会儿天留方便,让咱们在草地上好好躺了半晌。"杜丽娘有几分娇怯,也有几分怕羞,低头不语。柳梦梅又俯下身子,给她理理头发,端正了发饰,叮嘱道:"小姐,你可不要忘了今日之事啊!"说着,就闪下不见了。

disappeared.

Du Liniang opened her eyes. Liu Mengmei had gone and half asleep she said in a low voice, "Young scholar, are you really gone?" Then she turned over and went to sleep again.

Just then Madam Du accompanied by Chunxiang came to see her daughter. Finding her asleep during the day she was angry. She walked over to pat her on shoulder. "Liniang, how can you sleep at this time?"

Still half asleep, Du Liniang thought Liu Mengmei was calling her and murmured, "Young scholar." Fortunately Madam Du did not hear her clearly and Chunxiang hurried to wake her up.

"How are you feeling, my girl?" Madam Du asked.

Du Liniang, who had woken up completely, was frightened and cried out, "Oh, mother, you are here!"

"Liniang, why aren't you doing needlework or reading history? How can you sleep in broad daylight?" Madam Du scolded her daughter.

"I went to the garden early in the morning. The beautiful scenery upset me and I returned to my room not wanting to do anything. I fell asleep suddenly without realizing it. It was remiss of me not to come out to greet you. I hope you will forgive me, mother."

When Madam Du learned that her daughter had gone to the garden, she said seriously, "My daughter, the Back Garden is spacious and quiet. You shouldn't go there anymore."

"Yes, mother."

"Why didn't you go to class?"

"Mr. Chen asked for time off, so I am taking a break."

Madam Du sighed and said, "My daughter has grown and her mind is full of ideas but she won't tell me what they are. I'll just have to let things run their course." She left for her own room.

After her mother had questioned her, Du Liniang felt very frightened and now that her mother had gone she began to recall her dream: "Mother always urges me to study, but knows nothing about my need for love. I am glad to have met Liu Mengmei in my dream. How nice it is to be with the young scholar. Mother, you only let me read books. But no book can drive away the emptiness in my heart."

Night fell and Chunxiang saw that Du Liniang was still lost in thought. She went to help her take off her ornaments and make up her bed.

　　杜丽娘从梦境中转来,见柳梦梅已去,蓦然一惊,但仍未全然清醒,含含糊糊地低叫道:"秀才,秀才,你真的去了么?"翻转头来,又迷迷糊糊睡去。

　　正当杜丽娘好梦甜甜之际,春香陪着杜夫人来探视她了。杜夫人一见女儿居然白天痴睡,有些恼怒,上前拍着她的肩膀,低声呼道:"孩儿,孩儿,你怎在此瞌睡?"

　　杜丽娘乍然醒来,睡意朦胧,竟然以为是那书生叫她,口中仍呢呢喃喃地叫着"秀才",亏得杜夫人未曾听清,春香见状,赶紧将她拍醒。

　　杜夫人又问道:"孩儿怎样?"

　　杜丽娘此刻方才完全清醒过来,吓了一跳,惊呼道:"母亲到此!"

　　"我儿,你何不做些针指,要不就看看书史,怎能大白天在此睡觉?"杜夫人语含责备地问道。

　　"孩儿刚才在花园中玩耍,眼见一片春色,无端烦恼,因此回来。无可消遣,又一时困倦,不觉睡去。不知母亲前来,有失远迎,望母亲恕孩儿之罪。"

　　杜夫人听得女儿去游园,即刻板起脸来,严肃地告诫她:"孩儿,这后花园中太冷清,你不可再去闲走。"

　　"孩儿知道。今后再不去了。"

　　"孩儿,你怎不上堂读书去?"

　　"先生不在,所以才休息休息。"

　　杜夫人不禁长叹道:"女孩儿长大,就有许多情态,真叫人管不了,放心不下——唉,且由她去吧。"说罢,径自回房去了。

　　杜丽娘被杜老夫人这一喝问,吓了一身冷汗,见她离去,又独自回忆梦中之事,忽忽若有所失,依然倚几而坐,心想母亲只是要

Madam Du felt very uneasy after learning that her daughter had visited the garden and from then on often went to see her. One day, she walked towards her daughter's room after supper and finding Chunxiang sitting outside the house asked where Miss Liniang was.

Chunxiang was surprised to see her and said, "Madam, you're up very late. Is there something you wish me to do?" Madam Du insisted on knowing where Du Liniang was and Chunxiang pointed to the inner room. She said, "She talked to herself for quite a long while, then fell asleep. I think she is dreaming now."

Madam Du became very angry. "It is you who lured Miss Liniang to the Back Garden. What will we do if something happens to her?"

"It's all my fault. I'll never do it again," Chunxiang said obediently after seeing how angry Madam Du was. Madam Du still warned, "Chunxiang, don't you know that the Back Garden has been left untended for many years. Most of the pavilions and towers are dilapidated and people do not go there very often. Old people like me think twice before venturing in, so how can a young girl wander in when she wishes? What would I do if something happened to my dear daughter? I hope you will take good care of her rather than lead her astray." Madam Du stood up and Chunxiang hastily followed to see her off.

我去学堂看书,哪知自己情怀? 今日总算侥幸,在后花园中遇到书生,有这一番亲热,真是两情和合,千般爱惜,万种温存,哪知正待送那书生出门,恰恰母亲来到,唤醒我来,方知是南柯一梦。娘呵,你教我读书,哪一种书能消除我心中的烦闷呢?

天色暗淡下来,春香眼见小姐只是沉思,也不和人说话,便帮她卸了妆饰,伺候她早早安睡。

杜夫人自从得知小姐游园之后,始终放心不下,隔三差五地总要来女儿房中探视。这天晚饭后,她又缓缓走到杜丽娘绣房中来,只见春香在外房闲坐,杜夫人问她:"小姐在哪里?"

春香未免一惊,脱口而出:"老夫人,天色已晚,怎未安歇,来此有何吩咐?"杜夫人仍是追问小姐在哪里,春香用手指向内房,说:"她自言自语好一阵,后来就沉沉睡去了,大约正在做好梦哩!"

杜夫人闻言,怒气顿时爆发:"都是你这个贱人,引逗小姐去后花园闲耍。倘若有什么疏失,如何是了。"

"以后再不敢了。"春香见杜夫人动了真气,确也不敢再任性胡闹。杜夫人见春香已经认错,又惶恐之极,乃将板着的脸松弛几分,继续告诫她:"丫头,我不说你不知。后花园多年未整葺,亭台楼阁有大半倒落,平素少有人去。就是咱们老大年纪的人要去的话,还得考虑再三。一个年轻女孩儿家,怎么随意就进去闲耍? 要是有个什么三长两短,教我为娘的怎么办? 你也要尽心照管,不可再引逗她。"说罢,立起身来,春香赶紧将杜夫人送回。

CHAPTER FOUR

Du Liniang Draws a Self-Portrait

The next day Chunxiang rose very early and, after washing and dressing, went to ask Miss Liniang to get up. Then she went to the kitchen to make breakfast.

Du Liniang got up reluctantly. She sat in front of the dressing table and began to comb her hair. Soon the hand holding the comb stopped in the air and she sat there staring blankly. She said to herself, "Who is the young man I met yesterday in my dream? He is tender and soft like water. It seems that we knew each other very well. Now he is gone, leaving me alone and I feel so bored staying here all by myself."

"It's time for breakfast!" Chunxiang came in holding a tray on her palm. Her voice distracted Du Liniang from her thoughts.

"I'm in no mood to have breakfast. How could I swallow such food?"

"Madam Du said you missed your supper yesterday. Today you must have your breakfast."

Suddenly Du Liniang felt that she had a grudge against Chunxiang and said, "Oh, I don't have the energy to touch these bowls and plates. I ate yesterday, and I am not hungry now. You may eat it yourself." She waved her hand. Chunxiang had no choice but to leave taking the tray with her.

After she had driven Chunxiang away, Du Liniang wished that her dream would continue but it would not and she became more unhappy. Suddenly she had an idea. There was nothing for her to do that day, why not go to the Back Garden again and search for her dream without telling Chunxiang? She walked out of her room, turned several corners and came to the garden. Finding that the door was open and no gardener in sight she entered without any difficulty.

The scenery in the garden was as beautiful as before; the paths were covered with flower petals, the Chinese herbaceous peonies leaned on the

第四章
画像寄情

　　次日清早，春香便起身，她自己先行梳洗一番，然后打好洗脸水，催促小姐起床，自己到厨房去取早餐。

　　杜丽娘勉强起床后，独自一人坐到镜台前面懒洋洋地梳妆，才将一头乌发梳了两下，手便停在半空沉思起来：昨日园中闲游，梦中所见的究竟是何人？他那般一再顾盼，柔情似水，真好似平生知己。

　　"小姐吃早饭啦！"春香捧着托盘进来，一声招呼，将杜丽娘的注意力从沉思中唤了回来。

　　"有什么心情吃饭——这茶饭怎生吞咽？"

　　"老夫人盼咐，小姐昨天未吃晚饭，今天早饭要早。"

　　杜丽娘陡然怨恨起来："咳，哪有气力碰这些碗儿碟儿，我昨天吃过了。"说着连连挥手，春香无可奈何，只得捧起托盘出去了。

　　杜丽娘撵走了春香，企望旧梦再现，然而好梦难续，却平白添了一段新愁。想来想去，今天无事，何不背着春香，悄悄去花园看看，也许能重新寻到美梦也未可知。想罢，她就潜身而出，缓步而行，七转八弯，来到后花园。只见园门洞开，看园的花郎又不在，她也就无拘无束地走了进去。

　　园中的景致依然如昔，只是小径落满残红，芍药栏依畔着湖山石，那弯弯曲曲的流水缓缓地淌着，处处都逗引起她前梦的欢

rockery, and the winding stream ran silently. Everything in the garden reminded her of the happy time with the young man in her dream. A flower by the path caught her skirt made her think that like human beings, flowers also liked to hold onto beautiful things. "What a great waste of young life it is when I stay in the embroidery room all day long." She was lost in thought.

Let's turn to Chunxiang. After having had breakfast, she returned to the room to find that Du Liniang had disappeared. It frightened her, but she guessed that Miss must have gone to the garden and she hurried there. When she saw Du Liniang standing by the plum tree, she cried out, "Alas! Miss, you are here. How could you come here by yourself?"

Du Liniang tried to divert her with a vague answer. "I found a swallow in the painted corridor busy building a nest. Following it, I found myself in the garden."

"Let's go back, Miss. Madam will scold me if she knows you are here. I'll be blamed again," Chunxiang said, trying to convince her.

"Stop that nonsense. What's wrong with me visiting the garden occasionally?" Du Liniang said angrily.

"It's not me who talks nonsense. It's Madam Du's instruction. She said a girl should stay inside to do needlework, read books or practice calligraphy."

"Anything else?"

"She said the garden is desolate. There are flower and tree spirits here. If you want to get rid of boredom you'd better go to the front yard."

"I'll do as you say. You can tell my mother that I'll return soon." Du Liniang showed signs of impatience and Chunxiang left.

After she walked away, Du Liniang began looking for her dreamland. She thought to herself, "Alas! There is the rockery; the Peony Pavilion is over there; close to the pavilion is the Chinese herbaceous peony garden. In front of it is a willow tree. To its left stands a plum tree. The young handsome scholar led me to the rockery and then carried me in his arms to the flowering shrubs beside the pavilion. How happy we were when we were together! However, now the pavilions and towers are dilapidated; the garden is desolate; the grass and flowers have withered and there is no sign of human habitation. It is quite different from the scene I saw in my dream!" Looking around her, Du Liniang suddenly caught sight of a big plum tree. She moved towards it without thinking. It looked like a big umbrella, tall and straight and covered with green leaves and plums. In

畅。小径旁的灌木绊住她的裙边，使她顿然想到花儿也如同人一样，总是想牵住美好的事物。唉，整日关在绣房，岂不是辜负了这美好的时光！她不禁陷入了沉思遐想。

再说春香吃完早饭回房却不见了杜丽娘，心头一惊，继而一想，必是去花园了。就一路寻来，果然见杜丽娘独立在一棵梅树边。"呀，小姐，你在这里！——你怎独自一人来游园？"

杜丽娘见春香寻来，敷衍地答道："我在画廊上看见燕子衔泥而飞，随着它信步而行，不觉就到这园中来了。"

"回去吧，小姐。要是让老夫人知道，又要教训我'哪里去闲串？'我可担当不起！"这丫头学嘴学舌地劝诫小姐。

"哦，多嘴！偶尔来花园走走，就这么罗嗦。"杜丽娘恼火起来。

"不是我敢多嘴，这是老夫人之命。她说女孩子家，该到绣房中刺绣，或是看书写字。"

"还说了什么？"

"还说这花园荒废多时，难免有花妖木客，不如去前面院子中散心。"

"知道了。你到前面好好答应老夫人去。我随后就来。"杜丽娘不耐烦了。春香不得不应命前往。

杜丽娘见春香已出了花园，心想此刻正好寻梦。啊呀，那边不是湖山石么，这边就是牡丹亭了，前面是芍药栏，转过栏去，上面一株垂杨，左近一颗梅树。对了，正是那年轻英俊的书生，把我引到湖山石这边，又抱着我去牡丹亭旁。那是多么美好、多么欢畅的一刻啊！如今亭台倒败，园林荒凉，花谢草凋，寂无人迹，昨日今朝，景象大变，雨迹云踪，何处去寻？想到此处，不禁怅然若失。放眼四顾，似乎寻觅什么，忽然眼前突现一株大梅树，便挪步向前。这株亭亭而立的大梅树，像是一把太阳伞，罩住四周，树叶青青，果实圆圆，暗香飘动，依依可人。她

the breeze Du Liniang could smell a pleasant fragrance. But, when she thought that lovely plums had bitter kernels, a symbol of her own fate, she felt sad. She said to herself, "I would be happy if I was buried by the tree when I am dead."

She thought that there would be fewer unhappy people if everyone could control their own fate and love whoever they pleased. No one in the world would blame God or man. Feeling tired she leaned on the plum tree and rested. Her hand fondled the tree's root and she made up her mind that she would see the young scholar again no matter what happened.

After seeing Madam Du, Chunxiang came back to the garden looking for Du Liniang and finding her asleep tried to wake her up.

Half asleep, Du Liniang murmured to herself, "Looking at the boundless sky I feel sad. I am so sorry that I did not compose a poem for him!"

Chunxiang, who did not understand her, said, "Don't make me guess! Miss, let's go back to your room."

Du Liniang walked slowly towards her room supported by Chunxiang. She heard a bird singing and said sadly, "Listen, the cuckoo is saying 'let's go back'. Where can I return? I'm afraid I will not meet him in the garden again, unless in a dream or after my death." Ignoring what she said Chunxiang insisted on taking her back.

After her return to the garden to look for her dreamland, Du Liniang was disheartened and often went without food and sleep. As time went by, she became thinner and thinner. Chunxiang, who was very worried, said to her, "Since you've been to the Back Garden, you have no appetite and your nights are without sleep. You lose weight every day. How do you feel? Are you sick? No wonder Madam Du said you should not go there. Miss, from now on you should never enter it again."

"You don't know why I want to go to the garden. I put on bright clothes and make up with great care every day, but I only sit in the room all day long by myself. To whom can I express my feelings? How can I get rid of my worries?"

"Miss, after visiting the garden, you always shed tears. You're so sad all the time and you look wan and sallow. Madam Du will be very worried if she sees you."

Du Liniang walked to the dressing table and looked herself in the mirror. She was surprised to see that she had lost so much weight. "Alas!

想到这可爱的梅子，果仁却是苦的，这不正象征着自己的命运么？我死后，若能葬于此处，也算有幸了。

她又想到：如果生生死死都能由自己掌握，如果想爱谁就爱谁，一切都由自己做主，也就不会再怨天尤人了！想也想得远了，寻也寻不见了，走也走得累了，杜丽娘不觉倚在梅树下歇息，抚摸着树根，她又下定决心：拼却一命，也要与那书生在此重新相见。

春香去杜夫人处周旋一番后，放心不下杜丽娘，又回转花园来，正好见到小姐打盹，赶紧劝她回房。

杜丽娘仍在梦境中，自言自语地说："一时望眼连天，伤心自怜，我如今悔不与他题诗笺！"

春香听了这摸不着头脑的话，不禁问道："小姐，你和我打什么哑谜儿？快回去吧。"

杜丽娘在春香半扶半拽下，走走停停，忽然一声鸟啼，她又伤心地说道："听，这杜鹃声声'不如归'，难道除非梦中、除非死去，才能与他相会！"春香却不管她如何自怨自艾，只是尽力将她扶回绣房。

杜丽娘自从游园惊梦、园中寻梦之后，废寝忘食，意懒心灰，腰围日减，衣带渐宽，但犹不自知。倒是春香看在眼中，急在心里，不禁劝说道："小姐，你自游花园以后，寝食俱废，容貌日瘦，是不是受了凉，得了病症？怪不得老夫人说后花园不能去。"

"唉，你怎知道其中缘由啊！这都是无情无绪之故！你不见我，虽然精心梳妆，但也只是无聊独坐。我这片真情为谁表露？又有什么办法除尽忧愁？"

"小姐，游园之后，你的泪水儿就未曾干过，愁闷得如此花容憔悴，老夫人见了怕不心焦。"

杜丽娘听见春香这样讲，不禁走近镜台对着菱花镜一照，果

I used to be very beautiful. Now I am so thin and pallid." Her eyes were full of tears and Chunxiang comforted her, but failed to cheer her up. Both of them sat there, silent.

Suddenly Du Liniang said, "Chunxiang, fetch a piece of silk and a brush. I'll paint a picture."

"It's a good idea, Miss. What will you paint?"

"I'll do a self-portrait. I want to paint a portrait of myself while I am young. Otherwise I'll regret it when I'm old. Who would know Du Liniang was such a beauty if I died young?"

Chunxiang did not know what to say to the depressed girl and went to the inner room to get a piece of silk and a brush. Chunxiang thought to herself, "It's easy for Miss to paint her own portrait but it will be difficult for her to portray her sadness in the painting."

Before she began to paint, Du Liniang cried continuously and sighed. "I, Du Liniang, am only 16 years old. My life has only just begun. However I need to paint a self-portrait. It is really embarrassing!"

She thought for a while, began to clean the mirror carefully and looked at herself in it. Then she took a piece of silk, and started drawing with great concentration. Chunxiang who stood by could not help exclaiming, "Wonderful!"

Soon she had finished and Du Liniang allowed Chunxiang to hang it up. It was truly an excellent painting; there were elegant Taihu rockeries, weeping willows swaying gently in the wind, and green palm leaves. A slim, pretty girl leant on a willow tree with a plum branch in her hand.

"Does it look like me?" Du Liniang asked Chunxiang.

"It looks just like you. You're really a gifted painter. No one can compare with you." Du Liniang was also very satisfied with her work. Chunxiang sighed, "It's a great pity that there is not a young man beside you. After you get married, you may do a painting of a happy couple."

When she heard this, Du Liniang could not help telling Chunxiang everything. "I don't want to hide the truth from you. I did meet a handsome young man in the garden. However he was in a dream rather than in reality."

Chunxiang was surprised and asked if it was the truth.

Du Liniang said, "I met a young scholar in my dream. He broke off a willow twig and gave it to me. Does that mean I will marry a man

然消瘦许多,也不免吃了一惊,叹道:"哎呀,想我杜丽娘往日多么艳丽风光,何以瘦到如此地步!"不禁悲从中来,泪水盈盈。春香不断劝慰,似乎也无以消除她的烦愁。主婢二人只能默默无语,相对而坐。

半晌,杜丽娘突然开口道:"春香,你去将素绢、丹青取来,看我描画。"

"呀,小姐,作画倒好,不知小姐要画啥?"

"春香,我要替自己描绘下一幅肖像,趁着青春还在,留个形影,免得红颜一老,后悔不及,一旦死去,又有谁人知道杜丽娘有这般美貌啊!"

春香听了这番言语,也不知说什么好,只是遵命取来素绢、画笔等物,心中思忖着:"娇美容貌倒是容易画出来,她那一腔伤心又如何描摹得出?"

杜丽娘取过绢、笔,尚未描画,泪自先流,良久,叹息道:"想我杜丽娘年方二八,青春容颜,却待自家描画,这岂不令人难堪!"

沉思已罢,轻轻取来一副绢绡,将菱花镜细细揩抹一遍,又取过画笔来,对着镜中自家的容颜仔细审视、估量。只见她,一面对镜思忖,一面伏案运笔,或淡扫清描,或浓笔重染,春香在旁看得直是出神,失声叫好。

不一会儿,一幅少女肖像画就,杜丽娘吩咐春香将它张挂起来。只见一幅小小的素绢,画面上有透、瘦、皱、秀的太湖石,有迎风摇曳的垂柳,有绿叶碧翠的芭蕉,更有一位美艳的少女,倚在柳树旁,手中拈着一枝青梅,似有所待。

杜丽娘谛视良久,向春香道:"像不像?"

"啊呀呀,太像了。小姐这丹青工夫,是他人学不来的呀。"杜丽娘也觉得自己画得很到家,喜不自禁。春香接着说道:"好是好,只是少个姑爷在身旁——要是早早结了良缘,少不了画一幅和美

whose surname is Liu (Willow)? I have finished my self-portrait and told you everything about my dream. Shall I inscribe a poem on the painting?"

"That sounds good."

Du Liniang picked up her brush and wrote a poem on the painting. It read:

> Seen closely, she is an extraordinary beauty,
> And seen at a distance, she is like a goddess.
> One year she met a handsome young man from the moon,
> By a weeping willow rather than a plum tree.

As soon as she had finished, Du Liniang threw down the brush and sighed, "In ancient times some beautiful women were married when they were young and their husbands would draw portraits of them. Some beautiful women drew self-portraits and sent them to their lovers. No one was like me. I drew my self-portrait and have no one to send it to. Chunxiang, could you please ask the gardener to have this painting mounted?"

Chunxiang picked up the painting and left to look for the gardener.

夫妻游乐图了!"

　　杜丽娘听到春香此话,又触动了自己的心思。平素还不好向人诉说,此刻却倾泻而出:"春香,我也不瞒你,花园游玩时,倒有一个如意郎君,无奈只是个梦中人罢了。"

　　春香听了这话,吃了一惊:"小姐,怎的有这等事?"

　　杜丽娘也感到有些突兀,进一步诉说道:"梦中见有一个书生,折了一枝柳枝给我,不知道这是否预示我今后所嫁的人姓柳? ——画了像,说了梦。春香,我又成诗一首,题在画面上,好不好?"

　　"好哩。"

　　其实不待春香答应,杜丽娘已提起笔来,洒洒自如地在画卷上写下:

　　近睹分明似俨然,远观自在若飞仙。

　　他年得傍蟾宫客,不在梅边在柳边。

　　题罢,杜丽娘掷笔叹息道:"春香,古来有的美女早早嫁了丈夫,有丈夫替她描模画样;也有美人自己写照,寄给情人。哪有像我杜丽娘的,自己描画自家容貌,又留与谁人鉴赏? ——春香,你将此幅画像收拾起来,交代花郎送给一行家仔细裱好。"

　　春香奉命去找花郎寻人裱画。

CHAPTER FIVE

Du Liniang Dies for Love

Du Liniang became anxious and sick after going to the Back Garden. After almost six months she had not recovered. Sometimes she seemed better, sometimes worse, but there was no sign of complete recovery.

At 50 years of age Madam Du only had one daughter. Seeing her daughter become thinner and thinner made her very anxious. Du Liniang showed no signs of a chill or a temperature and Madam Du had no idea of what disease her daughter was suffering from. One day she decided to ask Chunxiang about the illness.

Chunxiang was a smart girl and knew what Madam Du would ask her. On her way to the hall she decided what to say to her. She knelt in front of Madam Du and said, "Humble maid Chunxiang pays her respects to Madam."

"Chunxiang, you wait on Miss Liniang every day. You must know what has made her ill. Tell me the truth!"

"I don't know anything at all, except that since Miss paid a visit to the Back Garden, she has not been well."

"How about Liniang's appetite?" Madam Du asked.

"All I can say Madam is that whenever I give Miss drink of tea or take in a meal, she always refuses it. She seems to be always in a trance, laughing and crying without reason. I'm afraid she is seriously sick."

"We have invited an imperial doctor to treat her, haven't we?"

Chunxiang said in a quiet voice, "She suffers from lovesickness. No doctor can cure her."

"What disease?" Madam Du had not heard what she said.

"I don't know. Maybe she has a chill," Chunxiang said cautiously.

Sensing that Chunxiang was hiding the truth, Madam Du raised her voice and said sternly, "Stop this nonsense. You know full well that she has not got a cold. Kneel down and tell me the truth!"

第五章
以身殉情

　　自从杜丽娘游园伤了情,画像又伤了神,从此罹疾在身,迁延半年,好一阵歹一阵,轻一时重一时,就是痊愈不了。

　　杜夫人年将半百,膝下只得这一个女儿,眼看她病成这般模样,忧虑异常,到底是什么症候,实在估猜不透。想来春香定然知道,便传春香上堂回话。春香何等精灵,闻知夫人此刻召唤,不外是询问小姐病情,腹中已打好底稿,急步上堂拜见杜夫人:"春香叩头。"

　　"春香,小姐如何得病,你自然晓得,从实说来!"

　　春香含糊地说:"只是小姐自从游了后花园,身体就不大舒服。"

　　"小姐近来茶饭用得多少?"杜夫人问道。

　　"回夫人,每逢请小姐饮茶用饭,她都懒得答应,总是精神恍惚,哭笑无端,怕是病得不轻。"

　　"不是早请太医了么?"

　　春香低声嘟噜着:"小姐这病呵,除非是最好的针法,能针断她的相思情,否则再好的丹药也治不了她这相思症。"

　　"生的什么病?"杜夫人只见春香嘴动,却听不清讲的什么话。

　　春香吞吞吐吐地说:"春香不知——想必是受了风寒!"

　　杜夫人见春香半吞半吐,不肯直言,大为狐疑,喝斥道:"胡说!受点儿风寒,岂能病到这步田地?还不给我跪下照实讲!"

When she saw how angry Madam Du was, Chunxiang fell to the ground and told her everything, "One day six months ago Miss went to the Back Garden. It was the very day that you happened to come to see her. She told me that she met a young man in the garden with a willow twig in his hand. The young man asked Miss to write a poem for him. It was the first time that Miss had met the young man, so she declined."

"What happened later?"

"Later ... later ... the young scholar took Miss to the Peony Pavilion."

"What did they do there?" Madam Du was alarmed.

"How do I know?" Chunxiang said. "Miss said it was only a dream."

"It seems that she ran into a ghost. Let me discuss it with the Master."

Chunxiang went to fetch Prefect Du and Madam Du told him everything about Liniang's sickness. She asked him to invite a wizard to drive the ghost away from Liniang.

Prefect Du blamed his wife. "I employed Mr. Chen Zuiliang to teach her and make her concentrate on books. But you, her mother, let her have her own way. Now she is sick as a result of a visit to the garden. In my opinion, she has just caught a cold. Let Mr. Chen take her pulse and write out a prescription. She will recover after taking medicine. We may also invite Nun Shi from the Ziyang Palace to chant scriptures to drive evil ghosts away."

One day after Du Liniang woke up Chunxiang helped her move and sit by the window. Chunxiang rolled up the curtain for her and a sweet smell greeted them. A pair of swallows flew freely in the sky.

"Chunxiang, I'm very sick and have become very thin and pallid. I am afraid I won't live very long. Now I'm very concerned about the young scholar I met in my dream. How is he?"

"Miss, he only appeared in your dream. Please stop thinking about him."

Du Liniang did not listen to her and was longing to see her young lover. She wished he would appear in her dream again and thought, "Maybe the young man really lives somewhere. But how can I find him?"

As Du Liniang was not listening, Chunxiang said, "Miss, a dream is not real. It's useless to think about him. You should think about your own health. Your illness is very troubling. It makes you muddle-headed all day long. Oh, when will you have a clear head?" Chunxiang

　　春香看到杜夫人变了脸,料是推诿不过,只好跪下,将杜丽娘游园得梦之事一五一十讲了出来:"就是老夫人来闺房撞着的那一天的事。小姐游园归来后对奴婢说,有个书生手里拿了柳枝,要小姐为她题诗。小姐说与这书生素昧平生,未曾给他题诗。"

　　"不题就罢了——后来呢?"

　　"后来,那、那、那个书生就和小姐一起走到牡丹亭上去了。"

　　杜夫人大惊失色:"去干啥?"

　　"春香怎么得知?——小姐说是做梦哩。"

　　"这样看来是被鬼冲撞了,快请老爷商量。"

　　春香奉命去将杜太守请来,自己回绣楼去了。杜夫人连忙将女儿去游园被鬼冲撞之事,一五一十地告知夫君,要他快请个懂法术的人来为女儿驱驱鬼。

　　杜太守不急着请人,倒先责备起夫人:"我请陈最良教她读书,为的就是拘束她的身心;你做母亲的倒纵由女儿闲游,这不游出事儿来了?我看,不过是些日晒风吹,伤寒感冒罢了。先请陈先生去看看她的脉息,再叫紫阳宫石道姑来念诵一些经卷驱驱邪鬼。"

　　再说杜丽娘午睡方醒,春香见她坐近窗前,便卷起湘帘。一片青翠扑人而来,双双燕子在微风中翻舞,主婢两人悄悄谈心。

　　"春香啊,你看我这一病,病得容颜憔悴,瘦骨嶙峋,不成模样,不知还能拖迁多久? 更不知道那书生现今如何了?"

　　"小姐啊,梦中的事,你想它做什么?"

　　杜丽娘不以为然,仍为梦里情景所牵萦,她希望旧梦重温,心想:也许那梦中的书生真在这世间,但是到哪里去找呢?

　　春香见小姐不说话,便又接着说道:"小姐,梦总归是梦,你也管不了他是谁人? 你的病却是缠人。你这单相思害得也不明不白,

was most anxious.

"Is Chunxiang in?" Their chat was interrupted by Chen Zuiliang who entered the room without waiting for Chunxiang to greet him. He had come to diagnose Du Liniang's disease as requested by Prefect Du. When she saw him, Du Liniang tried to get up. "Master, I'm sick and I cannot come to greet you. Please forgive me," Du Liniang said.

Hidebound Chen replied, "Miss, according to an old saying, a rich knowledge and great ability come from learning. You were sick after your visit to the Back Garden and since then you have neglected your studies. When I learned that you were sick, I was very worried. Fortunately today the Master allowed me to diagnose your disease and I have a chance to see you. I didn't expect to find you so thin. When will you get better and return to school? Miss, tell me what's wrong with you?"

Chunxiang tried to make him appear responsible for the illness and said, "Mr. Chen, it is all your fault. You explained the love poem from *The Book of Odes* in detail, asked Miss to recite it and learn it by heart. That's why Miss is sick."

"How come?" Chen Zuiliang could not believe what he had heard.

"You said, 'The modest, retiring, virtuous young lady/Makes an ideal mate for our prince.' She pines for the prince."

"Who is the prince?" Chen Zuiliang did not understand.

"No one knows who he is," Chunxiang replied defiantly.

As Chunxiang was being rude to Teacher Chen, Du Liniang cut in, "Mr. Chen, you may feel my pulse now."

Chen Zuiliang reached out and placed three fingers on the back of Du Liniang's hand and Chunxiang said bluntly, "How can you take Miss Liniang's pulse by feeling the back of her hand?"

Chen Zuiliang realized that was wrong and said, "Miss, you may turn your hand over." He felt Du Liniang's pulse with great diligence and cried out, "Alas! Your pulse is very weak. I had not expected you to be so seriously ill." He sighed and said to Chunxiang, "Chunxiang, you take good care of Miss. I'm going to prepare some medicine."

When she heard this, Du Liniang sighed and said sadly, "Master, I know myself well. Neither acupuncture nor medicine can cure me. Thank you very much for coming to see me." Tears ran down her face.

Chen Zuiliang and Chunxiang were also very sad but could say nothing. They comforted Du Liniang and told her not to think too much. "You just get better and don't worry. You'll recover after the Mid-Autumn

终日昏昏沉沉地似睡非睡,何日方好。"

"春香在么?"突然一声呼唤,打断她们俩人的谈话,原来是陈最良奉命来看视小姐病症了。听说是师父来了,杜丽娘挣扎着起来,抱歉地说道:"师父,学生有病在身,不能恭迎师父,失敬了。"

陈最良一昧迂腐,开口说道:"小姐,你不见古书上说过'学精于勤荒于嬉',你在后花园中被风吹日晒,怎不生病?生了病,不又荒废了读书工夫!为师的我,听说后也寝食不安。老爷请我来为你看病,小姐,我问你病症如何?"

"师父,你还问哩!都是你讲什么《毛诗》讲出病来的!"春香索性把病根安到陈最良头上。

"《毛诗》怎会生出病来?"陈最良不禁诧异地问道。

"你不是说'君子好逑'么?这病便是'君子好逑'逑上来的。"

陈最良乍闻此言,一时未曾领悟,便问道:"是哪一位君子?"

"谁知他是哪位君子。"春香没好气地冲了他一句。杜丽娘见他俩你一句我一句,谁也不相让,便婉言说道:"师父,还是诊脉吧。"

陈最良伸出手去切脉,岂知却糊里糊涂地错按了杜丽娘的手背,春香也顾忌不得礼数,直截了当地加以纠正:"师父,你把脉把错了,反转手来。"

陈最良这才恍然大悟,讪讪地"噢"了一声,又继续诊脉。"啊呀,小姐脉息细弱得很!"陈最良叹息着说道。然后立起身来,对春香说:"春香啊,小姐这病不易调理,你得好好服侍。我配药去。"

杜丽娘闻言,叹息一声,凄然地说道:"师父,我这病深入窍髓,料来针灸、药剂也难调理了。谢谢您老人家来看望我。"说到此处,不禁泣下数行。

陈最良、春香两人听得这番言语,也不禁伤感万分,只能劝慰而已:"病体要紧,不要心烦,安心养息,过了中秋就会好的。"

Festival."

After Chen Zuiliang left, Nun Shi from the Ziyang Palace arrived to drive the ghosts from Du Liniang. She asked Chunxiang what disease Miss suffered from.

Chunxiang did not like Nun Shi and said defiantly, "An embarrassing one."

"Where did she get the disease?"

"In the Back Garden."

Nun Shi struck a pose by raising three fingers then five. Chunxiang ignored her and when she saw Miss lying there, showing no response, she went close to her and heard her murmur, "My dear! My lover!"

"Listen," Nun Shi said to Chunxiang, "She talks incoherently. A ghost must have caught her." She took out a piece of yellow cloth and mumbled, "Go away wild ghosts and idle souls."

Nun Shi's voice woke Du Liniang who saw the yellow magic figure and said, "It does not work. My lover is not a young ghost attached to a flower or a tree."

"All right, if the magic figure does not work, let me call the palm thunder to hit him."

Though seriously ill, Du Liniang had a clear mind and tried to send the nun away politely. "Nun, I think you must be very tired from chanting scriptures. Could you please leave me alone and allow me to have a good rest?"

Nun Shi had to take her leave.

The Mid-Autumn Festival came. Thick black clouds hid the bright moon and the wind blew. There is an old saying that if it rains during the Mid-Autumn Festival, someone will die. With Du Liniang suffering from an illness at such a time, Chunxiang worried about how long she could live. The maid was determined to help Miss get up so that she could attend a family reunion for the festival. With her help Du Liniang sat down on a chair by the window.

Still sick, Du Liniang did not know which day it was and felt chilly as raindrops fell down the window. "Chunxiang, how long have I been sick? What's the date today?"

"It is Mid-Autumn Festival."

"Oh, it's a family reunion festival. I expect that my parents are worrying about me. Have they celebrated it?"

　　陈最良方才离去，那紫阳宫石道姑又奉杜老夫人之命前来替小姐赶鬼禳解。进得门来，就问春香："不知小姐害的什么病？"

　　春香见不得这不男不女的道姑，没好气地答道："尴尬病。"

　　"小姐从何处得此病？""后花园。"

　　石道姑便装腔作势地一会儿伸出三个指头，一会儿举出五个指头，她见小姐迷迷痴痴地躺在那边，便走去向小姐问话，杜丽娘也未听见她的问话，心心念念地呼唤着"我的人那，我的人那。"

　　石道姑趁势对春香说："你听，她那含糊不清的话语，可不是中了邪！"随手掏出黄布条做的符来挂起，口中念念有词："野鬼闲魂，快快离开！"

　　不断的吆喝声，惊醒了迷糊中的杜丽娘，她睁眼看见这道黄符，说道："咳，这符儿不灵，我那人儿呀，可不是依附花木的小鬼头。"

　　"好呀，符儿不灵，再请掌心雷打他。"

　　杜丽娘虽在病中，清醒时心中也还明白，便客客气气地打发掉这个道姑："姑姑，您也忙累了，又是挂符又是念经，请便吧。还是让我好好歇息歇息。"听了这番话语，石道姑只得无趣地别去。

　　每年一度的中秋团圆佳节已到，却不见天上月明，只见四方乌云密布，风雨萧条。春香见小姐在这秋风秋雨中挣扎，是否能摆脱病魔的控制，实不得知。且不管它愁煞人的风风雨雨，毕竟是团圆佳节，春香服侍小姐起床，扶她在窗前小坐。近来杜丽娘病情沉沉，既不知年月，更不晓节令，只觉轻寒扑身。又听着细雨敲窗，便开口问道："春香，我病了多日，也不知今夕是何夕？"

　　"八月半了。"

　　"哎呀，已是中秋佳节了！父母大人大概都为我的病担忧，不知二老有没有赏节？"

"Yes," Chunxiang replied.

"I remember when Mr. Chen came to see me last, he said I would have recovered by the Mid-Autumn Festival. Now that the festival is here my health has gone from bad to worse. What can I do? My illness must have spoiled your appreciation of the moon. Chunxiang, open the window. Let me see the bright moon."

"There is no moon tonight." Chunxiang gently pushed the window open.

Raising her head, Du Liniang saw dark clouds and no bright moon. She felt sad, sighed deeply and said, "Today is the Mid-Autumn Festival. Where do you hide yourself, bright moon? I feel so sad!"

Chunxiang who was standing by heard everything she said. She thought to herself, "Miss was cheated by a young scholar in a dream. I first thought that she would forget him. However as time goes by, she has sunk deeper and deeper into an abyss. She is such a beauty, but she will die for an unworthy man. I must go to comfort her." She helped Miss Liniang lie down and soon after feigned delight crying out, "Miss, the moon has come out. The bright moon will help you fall into a sound sleep. You'll have a good sleep tonight."

Chunxiang failed to cheer her up and she sighed deeply and said sorrowfully, "For a long time I have looked forward to Mid-Autumn Festival. However, when the festival comes, I cannot appreciate the moon. Probably I am fated to be afraid of it. Maybe my life will end with this autumn rain which goes on and on. Oh, even if there's a bright moon on the Mid-Autumn Festival I can only hear a plaintive whine in the distance, autumn insects chirping at night and the wind blowing through the Chinese parasol trees. All of this make my heart even heavier...." Before she had finished she became cold, shivered and her hands and legs became stiff.

It frightened Chunxiang. "Miss, Miss!" She cried at the top of her voice. And then she walked out of the door shouting, "Madam, could you please come right now? Miss is not well."

Astonished, Madam Du rushed to her daughter's bedroom. "My dear daughter, how are you now?"

"I have to tell you Madam, Miss is not well."

Finding that her daughter was unconscious, Madam Du could not help but weep. She held Du Liniang's cold hands gently and said, "Oh, my child, no one would believe that since you went to the Back Garden and dreamt, you have been in a state of delirium. If I had known earlier

"这还用说么！"

"上次病中,好像模模糊糊听陈先生说,到中秋节,我的病就会好转。但今天已是八月半,病势并未见好转,倒觉沉重,如何是好！为了我,累你们无心赏月。春香,你把窗子打开,让我看看月色。"

"哪有月色！"说着,春香还是轻轻打开一扇窗。

杜丽娘微微抬头目视窗外,并不见月华,却见乌云一片,似乎天助人怨,不由得更加烦闷起来,黯然叹道:"明月,明月,今天佳节,竟不见你一轮高照,令人心痛！"

春香在旁听着小姐这番自言自语,思忖着:小姐无端地受到春情哄骗,原以为不消多日便会清醒好转,哪知道却越陷越深。她这般轻盈身段,俊秀容颜,又为谁人而葬送！太不值得了,我得哄哄她。想罢,先扶杜丽娘回到床上,照料她躺下来休歇,稍稍停了一会儿,便走到窗前,故作喜悦地呼道:"小姐,月亮出来了。这轮明月要照着你美美睡一觉哩,伴你做个好梦。"

杜丽娘的心情也并未随着春香的惊喜而好转,长长叹息一声,哀哀诉说道:"平时盼望中秋,哪知到了中秋却身不由主,不能自行赏月,大概是奴家命中怕月,我这残生怕要在这绵绵秋雨中了结。唉,只听得天边哀鸿、草丛虫鸣、风吹梧桐,声声入耳,更令我心情沉重……"话语未完,便感到全身发寒,四肢软绵,难以动弹。

春香可吓坏了,连声惊呼:"小姐,小姐！"又急步走至门边,对外高呼:"老夫人,老夫人,小姐欠好哩！"

杜夫人闻得春香呼叫,也惊恐异常,三步做两步地赶来,边走边叫道:"我的儿,病体怎样了？"说着进了小姐闺房。

"禀告老夫人,小姐欠好。"

杜夫人听了春香这般言语,见女儿昏迷不醒,不禁哀泣起来,轻轻拍着杜丽娘冰凉凉的纤手,诉说道:"唉,儿呀！哪知道你去游

that you longed for a lover, I would have found a young man for you. Then you would not feel lonely, nor sleep by yourself every night. My baby, if you leave us, an old couple, I don't want to live either."

The bells hanging on the eaves rang in the wind, and Madam Du wept sadly by the bed. Du Liniang woke up. Seeing her mother she tried to get up but was so weak that she could not. When she spoke, she rambled. "Mother, I'm very grateful to you for bringing me up. You have given me boundless love since I was born. I'm not a dutiful daughter. I will not wait on you in your remaining years. Please don't be too sad over me. You must take good care of yourself." Her eyes brimmed with tears and Madam Du and Chunxiang both wept. They resented Heaven; it had destroyed some good things on earth and ruined Du Liniang's life.

After a while Madam Du wiped away her tears, lifted her head and said, "I have no sons, only you, my daughter. I have placed all my hope in you and thought that you would support your father and I when we are old. But now you're seriously sick. I'm so unlucky...." Madam Du stopped abruptly and comforted her daughter. "My daughter, don't be so upset, take a good rest."

Knowing that she would never recover, Du Liniang spoke of something that worried her. "Mother, I'm afraid I won't get better. Where do you plan to bury me?"

Though filled with deep sorrow, Madam Du immediately said that she would be sent to their hometown.

Du Liniang tactfully told her mother of her wish. "Though I miss my hometown very much, it is far away; I would like you to bury me here."

Her mother did not understand what she meant and said, "I'll try every way to ship your body back."

Du Liniang had to tell her frankly, "I have a wish. You must listen to me whether it is right or wrong."

"Go ahead and tell me. I'm listening to you."

"There is a plum tree in the Back Garden. I like it very much. You may bury me under it," Du Liniang said.

"Why do you want to be buried under the plum tree?" Madam Du did not understand.

Du Liniang answered her vaguely. "I'm not as lucky as Chang'e who lives among sweet-scented osmanthus. I love plum blossoms very much. I do hope you will bury me under the tree. It's my last wish."

园做了个糊里糊涂的梦,从此神志再也不能清醒,只是昏昏沉沉地睡。唉!要是早早招个乘龙佳婿,也不会让你夜夜孤眠,一病不起,唉,儿呀,你若有个好歹,为娘的也活不成了!"

窗外风吹铃声,床边杜夫人泣声,终于催醒昏迷中的杜丽娘。她眼睛睁开一丝,见到杜夫人在旁,想挣扎起来,却又重重倒下,大口喘气后方才断断续续说道:"母亲,我从小就得到您的百般爱护,但女儿不孝,不能终生孝顺您老人家,请母亲不必伤悲,保重身体要紧。"杜丽娘说着流下了眼泪,杜夫人、春香更是泪流满腮,三人都怨恨老天,为何好端端地摧残人间好事,断送佳人性命!

良久,杜夫人方才从悲痛中回过神来,哀泣道:"老生无儿,好不容易生了你这个娇娘,膝下承欢,指望你长大成人,替老身送终。哪知道老身命孤运穷……"说到此际,又顿然停住,转而劝慰道:"儿呀,你却不要心烦意乱,好好休歇。"

杜丽娘心知自家将一病不起,既然母亲在旁,便说出自家心事:"娘呀,女儿这病怕难治了,你老准备如何处置女儿后事?"

老夫人虽然哀痛万分,但对这个问题却毫不犹疑地回答:"儿呀,将你送回家乡。"

杜丽娘听了杜夫人的话,委婉地说道:"娘呀,我虽然也盼望回到远在千山万水的家乡,但还是请娘把我的棺木寄在此地吧。"

"便是再远也运回去。"杜夫人错解了小姐的心事。

杜丽娘不得不直诉胸臆了:"娘呀,儿有一句话,不知对不对!盼娘不管怎样也听儿一句。""你说,说呀!"

"后花园中有一株梅树,是儿心所爱,把我葬在梅树下面就行。"

杜夫人不解:"这却为的啥?"

杜丽娘含含糊糊地答道:"我命不好,不能做月中嫦娥,长在桂花丛中讨生涯,我这把枯骨却喜爱埋在梅花树下。"

Madam Du was too sad to know what to say. She hated to hear the words spoken by her dear daughter, but she had to face reality. She thought she should tell her husband immediately. After instructing Chunxiang to take good care of her daughter, she went to see her husband.

After Madam Du left Chunxiang was alone with Miss who beckoned her to the bedside and said, "Chunxiang, we have been congenial companions for many years. After I die, you must take good care of my parents for me."

"That's the least I can do," replied Chunxiang.

"Chunxiang, may I entrust you with another thing?"

"I'll do everything you want."

"I wrote a poem on my self-portrait. I don't want any one else to see it. Could you please place the portrait in my purple sandalwood box and hide it under the Taihu Rock."

"Why do you want me to put it under the rock?" Chunxiang did not understand.

"I drew a self-portrait with great care just for a man who will be my lifelong companion."

Chunxiang thought that she should not discuss arrangements that would be made after Miss Liniang's death. She tried to comfort her. "Miss, you take it easy and rest. I'll speak to the Master. We'll find a young man for you; whether he is Mr. Mei (Plum) or Mr. Liu (Willow), he will be your lifelong partner. Does that sound good?"

"I'm afraid I will not see the day. Oh, oh!" Probably tired after talking so long, Du Liniang felt heart pain. "Chunxiang, will you miss me often after my death?"

This made Chunxiang very sad and before she could reply Du Liniang lost consciousness again. Shocked, Chunxiang shouted, "Master and Madam, come quickly! Miss has passed out!"

Prefect Du and his wife had had a premonition that their daughter was dying and, when they heard Chunxiang, they lost no time in coming. They wept as they walked and cried out, "My dear daughter, how can you abandon your old parents!" Standing by the bed Prefect Du shouted, "Please come to, my dear. Your father is here."

After a while Du Liniang regained consciousness and said in a low voice, "Father, I'm dying. I hope you will set up a tablet in front of my tomb...." She died and her parents' sobs choked them.

Prefect Du, his wife and Chunxiang grieved deeply. Chunxiang cried

听了女儿这番话语,杜夫人不知说什么是好,恨不得自家先女儿而亡,便不会看到这种令人心碎的场面。心想:老爷还不知道,待先去向他报信。便吩咐春香尽心照顾,她暂时别去。

杜丽娘见杜夫人已走开,悄悄对春香说:"春香,你从来事事依从我,我与你也情意相投,我走了,你可要小心服侍老爷夫人。"

"这是该做的了。"

"春香,我还记起一件事。"

"你说,尽管吩咐奴婢。"

"我那幅画像,上面题了诗,让他人看见不雅,我葬了之后,你将它放在那只紫檀盒子中,藏在太湖石下。"

春香不解她的意思:"这样做,又是为什么?"

"唉,你哪知道啊!我尽心尽意描绘自家容颜,就是为了碰上一个知心的人!"

春香觉得不该与小姐谈论身后之事,便劝慰道:"小姐,放宽心,好好休息。待禀告老爷,不管姓梅的还是姓柳的书生,替小姐招来做夫婿,将来同生同死,岂不是美事!"

"我怕等不得这一天了!"大约讲了半晌话,伤了神,心前一阵痛,稍歇后杜丽娘又说:"春香,我亡过,你可要常常念叨我啊!"

春香听得此话十分伤心,还不及答话,见杜丽娘又昏迷过去,大惊失色,高呼道:"不好了,不好了,老爷,夫人快来!"

杜太守和夫人,听得春香呼叫,知道女儿命在旦夕,连忙相扶而来,边走边哭:"我的儿呀,你怎能抛下双亲!"走近床前,杜太守连连呼叫:"女儿,快快醒来,爹爹在这里。"

杜丽娘在千呼万唤中苏醒过来:"爹爹呀,儿是不济事了。再不能好转了,盼爹爹在女儿坟头立一块小小的断肠碑……"在父母哽咽声中,杜丽娘终于撒手而去。

and said, "Miss, how sad I am. No longer can I burn joss sticks, light candles, pick flowers, feed birds or move the mirror for you. You often did needlework until midnight and got up early to paint...." She remembered Miss Liniang's instructions before her death and put the portrait in a purple box. Nun Shi and Chen Zuiliang arrived soon after and cried bitterly.

Just then the housekeeper came in to say that an edict had arrived. Prefect Du received it and ascertained that it was an imperial edict passed on by the Ministry of Personnel. It read: "The Kin troops are invading our border. Prefect Du Bao of Nan'an is promoted to Pacification Commissioner of Huaiyang. Du Bao will set out for his new post immediately. This is an order from the emperor himself." Though Prefect Du had been promoted, he was not at all happy. His dear daughter had just passed away, and he had not yet made arrangements for her funeral. However he dared not disobey the emperor's order and after a deep sigh sent for Chen Zuiliang.

Chen Zuiliang was waiting at the outer room and, when he heard his name mentioned, hurried in. Prefect Du said, "Mr. Chen, my daughter has gone." Chen Zuiliang said sorrowfully, "Now that Miss Liniang has gone, I have lost a student. Master Du has been promoted so I have no one to rely on."

Prefect Du had no time to listen to him and said, "Mr. Chen, I have something to discuss. At the emperor's command I will soon leave for the post. My daughter had a wish. She wanted to be buried under the plum tree in the Back Garden, but I'm afraid this does not suit the new prefect of Nan'an, so I told my housekeeper to build a nunnery in the Back Garden. It will be called the Plum Blossom Nunnery and will house my daughter's tablet." He turned and said to Nun Shi, "Could you please stay in the nunnery to take care of it?"

Nun Shi was pleased. She knelt on the ground and said, "I'll take good care of the nunnery."

Prefect Du also allocated one hectare of land to Mr. Chen and told him that he could share the harvest with Nun Shi after they had paid the costs of the Plum Blossom Nunnery. Chen Zuiliang and Nun Shi were delighted. Finally Prefect Du urged them again and again to take good care of his daughter's tomb and offer her a bowl of rice on the Pure Brightness Festival every year. Too sad to continue Prefect Du left, supporting his wife.

　　老俩口悲伤自不必说，春香也是悲痛欲绝，放声痛哭："我的小姐呀，这不痛煞小春香了！小姐呀，再不能与你烧香、剔烛，也再不能与你拈花、喂鸟，更不能为你移镜、点唇。想起你深夜做女工，清晨临画稿……"哭到这里，忽然记起杜丽娘临终嘱咐，赶紧将画像收拾好。石道姑与陈最良也闻讯而来，陪着哭泣。

　　正当此际，管家进来禀报，有朝报送来，杜太守接过一看，只见吏部转发圣旨一道："金寇南窥，南安太守杜宝，可升安抚使，镇守淮扬。即日起程，不得违误，钦此。"虽是升官喜事，但正值女儿亡故之时，杜太守也高兴不起来。君命不可违，女丧尚未处置，便长叹一声，吩咐管家快请陈最良说话。

　　陈最良正在外屋等候，听得传呼，立即抢步过去，杜太守先招呼道："陈先生，小女去了。"陈最良借此哭道："正是。小姐仙逝，使得陈最良无人照顾；老相公高升，陈最良更失依傍。"

　　杜太守也顾不得陈最良诉说自家困境，开口便道："陈先生，请你来有事相商。我奉旨赴任，不能久停。因小女有话，要葬在后花园梅树之下，这样恐怕要影响继任官员居住。我已吩咐家人，将后花园分割出去建一座梅花庵观，安置小女神位。"说着转过身来，对立在一旁的石道姑说："就请你在里面修性看守，你可能承担下来？"

　　石道姑巴不得有此美差，连忙跪下应承，说道："老道婆添香换水，自然做得。"

　　杜太守又拨了一块祭田，交由陈最良经管，收下的粮食，除去杜丽娘的香火花费外，一概给陈最良和石道姑享用。这样一来，陈、石二人的生计无忧虑了，自然是欢喜不尽。杜太守最后叮咛道："陈先生、石道姑，咱老夫妻就指望你们照看小女孤坟了。逢上清明寒食，替咱老夫妻供上一碗水饭。"说到此处，已伤心得说不下去了，便扶着杜夫人别去。

CHAPTER SIX

Liu Mengmei Visits His Friend

After Liu Chunqing dreamt of meeting a beauty under a plum tree, he changed his name to Liu Mengmei. Although he had been disappointed to find himself alone after waking up, he remembered clearly that the beauty in the dream had said that he would gain fame and fortune. He had studied hard for many years and had thought that it would not be difficult to get an official post. After being an official it would be easy for him to find a beautiful wife.

However reality was quite different. He was poor. The grandson of Hunchback Guo supported him by growing trees. Life dragged on and Liu Mengmei was very lonely. He did not have any close friends with whom he could converse in the city except for Han Zicai. Both Liu and Han were descendants of famous writers in the Tang Dynasty. Liu's ancestor was Liu Zongyuan while Han was descendant of Han Yu. According to Han Zicai, his ancestor, Han Yu, had been demoted to Chaozhou in south China because he offended the emperor by submitting a petition. On the way to Chaozhou, he had been delayed by heavy snow in Languan, Shaanxi Province, and his horse could not go on. Han Yu thought that it was not a good omen. Suddenly one of the Eight Immortals in the form of his nephew, Han Xiangzi, came to see him. Han Yu, more depressed and in low spirits, picked up his frozen brush, softened it by blowing on it and wrote a poem at the thatched post of Languan:

A petition was submitted to the emperor,
And I was demoted to Chaozhou 8,000 li away.
To help the emperor correct his errors,
I would devote my remaining years.
Where is my home? Mount Qinling is covered by clouds
And my horse is held by heavy snow in Languan.
I know why you come here from afar.

第六章
梦梅访友

　　书生柳春卿自从梦中在梅花树下艳遇美人之后，就改名为柳梦梅。梦醒以后，仍旧是孑然一身，梦中佳人不知何在。他想：梦中佳人曾预言说自己遇到她后就能发迹。细细想来，凭自己多年苦读，挣个功名，谋个官职，也不是难事。那时节走马市曹、夸官游街，还怕没有仕女与自己缔结良缘！

　　这种花团锦簇的想像毕竟不能改善依赖驼孙种树糊口的困窘生涯。岁月悠悠，生涯寂寂，平素能够交谈的友人也很少，只有一个韩子才还有些谈吐。说起韩子才其人，倒有些来历，他也像柳梦梅是唐代大文人柳宗元之后一样，他的先人是唐代大文人韩愈。据他自述，他的公公韩愈，字退之，只为上了破佛骨表，得罪了宪宗皇帝，一贬就贬到南方潮州来。离开京城不远，在陕西蓝关地界因雪受阻，马不能前。韩愈公公暗想这个兆头不好，正不知如何办时，忽然侄儿韩湘子（传说中的八仙之一）来见。韩愈公公心里更加不快，就用口中的热气呵开已冻僵的毛笔，在蓝关草驿题诗一首：

　　一封朝奏九重天，夕贬潮阳路八千。

　　欲为圣明除弊事，肯将衰朽惜残年。

　　云横秦岭家何在，雪拥蓝关马不前。

You came to gather my bones by the river.

The last two sentences referred to Han Xiangzi and, when he saw the poem, the Immortal Han Xiangzi burst out laughing, tucked the poem into his sleeve and left on a cloud. Later Han Yu died of miasma in Chaozhou. As he had no relations in Chaozhou, Han Xiangzi, who already knew of his uncle's death, came on a cloud and buried his body. Then the Immortal Han Xiangzi went to the county government office and found no one there except for a woman who became his lover. She gave him a look of love, he was moved and spent a night with her. Later the woman became pregnant and gave birth to a son. Han Zicai was a descendant of both Han Xiangzi and the woman. Later, when war broke out, Han's descendants wandered destitute from Chaozhou to Guangzhou. As Han Zicai was a descendant of Han Yu, the local official of Guangzhou submitted a memorial to the court suggesting that he be given a post. Later Han Zicai was appointed a petty official in charge of sacrificial rites at the Changli Shrine and lived on the Prince Yue Terrace built by Zhao Tuo.

Both Liu Mengmei and Han Zicai had passed the imperial examination at the county level and lived in the same city. Though Liu Mengmei looked down on Han Zicai, just a person in charge of joss sticks and candles, they had some things in common and often visited each other. One day, when Liu Mengmei was still quite upset over the dream he had had a few days earlier, he had nothing in particular to do. As he could not concentrate on books, he walked slowly towards Prince Yue Terrace. Han Zicai was doing nothing except looking into the distance from the terrace. Seeing Liu Mengmei coming, he greeted him, "Hello, I haven't seen you for quite a long time. What wind has blown you here today?"

"I had nothing to do at home, so I came to see you." While climbing the terrace Liu Mengmei made an obeisance by placing his hands together before his chest.

"You'll get a good view from the terrace," Han Zicai said proudly.

Liu Mengmei knew that the terrace gave a panoramic view but he was low in spirits and said, "It does not make me very happy to climb up."

Han Zicai, who did not know what he was implying, said in great delight, "I'm living in ease and comfort here."

"I believe those who are not intellectuals live a happier life than we do," Liu Mengmei said expressing dissatisfaction.

知汝远来应有意,好收吾骨瘴江边。

这后两句就是指的韩湘子。湘子见了这首诗,长笑一声,袖了这首诗,腾空而去。后来韩愈公公果然在潮州受瘴气而死。又无亲人在旁,韩湘子得悉,想起前诗,乃落下云头,收拾韩愈骨殖。又去衙门,四顾无人,仅有湘子原妻一人,四目相视,湘子不禁动了凡心,当下生了一子,就留在水潮地方,后来就承传不绝。韩子才就是这支的后裔。因逢乱离之世,就从水潮地方流落到广州。当地官府念他是韩愈后人,就奏请朝廷敕封他为专门祭祀先人的"昌黎祠"的香火秀才。平常就住在赵佗所筑的越王台上。

这两个大文人之后,同为秀才,又同住在一个城市里,虽然柳梦梅并不太看得起韩子才这个香火秀才,但总算还谈得来,所以彼此之间也有些往来。这天,柳梦梅无什么要紧的事,又因日前梦中之事骚扰心境,坐不下来读圣贤之书,便信步闲走,一走就走到越王台。那韩子才也是终日无事,在台上闲眺,老远就看见柳梦梅来了,首先招呼道:"啊呀,这不是柳兄么,好多日子未见,是什么风把老兄吹来的?"

"偶尔无事得闲,乃前来台上游耍,看望老兄。"柳梦梅边拱手行礼,边走上台来。

"这台上的风光倒不错。"韩子才不无得意地说。

柳梦梅虽明知台上风光不错,但心情不好,没好气地说:"只是登临不快啊!"

韩子才并未听出话外之音,仍兴高采烈地说:"小弟在此,倒颇享福。"

"我想起来了,倒是不读书的人比咱们享福。"柳梦梅此刻正一肚子牢骚,借这个话题发泄出来。

"那是谁?"

"Who in particular are you talking about?"

"Zhao Tuo who had the Prince Yue Terrace built is a good example."

"What makes you think that?" Han Zicai still could not understand.

"Originally Zhao Tuo was only commandant of Nanhai. After Emperor Qin Shihuang died, the country fell into great disorder and many heroes rose up. Zhao Tuo, relying on natural defences, set up a separatist regime by force of arms and called himself emperor. After that he had a grand palace built and lived there happily in his remaining years. Look at us. Though we have read thousands of books, we cannot gain a foothold." Liu Mengmei became more indignant and said, "Our ancestors said, 'One who has read the first half of *The Annalects of Confucius* can occupy the country, while one who has read the second half of the book can administer it.' However I have read the book time and time again, but I haven't found a way out for myself." He paced back and forth on the terrace, now looking ahead, and now standing still. He turned to Han Zicai and said, "It is no use us worrying about the present and cherishing a memory of the past. Brother Han, look! Only a few ancient trees can stand the wind and rain around the terrace."

As a long-standing friend of Liu Mengmei, Han Zicai knew that Liu was rather conceited and fancied himself as a gifted scholar. When he heard him grumbling, Han Zicai tried to talk him out of it. "Lord Changli once said, 'Be concerned that your article is good enough rather than worrying that officials do not understand you. Be concerned that you are not an outstanding scholar rather than worrying that officials do not know you.' Brother Liu, I think the reason why you have not started on your official career is that you have not worked hard enough."

Liu Mengmei was not convinced and continued, "Brother Han, what you say is not right. For instance, both my ancestor Liu Zongyuan and your ancestor Han Yu were learned scholars. Your ancestor Han Yu offended the emperor by submitting a memorial and was then demoted to Chaozhou; my ancestor Liu Zongyuan frightened the emperor when he was playing chess with Prime Minister, Wang Shuwen. He was sent to be commander of Liuzhou. Both Chaozhou and Liuzhou are in the border areas far away from the capital. Han Yu and Liu Zongyuan traveled together at that time and whether they were on a boat, or on horseback, they always kept their books. Every night they sat up late to read books and discuss

"远的不说,眼前建这越王台的赵佗就是一个。"

韩子才依然不明白:"何以见得?"

"那赵佗,原不过是个南海尉,自从秦始皇一死,天下大乱,群雄并起,他就依着天险,割据一方,称孤道寡。自从他做了皇帝,就大造宫殿,尽情享受。像咱们读书破万卷,可有立足之地么?"柳梦梅越说越气,愤愤不平,继而又说:"前人说'半部《论语》得天下,半部论语治天下'。咱们把《论语》不知熟读了多少遍,可是哪有什么进身之路?"说罢,在台上一会儿走来走去,一会儿放目四顾,又立定脚跟,对韩子才说:"咱们在这儿攀今吊古,也是徒然,无济于事。韩兄,你看,这一片荒台就只有几棵古树经历着风吹雨打。"

韩子才与柳梦梅交往有年,平素就知道他颇以才子自负,此刻听他这番议论,知道他又在发牢骚了,就劝慰他说道:"先祖昌黎公曾经说过'不怕当官的不明白,只怕自己的文章不精妙;不怕当官的不知道,只怕自己的经书不通晓。'柳兄,你之所以还没有弄个一官半职,只怕你的功夫还不曾到家。"

柳梦梅颇不服气,滔滔不绝地议论起来:"韩兄,你这话就说得不对了。比如我公公柳宗元,与你公公韩愈,都是饱学之士,却也时运不好。你公公错题了佛骨表,得罪了皇帝,被贬到潮州。我公公则因为在朝阳殿中与丞相王叔文下棋,惊了圣驾,也被贬到柳州做司马。这两处都是海边烟瘴地方,离京师十分遥远。那时,你公公与我公公一路同行,不论是行舟走马还是驿舍住宿,都在一起挑灯夜读,细细论文。"他描绘当时的一番情景时,就好似自己在场,亲眼目睹一般。他越说声音越高:"当时你公公说'宗元,宗元,论起我和你两人的文章来,真可谓旗鼓相当,半斤八两;我有《王泥水传》,你便写《梓人传》;我有《毛中书传》,你便写《郭驼子传》;我写《祭鳄鱼文》,你便有《捕蛇者说》。这也就罢了。当我写

articles." Liu Mengmei described their ancestors in great detail as if he had seen them himself. As he spoke he became more excited and said in a high voice, "As for the articles they wrote, they were well-matched. Han Yu said to my ancestor, Liu Zongyuan, 'I wrote *Biography of Wang Nishui*, and you followed suit and created *Biography of Ziren*. Later I wrote *Life of Palace Secretary Mao*, and you *Hunchback Guo*. I wrote *A Funeral Oration for Crocodiles*, and you *Snake Catcher's Words*. I once wrote an article praising the emperor. So did you. You always compete with me. Now I am sent into exile and you keep me company. Are we fated always to be together?' "

After a while Liu Mengmei calmed down and said gently, "Brother Han, let's forget the past. But why are we treated coldly by the court? My ancestor once wrote an article called 'Begging for Skills.' So far I haven't gained any skills for my career. Your ancestor once wrote an article 'Sending Away Poverty' and you haven't rid yourself of poverty yet. Both of us have had bad luck."

Moved, Han Zicai said, "What you say is true. You studied very hard all of those years and spent your family property on books but your knowledge is not worth a penny. However Lu Jia was also a Confucian scholar. When Emperor Gao Zu of the Han Dynasty (206 B.C.-220 A.D.) sent him here to make Zhao Tuo Prince Nanyue, Zhao Tuo held him in great esteem and gave him lots of gold. After he returned to the court, he was promoted to Grand Master."

Both young men envied Lu Jia very much. Han Zicai said, "Lu Jia was a scholar who had good luck. Emperor Gao Zu of the Han Dynasty had a strong dislike of scholars. Whenever a Confucian scholar came to see him, he would take the scholar's scarf and urinate on it. One day when Lu Jia went to see the emperor in a robe and scholar's scarf, Emperor Gao Zu could not help saying, 'Another scholar is sending his scarf for me to pee on.' Lu Jia pretended not to hear him and continued walking towards the emperor. The emperor looked at him and shouted, 'I won the country by military force. I don't need any scholars like you.' Instead of becoming angry, Lu Jia, a very capable and brave man, said, 'Your Majesty, you can win the country with your skills on horseback. However can you administer the country with the same skills?' Emperor Gao Zu, who had not expected Lu Jia to reply, was rendered speechless. After a pause, he smiled and said, 'All right, that sounds reasonable. If you have any good articles, please read them out to me.' Lu Jia was happy to oblige and

《进平淮西碑》歌颂朝廷时,你也不放过,又进个平淮西的雅。我有一篇,你就有一篇,一篇都不放过我。就是如今贬职流放烟瘴地方,也同时而行。这是时乎,运乎,命乎!'"

柳梦梅说到这里,气愤渐平,语气平和了:"韩兄,过去的事不提了。现今以我和你的遭遇来看,难道应该受这般寒苦冷落!为什么我公公写了一篇《乞巧文》,到我二十代元孙,也不曾乞得一点儿巧来?便是你公公下决心写了篇《送穷文》,到你老兄二十几辈的人了,也还不曾将穷送走!算来算去,总是时运不好。"

韩子才倒被他这番话说动了,附和地说:"是呀,柳兄,你耗尽家财,努力攻读,哪曾知道学成之日学问又不值钱。你看陆贾,也只是儒生。当时汉高祖派他来这里封赵佗为南越王,赵佗王那么尊敬他,赏他多少黄金,回朝以后,又升了官,被封为大中大夫。"

说到陆贾,更令他们歆羡不已:"陆贾这个儒生真是好时运。当时汉高祖十分讨厌读书人,有儒生来求见的,他都要将儒生带的头巾取来溺尿。可是这个陆贾,居然带了儒巾,穿着大摆长袍去见汉高祖。那汉高祖见了,连忙呼道:'又来了一个尿壶!'陆贾装作未曾听见,继续向前走来,汉高祖十分不耐烦,迎着脸骂道:'你老子我靠马上功夫得天下,哪里用得到你的诗书?'那陆贾十分有能耐,修养极好,毫不生气,也不应他这话,只回了一句:'皇上靠马上功夫得天下,能以马上功夫治天下么?'汉高祖倒未曾想到陆贾有此一问,愣了一会儿,回过神来,作出一副笑容,对他说:'好呀,算你说的有理。你有什么高招,有什么文章,念出来与寡人听听。'这么一来,陆贾心中有了底,不慌不忙地从衣袖中掏出一卷文章来,那是他平日熬夜纂集的《新语》十三篇,舒张开来,抬高声音,不急不忙地念起来。汉高祖才听了一篇,就觉得到底不同凡响,很有见解,因而龙颜大喜。陆贾念完一篇,汉高祖喝采一篇。等

75

calmly took a roll of 13 articles from his sleeve. He had written them with painstaking effort and opened and read them in a loud voice. The emperor was very pleased as the articles had many new ideas and he thought them extraordinary. The emperor praised him at the end of the first article, but, after Lu Jia had finished reading all of them, Emperor Gao Zu appointed him a marquis. Scholar Lu did well that day. All the officials and officers at the court were most delighted that the emperor had found a gifted scholar."

Liu Mengmei knew the story and was very depressed by Han Zicai's description of how Lu Jia read his articles to the emperor. He said, "Oh, I'm so unlucky. I've also written many articles, but I have no one to read to."

"Brother Liu, how do you make a living?" Han Zicai asked.

"I have no choice other than to depend on my gardener, the grandson of Hunchback Guo."

Liu Mengmei was at the end of his tether and Han Zicai suggested that he ought to visit some well-known people who might give him a chance.

"Brother Han, don't you know that it's very hard to find someone who is willing to help me."

"Brother Liu, Mr. Miao is an imperial envoy in charge of treasures. He is experienced and prudent, and always ready to help others. I have been told that his term of office will end this coming autumn, and he will hold the Treasure Exhibition Assembly at the Duobao (Numerous Treasure) Temple in Xiangshanao. Why don't you go there in autumn to meet him?" Han Zicai suggested this with great sincerity.

Liu Mengmei was persuaded and said, "Thank you very much for your advice. I'll go there and meet him." He took his leave.

After Liu Mengmei had returned home, he thought to himself, "As a result of my hard study in the past 10 or so years I'm now the most outstanding scholar in Guangzhou, but my knowledge has not earned me any rewards and I still live in a vegetable garden relying on my gardener. I am ashamed of myself." The more he thought about it, the more sensible Han Zicai's suggestion seemed. He was determined to walk out of his house and hew out his own path. He hoped that he would be fortunate.

He began preparing and one day called in his gardener, the grandson of Hunchback Guo, saying that he wished to speak to him.

他全部念完后，汉高祖立刻封他为关内侯。那一天陆贾好不风光！不要说汉高祖高兴异常，就是朝中的两班文武，都欢呼万岁得人！”

陆贾的风光，柳梦梅不是不知道，此刻听见韩子才绘声绘影的一番渲染，心中更不是滋味，讷讷地说道："唉，真倒运。我写的文章连篇累牍，可就是无人赏识！"

"再问柳兄，你近来何以为生？"韩子才试探地问道。

柳梦梅觉得韩子才此问，似有所建议，乃如实答道："无可奈何，仍靠园丁郭驼供食。"

韩子才见他已到了山穷水尽的地步，就大胆建议说："依小弟看来，不如去拜求一些有地位的人，或许可以得到引进。"

"韩兄，你不知道，如今肯帮人忙的人可不多哩。"这倒是实情。

"柳兄可知道，有个钦差大人识宝使臣郎中苗老先生，是个老成持重、乐于助人的人。听说到秋天，他的任期已满，照惯例回京之前要在香山嶴的多宝寺中赛宝。到那时，柳兄去走一趟，如何？"

柳梦梅知道韩子才出自真心，也就坦诚地表示同意："谢谢韩兄指点，届时必当前往。"两人就此别过。

柳梦梅被韩子才一席话说动了心，回来之后日思夜想。想想自己在广州秀才群中也是数一数二的人物，是全靠自己严寒酷暑一味苦读换来的。可是这份荣耀并未带给自己富裕的生活，如今仍然藏身在菜园中，依赖仆人驼孙种树为生，不免羞愧惶恐。越想越觉得韩子才的话不无道理，还是去外地他乡，闯闯运气，兴许能有个机遇也未可知。

拿定主意后，他便稍做安排，叫来驼孙，吩咐道："园公，我与你商量一事。"

"What is it?"

" I'm over 20 years old without any hope of gaining fame or fortune. You work very hard to support me all the year round and both of us live a poor life eating simple food every day. Though young, I already know how inconstant human relationships are, and after careful consideration I have decided that I should not waste my youth carrying firewood and water every day. I'll have much to do...."

The gardener interrupted him saying, "Young Master, although I am not a man of great ability, I've done my best."

"I am not blaming you. I am going to give you all of the fruit garden."

The grandson of Hunchback Guo was very upset and said, "Then where will you make your living?"

"There's an old saying, 'Eating three meals a day without toiling at home is not as good as making a living outside it,' " Liu Mengmei said.

"But, Young Master, it's not a good idea for you to make a living somewhere else. I think you'd better concentrate on your studies and try to pass the imperial examination at the provincial level. Then you'll bring honor to your ancestors." The gardener tried to advise him, but Liu Mengmei had made up his mind, and said bluntly, "Please don't stop me!"

Left with no choice, the gardener began to pack for him and before Liu Mengmei went he asked him many times to return after he had gained fame and fortune. The gardener would be waiting there for him.

Liu Mengmei started his journey with a bundle wrapped in cloth on his back.

Imperial Envoy Miao Shunbin's term of office had expired. Before leaving for the capital to make a report to the emperor he intended holding the Treasure Exhibition Assembly at the Duobao Temple.

Located in Xiangshanao, Guangzhou, the Duobao Temple had been built from funds raised by foreign business people to welcome the treasure-collecting official who had been sent by the court. The temple had a bishop and joss sticks and candles burned every day. Before the Treasure Exhibition Assembly, the bishop, who had received notice from the imperial envoy, made various preparations. Early on the morning of the opening ceremony, he made another tour of the temple to see if everything was ready. Then he walked out of the temple to greet the imperial envoy.

Mr. Miao Shunbin soon appeared, climbing the flight of stone steps

"什么事？"

"想我已过了二十岁，苦读到今天，也没个发迹之期。一直靠你种树供养，吃尽了咸菜黄饭，尝遍了人间炎凉。思前想后，前路正长，我不能老是郁郁不乐地在这儿搬柴运水，消耗年华……"

驼孙不待他说完，便惶恐不安地说道："公子，我的能耐有限，但我已尽力而为了。"

"谁怨你？找你来商量，就是想把这园中果树都归属给你。"

"那，那你去何处求生？"

"俗话说得好，'坐食三餐，不如走空一棍。'"柳梦梅打起哑谜来。

"什么？什么叫做'一棍'？"

"呀，就是'打秋风'的混名啊！"

"咳，公子，你费工夫到他乡外地，撞府闯州去'打秋风'有啥好处？不如守依本分考科举，求得春风及第不好？"驼孙不以为然地劝说。可是柳梦梅主意已决，也不再解释，直截了当地告诉驼孙："你休得阻我！"

驼孙见劝阻无效，便为他准备了一些衣物，叮嘱他发迹之后一定要回来，他在此专等公子衣锦还乡。

柳梦梅背了一个布包袱就上路去了。

且说韩子才向他提到的钦差大人识宝使臣苗舜宾目今三年任期已满，回京复命之前，先要办一个赛宝大会。大会在多宝寺举行。

多宝寺位于广州府香山岙，是洋商集资建造的，用来迎接朝廷委派的收宝官员。平常香火依旧，也有住持。赛宝之前，住持已接到识宝大臣属下干办人员的通知，按照常例做好各项准备工作。开幕那天，他再次巡视一番，看看有什么不到之处。一切就绪后，就去山门外迎接识宝大臣。

to the temple followed by an interpreter, a retinue and many foreigners. The bishop went to him and fell on his knees. Then he got up and led Mr. Miao to the main hall. Everything was ready and Mr. Miao smiled with satisfaction. After he had taken a seat, he allowed the foreign merchants to show their treasures. The foreigners vied with one another to guide the imperial envoy to their sandalwood shelves on which rare treasures were placed.

Mr. Miao walked slowly by the shelves examining them with great interest. There were so many rare treasures that Mr. Miao, an expert judge, was full of praise and said, "All the rare treasures of the world are gathered here. The Duobao Temple deserves the reputation that it enjoys." Soon Mr. Miao came to the statue of Avalokitesvara. He asked the bishop to burn some joss sticks for him and standing in front of the statue he bowed deeply several times praying that Avalokitesvara would bless and protect the coastal areas and territorial seas and that foreign merchants would keep coming to China to present their treasures.

When Mr. Miao looked back, he saw that many merchants from the West and Arabia were looking at him intently and he was moved. He asked the bishop to pray for the foreign merchants in front of the Buddha and the bishop, who was good at singing praises and blessings, spontaneously recited:

The sea holds numerous treasures,
But boats will meet storms at sea.
Merchants who bring precious treasures with them
Are afraid of traveling on the sea.

Then the bishop turned to the foreign merchants and said, "Gentlemen, if you encounter a storm at sea, you will be safe from danger only by repeating over and over again, 'My infinitely merciful Avalokitesvara.' Be sure to remember this!"

When the Treasure Exhibition Assembly was almost over, Liu Mengmei arrived at the gate of the temple. He was determined to meet the imperial envoy and hoped to persuade him to help him in his official career. Though the guards in front of the temple stopped him, he insisted that they report his coming to the imperial envoy. He said to one of them, "Brother, could you please inform the imperial envoy that Liu Mengmei, a student of the Academy of Guangzhou, asks to see the treasures."

不一会儿,苗舜宾大人在翻译、随从、洋商的簇拥下登上石阶走进山门。住持趋步向前,拜倒在地,起身后紧跟在苗大人身旁,一面指引,穿堂入殿;一面禀报,诸事俱备。苗大人十分满意,落座后即吩咐洋商献宝,众多洋商早有安排,听得钦差大人此话,争先恐后引导他鉴赏自家所献的奇珍异宝。

苗大人依次在陈列宝物的檀架前观赏。见所未见、闻所未闻的各种宝贝,连一向识得宝物的他也看得眼花缭乱,赞不绝口地说:"真是天下奇宝啊!一齐汇集于此,多宝寺名不虚传矣!"边赞叹边观看,不觉走到正殿观音菩萨像前,苗大人吩咐住持上香,然后他深深拜了几拜,祝愿菩萨保佑海疆无事,让海外洋商不断前来献宝。

苗大人拜毕,回顾身边那些来自西洋的商人和来自阿拉伯的商人,见他们个个都以企求的眼光热切地注视自己,于是吩咐住持替这些洋商在菩萨面前祝赞一番。住持在此寺多年,对于颂赞祝福之事,可谓驾轻就熟,听得苗大人吩咐,脱口念出赞词:

"大海宝藏多,船舫遇风波。

商人持重宝,险路怕经过。"

念毕,又对周围的洋商告诫道:"诸位,若是海上遇到风暴,你们只要及时口念我佛观音,立时就能解脱危难,切记!切记!"

正当祭宝大会行将结束之际,柳梦梅恰好赶到山门处,想拜见钦差大臣,以自己的三寸不烂之舌,说动大臣,求得他的帮助,图个上进机缘。因此,一进山门,不顾家丁阻挠,向随从高声求道:"大哥,烦你通报一声,广州府学生员柳梦梅,特地前来求看宝物。"

随从知道苗大人平素对读书人十分礼遇,听得"府学生员"身份,怜惜之情油然而生,大开方便之门,立刻向钦差通报。苗大人

The guard knew that Mr. Miao was very fond of scholars and when he heard that Liu Mengmei was a student of the Academy of Guangzhou, he was more favorably disposed and went inside to report. Mr. Miao heard that the scholar wanted to come in to appreciate the treasures and automatically said, "These treasures belong to the court. All and sundry are not allowed to see them." After a while he changed his mind and said that since it was a scholar he could make an exception.

Liu Mengmei walked in and bowed to Mr. Miao and before he had had time to say anything Mr. Miao asked him why he had come to the assembly that day.

"My name is Liu Mengmei. I am a poor scholar. I am bored to death at home. When I learned that Your Highness was holding the Treasure Exhibition Assembly here, I made a special trip to see the treasures and enrich my knowledge," Liu Mengmei replied.

"If that is so, you may start appreciating the treasures." Mr. Miao stood up and led Liu Mengmei to the shelves. Liu Mengmei was most surprised.

"I know something about pearls and jade but compared with you I'm only a pupil. What are the names of the treasures on the shelves? You're experienced and knowledgeable, could you please tell me about them?" Liu Mengmei was courteous and very modest.

Mr. Miao, who was immensely proud, said, "This is a magic grit. That is the Sea-Boiling ruby. Over there is the cat's eye, and the emerald...." Liu Mengmei praised his knowledge and after a tour of the exhibition hall, Mr. Miao allowed him to sit down and his attendant served tea.

Liu Mengmei sat with ease and confidence and after sipping tea, he thanked Mr. Miao. "If I had not come today how else could I feast my eyes on so many treasures? I'm very grateful to Your Highness for giving me such an opportunity."

Mr. Miao replied courteously. Realizing that the imperial envoy was not arrogant and rude Liu Mengmei said, "May I ask Your Highness from how far away these treasures came?"

"It all depends. The farthest is 15,000 kilometers and the nearest is over 5,000 kilometers."

"Did they fly or walk here?"

Mr. Miao could not help laughing at such a ridiculous question, but replied earnestly, "How could they fly or walk here? The court bought

乍闻之下，脱口而出："这些宝物都是朝廷专有，哪容闲杂人员任意观看！"继而一想，又吩咐随从说："既然来的是个读书人，就让他来见识见识吧。"

柳梦梅因此得以面见钦差大臣，拜揖行礼方罢，苗大人先行开口问道："敢问公子为什么事赶到此处？"

"小生柳梦梅，生计艰难无告，百无聊赖。听见老大人在此赛宝，特来请求观看，以增识见。"

"既然如此，我又何必秘不示人，就请公子随意观赏。"说罢，苗大人站起身来，亲自导引，这倒也出乎柳梦梅意料之外。

"明珠美玉，小生也识得一些。但哪能与老大人相比？架上有一些宝物，不知何名？老大人见多识广，烦请大人一一指教。"柳梦梅一副谦恭礼敬的神态。

苗大人颇为得意，神采飞扬地告诉柳梦梅：这是星汉神砂，那是煮海金丹，那是猫儿眼，这是祖母绿……钦差说一句，柳梦梅赞一声，好一会儿工夫才观赏完毕，彼此落座，苗大人吩咐家丁给柳梦梅上茶。

柳梦梅倒也大大方方地与苗钦差分宾主坐下，呷了一口茶，对苗大人再次表示感谢："小生今日不游大方之门，怎能见到这些宝物？真要谢谢苗大人，让小生亲眼目睹大场面。"

苗大人出自礼貌，也略略谦逊几句。柳梦梅观察这位钦差大人倒也不是倨傲无礼的官员，乃趁机游说："禀问老大人，这些宝物从海外运来此地，有多远路程？"

"远的三万里，近的至少也有一万多里程。"

"这样远的路途，宝物是飞来的，还是走来的？"

苗大人听到柳梦梅问出这样的问题，觉得非常荒唐，不禁哑然失笑，但仍然诚恳地告诉他："哪有飞来、走来的道理！这些宝物

some at a high price, and others were contributed to the court by foreign merchants."

Liu Mengmei sighed and said, "Your Highness, these lifeless treasures can come from afar without feet. I am a student of the Academy of Guangzhou and have much knowledge. It is only 1,500 kilometers from Guangzhou to the capital, but no one is willing to buy me, which means that though I have feet, I can't walk. I cannot help wondering whether the official at the Maritime Trade Commissioner in charge of foreign trade can really find treasures for the court."

Mr. Miao, who didn't understand the meaning of Liu Mengmei's words, said, "You don't suspect that these treasures are false?"

"No, they are real, but they cannot be eaten when we are hungry, and they cannot be used as clothes when we feel cold. What's their use?"

"Then, what, in your eyes, are real treasures?" Liu Mengmei expected this question and replied loftily, "I would not dare cheat Your Highness. If you want to see a real treasure, I am one of the world's rarely seen treasures."

Mr. Miao thought that Liu Mengmei was boastful and sneered at him. "I'm afraid that the court has too many rare treasures like you."

"Please don't tease me, Mr. Miao. A rare treasure like me can even win the championship at the Lintong Treasure Competition held by Lord Mu of the Qin Dynasty (221-206 B.C.)."

Realizing that Liu Mengmei was serious, unlike some poor scholars who cheated others for their food and drink, Mr. Miao assumed a benevolent look and said, "According to what you say, treasures like you can only be presented to the emperor. Is that right?"

Liu Mengmei knew that he must grasp this critical moment if Mr. Miao was going to help him. He said, "I can say to Your Highness, if it's hard for poor scholars like me to meet local officials, how dare I dream of meeting the emperor?"

Mr. Miao told him the truth. "There's an old saying, 'The lackeys are even more difficult to deal with.' It will not be very difficult to see the emperor."

Liu Mengmei then gave an account of his situation. "The capital is 1,500 kilometers from here. I have no way of finding money for the journey."

"It's easy. In ancient times the gentry often gave gold to heroes. I can give the regular silver I draw from the government to pay your expenses

都是朝廷重价求购,洋商方持之以来向朝廷贡献的!"

柳梦梅故作长叹道:"老大人,其实这些宝物并无知觉,远在三万里之外,还能无足而至——想我柳梦梅,虽是府学生员,却满腹奇才,到京城临安也不过三千里之近,倒无人收购,可谓有脚不能飞了!我不能不怀疑那些管理海外贸易的市舶司的官员,能否为朝廷购得真正的宝物!"

苗大人一时尚弄不清柳梦梅这话的真正含义,问道:"你难道怀疑这些宝物是假的?"

"这倒不是。老大人,这些宝物便是真货,饥时不可用来吃,寒时不可用来穿,又有什么实际用场!"

"那么,依公子说,什么东西才是真正的宝物呢?"柳梦梅正等着钦差大人这一问话,气宇轩昂地回答道:"不敢欺诳老大人,若说真宝,小生倒是个真正的罕见于世的现世宝!"

苗大人初闻此话,觉得这个柳梦梅也未免大言不惭了,不无讥讽地说道:"只怕朝廷之上,像这样的现世宝也太多了!"

"老大人不要取笑。像我这样的现世宝,即使在秦穆公举办的临潼斗宝会上也可夺魁。"

苗大人眼见这个柳梦梅口气硬朗,倒不像那些骗吃骗喝的穷儒,便又和颜悦色地问道:"照这样说,你这等宝物只好献给朝廷了?"

柳梦梅知道话说到这一地步,已到紧要关头,乃和盘托出自己的打算:"禀告老大人,一介寒儒,连伺候地方官府还不能,如何能见到皇上?"

"你这就不知行情了,俗话说'阎王好见,小鬼难当'——倒是圣上好见。"苗大人倒也不打官腔,以实情相告。

柳梦梅也以实情相求:"只是到京城三千里,一路盘缠无处可求。"

on the way to the capital." Mr. Miao was very generous.

Overjoyed, Liu Mengmei bowed low to Mr. Miao and told him that as he had no parents or wife to care for, he could leave for the capital immediately. He stood up and took his leave. Mr. Miao asked his servant to take out some silver to give to him and offered him a cup of wine, wished him a good trip and hoped that he would achieve his desires.

Before Liu Mengmei accepted the wine cup, he said, "Mr. Miao, I'm still worried. Although the emperor is wise, high-ranking officials around him will not appreciate my talents."

Mr. Miao comforted him. "Don't worry, there are people around the emperor who can tell good from bad and know what's what. Please drink this cup of wine and I hope that your talents will be useful to the imperial court."

Liu Mengmei went home, picked up some clothes, packed them and left Guangzhou holding an umbrella. He first took a boat and then crossed Mount Meiling on foot.

"这倒不是什么难事。古人以黄金赠壮士,我就将衙门分给的一份常例银子送你做盘缠。"苗大人十分慷慨地解囊相助。

柳梦梅大喜过望,深深拜谢,并且表示自己也无父母妻子牵累,说行就行,当即辞别。苗大人也爽快,吩咐随从取来银两赠作路费,又请左右斟上酒来,为柳梦梅送行,并祝他一路顺风,如愿以偿。

"大人,我有些担心,皇上有眼,而左右大臣却没有波斯人那样识宝的眼力。"柳梦梅临行之际,未免有些忐忑不安。

苗大人安慰他说:"你也不必担心,真假从来是分明的,识货的人总能区别。请饮下这杯酒,祝愿你胸中的宝物能货与帝王家!"

柳梦梅回到住处,收拾了几件换洗衣服,打了一个包袱,又携了一把雨伞,就此上路。先搭便船离开五羊城广州,然后舍舟登岸,一路步行过了梅岭。

CHAPTER SEVEN

Liu Mengmei Falls Ill

Liu Mengmei had lived south of Mount Meiling for many years and had never traveled far. He did not know that the weather north of Mount Meiling was quite different from that of the south. To the south it was like spring all the year round and there was no snow in the winter; the north had distinct seasonal changes with rain and snow in winter. When Liu Mengmei took his leave from Imperial Envoy Miao at Xiangshanao, it was autumn and after he arrived north of Mount Meiling he encountered cold winter weather and a strong wind from the north.

Liu Mengmei was eager to start his official career and traveled from dawn to dusk often braving wind and rain. Before he knew it he had caught a cold and shivered all over. He had not realized how difficult a long journey was and wished that he was at home south of Mount Meiling. But when he thought of his hard-earned funds, he was determined to go ahead. Fortunately the city of Nan'an was not far away.

The strong wind broke his umbrella, his old scarf was almost blown away and snow fell in large flakes. Shivering all over Liu Mengmei struggled along the rough and bumpy snow-covered paths between the fields. Looking around he saw that there were no houses nearby for him to stay the night. He had to walk towards the city, braving heavy snow.

The snow blotted out the sky and covered the earth. Liu Mengmei took each step with great care. Soon he came to a river, over which there was a broken bridge. How could he cross it? He was at the end of his tether and walked back and forth carefully surveying the broken bridge. Finally he decided that he could cross the river with the help of a willow tree by the bridge. The challenge of crossing the river preoccupied him and he had not expected the surface of the bridge to be so slippery. He fell from the bridge into the river crying "Help! Help!" at the top of his voice.

第七章
病困旅途

　　柳梦梅长期住在梅岭之南,很少出门远行,哪知梅岭南北,气候大不一样,岭南四季如春,冬季不见雨雪;岭北却四季不同,冬季雨雪交加。柳梦梅在香山嶴告别苗大人时正值秋季,涉水登山,一路行来,过了梅岭已是严冬,北风凛冽。

　　柳梦梅一心想着功名,起早带晚地赶路,不免冒风冲寒,未曾防备,路上感了寒疾,四肢发冷,满脸病容。此际方知世上人间行路难,恨不能回到岭南,但继而一想好不容易谋得资助,怎能舍此难得的机遇扫兴回乡?眼见南安城在望,便勉力挣扎前行。

　　旷野风大,把一柄破伞吹得呼呼作响,一顶旧头巾也吹得歪倒一旁;鹅毛大雪扑面而来,湿透单薄衣裳,全身作寒。田野小路原就坎坷不平,又积满冰雪,更是滑溜难行。放眼四望,周围白茫茫一片,少有人家,无处借宿,只得冲风冒雪向城里赶去。

　　那满天风雪,已是铺天盖地。他寻路而去,前行不久,突然路断,原来是被一条小河隔开,河面上虽有小桥一架,却已断裂,怎能过渡?柳梦梅不禁犯难。前看看后觑觑,左瞧瞧右窥窥,围着小桥绕行几遍,总算见到断桥之旁有一株柳树,或许可以攀沿而过。说不得安全不安全了,柳梦梅只能拼命过桥了。岂知脚底冰凌,踩着即滑,一个不当心,柳梦梅滑跌在冰雪之中,不禁呼叫:"哎呀!"

Usually there would have been no one around in such an open area and on such a bad day. Maybe he was not destined to die for his shout was heard by a man. It was none other than Chen Zuiliang, who used to be the tutor of Du Liniang, daughter of Prefect Du.

As it turned out, after Du Liniang died and Prefect Du Bao had been transferred to north China, Chen Zuiliang received no regular income and, although he was in charge of one hectare of land, he often ran short of money. When he learned that a village school was looking for a teacher, he rode a donkey and braved heavy snow to apply for the job. Suddenly he heard a voice from the river and said to himself, "Where is the voice coming from in such a bad weather?" He got off the donkey and near the broken bridge found a man struggling in the river.

"Help! Help!" Liu Mengmei caught sight of him and shouted at the top of his voice.

"Who are you? How did you fall into the river?" Chen Zuiliang asked.

"I'm a scholar."

On hearing that it was a scholar Chen Zuiliang was determined to save him and said, "As you're a scholar, let me help you." He walked with great care towards the end of the bridge but he was over 60 and he had great difficulty helping Liu Mengmei out of the water. He stretched out his hand and was just about to grasp Liu's hand when he fell on the ground himself. Fortunately Liu Mengmei was near the shore and finally escaped from the river helped by Chen Zuiliang.

When Liu Mengmei was out of danger, Chen Zuiliang asked him where he was from.

"I'm from Guangzhou."

"Where are you going?"

"To the capital, Lin'an."

"What for?"

"To present a treasure."

"What treasure?"

"I am a rare treasure. I'm braving wind and snow to take a trip to the capital, seeking an opportunity." After Liu Mengmei had been unexpectedly rescued from a desperate situation, he began to boast.

Chen Zuiliang had his doubts and said, "You must be very sure that you'll pass the imperial examination or you would not hurry on such a journey in the freezing cold winter."

旷野风雪,本无人烟,也许是柳梦梅命不该绝,他的呼叫声居然被刚刚走到附近的一个行人听见。这个人不是别人,就是曾任南安府杜宝太守府中西席的陈最良。

原来自从学生杜丽娘病逝、杜宝太守升迁北调以后,陈最良虽然管着两顷祭田,但别无收入,手头也不宽绰,总想找一个进财之道。前日听说附近有一村学,要请教馆先生,他为谋取这一教席,才在这天寒地冻时骑一头毛驴赶来的。偏偏柳梦梅求救的叫声让他听到。他不禁自言自语地说:"这鬼天气,哪里来的人声?"翻身下驴,在断桥附近张望,发现前面小河中陷落了一个人。

"救人呀,救人。"柳梦梅也看见了他,更是高声呼救。

陈最良走过去问道:"你是什么人,怎么在此失脚跌倒?"

"我是个读书人。"所谓"斯文骨肉",陈最良被这"读书人"三字打动:"你若真是读书人,我却要扶你起来。"说罢,就一脚高一脚低地向桥塊摸着前去。他也是六十开外的人了,扶持这个柳梦梅并不容易,刚刚拽住柳梦梅的手,自己就滑跌一跤,两人滚在一处去了。幸亏他在岸上,柳梦梅在水边,你拽我爬地总算拉上岸来。

陈最良见人已救上岸,再无危险,又问道:"请问你从何处来?"

"我从广州来。"

"到何处去?"

"去临安。"

"你去京师临安有何公干?"

"去献宝呀?"

"你有何宝?"

"我本人就是现世宝。单身上路,冲雨雪,冒风寒,为的就是去京城一试。"柳梦梅绝处逢生,又信口卖弄起来。

陈最良不无疑惑地说道:"你大概有必定考中的把握,才受这

93

When Liu Mengmei realized that Chen Zuiliang doubted him he boasted, "To tell you the truth, I'm an extraordinarily learned man, like a white jade pillar supporting heaven or a purple-golden beam of the sea."

Chen Zuiliang burst out laughing and said, "Alas, heaven has no eyes. It has almost broken the pillar that supports it and the purple-golden beam!" Then he turned to Liu Mengmei and said with great concern, "I'm just kidding you. I know something about art of medicine and your hands are freezing which means that you are suffering from cold. The Plum Blossom Nunnery is not far from here and, if you go there with me, you could live there for the time being. You could continue your journey north after winter, what do you think?"

Liu Mengmei knew that he was too weak to continue his journey and happily accepted Chen Zuiliang's invitation. He thanked Chen Zuiliang. The pair stumbled on through the snow supporting each other.

After saving Liu Mengmei from the river, Chen Zuiliang took the young man to the Plum Blossom Nunnery and allowed him to live there. As time went by he gradually recovered under the careful medical treatment of Chen Zuiliang and soon had no difficulty getting about.

Before very long winter passed and spring arrived. One day when Liu Mengmei woke up, he was pleased to find the room full of sunshine. He had lain on the bed for a long time and now found it better to get up and move around. He jumped up and took up the bundle which he had thrown in the corner of the room many days ago. His winter clothes still had stains of rain and snow and he hung them up by the window to dry.

He was not in the mood to read books and pulled a chair over by the window and sat on it. The warm spring sunshine made him drowsy and he yawned again and again. He was bored but had no idea how pass the time. Just then Nun Shi, the head of the nunnery, visited him. "Young Master, how are you getting on these days?"

"Thank you very much for coming to see me. I'm much better now but I do feel very bored. Look, without having anything to do, I have to sit in the sun." Liu Mengmei usually had no one to talk to and was very happy to see Nun Shi. He said, "Aunt, the nunnery is not small. Does it have a garden or a pavilion? I would like to spend some time in it."

There was a pause, then Nun Shi replied, "There is a garden at the rear. However, as the pavilions and towers have not been renovated for years, most of them have collapsed. The flowers, trees and grass grow thickly but you

番辛苦的罗。"

柳梦梅见他有几分不信，又夸口说："不瞒你说，小生实怀抱绝学，真可谓擎天白玉柱、架海紫金梁。"

陈最良放声笑道："啊呀呀，天也不长眼，怎么就冻折了擎天柱，扑倒了紫金梁？"笑了一阵，又关切地说："说笑归说笑——老夫颇通医术。摸摸你的手，冰凉彻骨，显然是风寒所侵，前面不远处有座梅花观，待老夫与你前去，你就暂时住下调理调理，且过了残冬再北行，你看如何？"

柳梦梅也知道自己的病体不宜再远行，既然得到陈最良邀请，哪有不允之理？立即表示同意，并致谢意。两人相伴，踏着积雪，高一步低一步地向梅花观走去。

柳梦梅被陈最良救起带回梅花观中养病多时，又经过陈最良尽心调治，渐渐痊愈，行动也自如起来。

不觉冬去春来，久困思动，今日醒来，阳光照屋，精神为之一振，扔在房角的包袱一直未曾打开，趁天气晴朗，一把拎了过来，抖出冬天换下的衣衫，上面尚有点点雨渍雪痕，便将它摊在窗前晒起。

晒好衣衫，便拉过一张靠椅，当窗而坐。春阳温和，坐了一会儿，春困上来，呵欠连天，不知如何打发这无聊的日子。正当此时，观主石道姑到院中来探视他了："公子，近来安稳么？"

"谢谢姑姑，近来病情倒是好转不少，只是天长日久，闷得慌。你看，我无事可干，只得坐在这里晒太阳。"柳梦梅难得有谈话机会，见了石道姑也就尽情诉说了："喂，姑姑这座梅花观倒不小，难道没有些园亭么？如果有几座亭台，也好消遣消遣。"

石道姑沉吟了一会儿，答道："后面倒有一座花园，亭台楼阁长久无人修葺，大半倒塌了，不过花草树木倒还郁郁葱葱。你去散

could go there to relieve boredom. But please don't feel sad."

"How could I feel sad walking in a garden?" Liu Mengmei did not understand.

After sighing deeply, Nun Shi said, "I only made a casual remark. Please don't take it seriously. Go there and enjoy yourself. Walk along the painted corridor in the west and you'll see a bamboo gate about 100 paces in front of you. It is the gate to the garden which is about 1.5 kilometers in circumference. You can spend a whole day there. I'm sorry that today I'm too busy to go with you."

Liu Mengmei dismissed from his mind what Nun Shi's had first said and was eager to find a diversion. He said happily, "As there is a garden, I'm going there right away." He said good-bye to Nun Shi and headed for the garden along the painted corridor.

Soon he came to a bamboo door surrounded by bushy trees; one part of the door lay on the ground. He pushed the door open and entered. "Oh! What a huge garden!" He was delighted. Preoccupied by the scenery, he did not notice green moss beneath his feet and slipped and fell. The garden, he thought, must have been neglected for quite a long time.

Walking along a narrow path, he came to another bamboo door which was bolted. He reached out, took off the bolt and walked in, and when he saw the groves of bamboo, small lake, wild flowers in full bloom and thick grass, he became suspicious. There was only one nun at the Plum Blossom Nunnery, how could such a small place have such a large back garden? The more he thought about it, the more he wondered.

However he wanted to see all of the garden and stopped thinking about it. Following a path he went deep into the garden and found pavilions by the water, all of them collapsed, a pleasure boat by a leaning pavilion and a swing hanging in the air. What a scene of decay he thought. There had been no war recently, why was it so desolate? Was there a sad story connected to it?

As he could find no answer to his questions, he simply gave up and started to enjoy the scenery. Soon after turning several corners he came to a rockery made of Taihu rocks. It was oddly shaped but elegant and he liked it so much that he walked round it again and again, examining it with great care. Finally he found a cave and without hesitating entered. One of his feet kicked something hard and he looked down to see a sandalwood box on the ground. He bent down, one hand holding a stone, and picked it up. When he opened it, he was surprised to find a portrait of

散心是可以的,但不要伤心。"

柳梦梅不免有些诧异:"去花园闲走走,怎会伤心?"

石道姑长叹一声,口不应心地说:"这么说说罢了。你自个儿去游赏便了。从西边画廊沿着这粉墙出去,不过百步,便是篱门,池馆园林,约在三里范围,尽够你整天玩赏的。我就不陪你去了。"

柳梦梅也不管石道姑的弦外之音,急于解闷,高兴地说道:"既然有个后花园,我立刻就去。"说罢,与石道姑拱手告辞,径自沿着画廊而去。

行不多时,果真见到两扇篱门,被一片葱翠环绕,可惜倒了一扇,推门而入,另有一番景象:"哟,好大的一个花园。"柳梦梅只管观赏景致,也不顾脚底苍苔,"滑擦"一声跌倒在地,这园林实在久无人迹了。

沿小径转去,又是一道双扇的篱门,门却闩着,柳梦梅伸手取下门闩,信步而入,只见一片竹林,一湾流水,野花砌地,荒草连天。见到这种境况,柳梦梅方才起了一些疑心:这桩事儿有些怪异,梅花观中不过一个老道姑,怎么建这么大一座花园?实在令人不解。

不过,柳梦梅此刻急于游赏,也无心深究。他沿着花间小路向园中深处走去。只见几座水阁散在园中,可惜都已倒败,不能登临;小阁边泊着一艘游船,船身倾斜,绘采剥落;草地上悬挂的一架秋千,索儿无力地垂着……近来又没有兵火发生,怎么这般衰败?难道园中发生过什么伤心事吗?

柳梦梅解不开这个谜底,索性不去管它,依旧自行寻乐,随处观赏。左转右弯地走到一座湖山石前,这座太湖石叠成的假山,倒也具有皱、秀、瘦、透的特色,十分难得。他不禁停下脚步,仔细鉴赏。一会儿沿着湖山石绕行,一会儿探身进入假山洞中。脚尖忽然

Avalokitesvara and could not help shouting, "Wonderful! Wonderful! The portrait is so magnificent. I'll take it to my room, hang it up and worship it every day." He left the garden in high spirits and headed for his room where he put the sandalwood box on the table, planning to burn joss sticks and pay genuine homage to it.

Nun Shi knew that Liu Mengmei had come back from the garden when she heard a sound in his room. She had nothing to do and had returned to Liu Mengmei's room; she liked talking to the young scholar and said, "Young Master Liu, are you back?"

"Yes, I am back. Aunt, you said I would feel sad if I visited the garden. Could you please tell me which place would make me happy?" After exchanging casual remarks, Nun Shi took her leave and Liu Mengmei went to bed.

It drizzled for more than 10 days after Liu Mengmei visited the Back Garden. As soon as it cleared up, he opened the sandalwood box, carefully unfolded the portrait and looked at it again and again. He thought that he was very lucky. It was said that Avalokitesvara used to be on Mount Putuo in Zhejiang Province. People in Guangzhou seldom had a chance to see her, but he, a man living to the south of Mount Meiling, had obtained a portrait of her. It was a good omen. Also, the portrait had been painted with great care and was extraordinarily beautiful.

He could not keep his eyes off it and examined it carefully. Finally he spotted something that was not right; Avalokitesvara should have had natural feet while the beauty had three-inch feet deformed by foot-binding. He started to doubt that it was a portrait of Avalokitesvara and then concluded that it was not.

He continued looking at it and found the woman's elegant shape was just like that of Chang'e, a goddess in the moon. "Since she is a goddess who has come down to the world, I should prostrate myself before her," he said to himself. He wished that he could be one of the goddess' lovers on the moon. He took a step back to view it at a distance and saw that it was not Chang'e. There were no auspicious clouds around her and the beauty leant on a willow tree rather than a sweet-scented osmanthus tree. (Legend has it that there were only sweet-scented osmanthus trees on the moon.)

She was neither Avalokitesvara nor Chang'e. Who was she then? Liu Mengmei was attracted by the girl and thought that there was nothing on earth to equal her beauty. Looking up he stared at the girl's face. Oh,

触到一样硬的东西，低头一看原来是个檀香匣。他一手扶着山石，俯身下去，一手拾起匣子，打开一看，原来是一幅观世音菩萨像。不禁呼道："好啊，好啊! 这幅观世音像，真太妙了。待我捧回房中，顶礼供养，也比埋在此处强。"说罢，他就喜孜孜地离开花园。回到房中，他小心翼翼地将檀香匣捧上案去，准备点上香火，虔诚礼拜。

石道姑听见客房中已有动静，知道柳梦梅回来了，信步走到客房门前，与书生闲话，石道姑问道："柳公子，回来了。"

"回来了。姑姑，你说游园不可伤心。你再替我找一个可以不伤心的地方游耍游耍。"彼此无话找话，闲话几句，石道姑别去，柳梦梅安歇。

柳梦梅游园以后，天公不作美，绵绵春雨，滴滴答答下了十余日。好不容易雨霁天晴，方将上次拾得的檀木匣子打开，将那幅观世音像轻轻展开，细细鉴赏。想来真是十分幸运，传说观世音原在浙江普陀，久居岭南的人居然得以一睹真容，真是难得的幸事! 何况，这一幅观世音像画得又十分好，无处不精妙。

柳梦梅一时倾倒在观世音像前，仔细端详，忽然看出破绽来了! 观世音本是一对天脚，画上怎的变成一副凌波小脚? 他不由得不怀疑起来，这是观世音么? 不像。

再一细看，画中的人又像是天上的嫦娥仙女——既然是仙女下凡，更该顶礼膜拜了。他真想问问嫦娥，折桂的人中有没有自己? 就这样发一会儿傻想，又看一会儿画像，又看出毛病来了。怎么嫦娥身下没有祥云烘托，她倚着的分明是柳树，并不是桂树。看来又不是嫦娥了。

不是观音，不是嫦娥，那么又是谁呢? 柳梦梅思忖着：这样的美女，人间怎能有? 他不由得盯着画上脸庞儿多看了几眼，一时惊

she looked familiar. "I must have met her before. But where have I seen her?" Liu Mengmei asked himself. "Was the portrait done by a master painter or by the beautiful girl herself?"

The beauty in the portrait was vivid and life-like. No painter in the world could create such a natural and wonderful painting. It must have been painted by the beauty herself. The girl must be extremely intelligent and a skilled artist.

After some thought, Liu Mengmei went closer to the portrait, examining it carefully. He was surprised to find that a four-line poem was written on it. It read:

Seen closely, she is an extraordinary beauty;
And seen at a distance, she is like a goddess.
One year she met a handsome young man from the moon,
By a weeping willow rather than a plum tree.

After reading the poem, Liu Mengmei was more surprised and thought, "How strange it is! The poem mentions willow and plum trees. The beauty leans on a willow tree holding a plum twig which are related to my own name. In addition, it seems that I have met her before. Is she really the girl who once appeared in my dream?"

The beauty in the portrait reminded him of his dream and he remembered the beauty saying, "Only if you meet me, will you have a happy marriage and gain fame and fortune." He said joyfully, "Are you the beauty? If it is true, good luck is not far away."

The more he looked at the portrait, the more he was attracted by the elegant beauty. Holding a plum twig the girl looked at him with tenderness and love. Liu Mengmei longed to hold the beauty's hands but it was only a daydream. He had no choice but to pick up a brush and write another poem on the portrait expressing his feelings.

The surpassing quality of this painting is natural;
The beauty in the picture must be a goddess.
If you would like to accompany a man from the moon,
You may find him by a willow or plum tree in spring.

After writing the poem on the painting, Liu Mengmei threw his brush aside and sat down.

愕起来:这面孔好熟悉！似曾相识,仿佛在什么地方见过。柳梦梅又自语道:这画儿是画工画的,还是美人自描的?

呀,这个美人像画得真是活色生香,这样的画像,是画工所不能绘出的,大概是这个聪明绝顶的美女自己能描善绘的。

柳梦梅沉思半晌,又走近画前,细细鉴赏,忽然看见画端有数行小字,原来是一首绝句,不觉念了出来:

近睹分明似俨然,

远观自在若飞仙。

他年得傍蟾宫客,

不在梅边在柳边。

念罢,柳梦梅越发惊异了:"奇怪,奇怪!诗中写的柳与梅,画像上又执梅倚柳,处处都与自己的名姓相连,而且春容好似见过。难道真就是梦中相遇的人儿?"

他模糊记得梦中一个大花园的梅树下,站着一个美人,美人对他说:"你遇到我才有姻缘,也才能发迹。"于是他高兴地说道:"美人,真的是你!今日既然相逢,我的好运必不远矣。"

柳梦梅看得越仔细,想得越深远。呀,她一枝青梅在手,逗得人春心蠢动。我与画儿相对,她是望梅止渴,我是画饼充饥,怎能得到这个美丽动人的少女呢?呀,不若先用她的诗韵,和作一首,也可略略抒发一己情怀。想罢,他提笔沉吟,随即挥笔:

丹青妙处却天然,

不是天仙即地仙。

欲傍蟾宫人近远,

恰些春在柳梅边。

写就,掷笔而坐。

继而柳梦梅又发奇想:"这个人儿真不平凡,既能绘画,又善

He thought to himself that the woman in the portrait was not only beautiful; she could paint pictures and compose poems. The more he thought about it, the keener he was to hold the beauty in his arms. He could not help saying to himself, "Beauty, beauty! Sister, sister! In your company from now on I shall lead a happy life and worship you day and night."

吟诗。"这越发增强了他渴望得之的心情,不禁对着画像高呼:"美人,美人! 姐姐,姐姐! 今后有你陪伴,我当早晚看之,拜之,叫之,赞之! "

CHAPTER EIGHT

Du Liniang Meets Liu Mengmei

It was close to the third anniversary of Du Liniang's death. Entrusted by Du Bao and his wife, Nun Shi of the Plum Blossom Nunnery was busy preparing for a rite to save her soul. An auspicious day had been chosen. On the day Nun Shi got up very early; a flag was hung outside the nunnery to call back her spirit and a yellow notice pasted to the wall. A sacrificial altar had been set up as well. When everything was ready, Nun Shi began the ritual. At the time two nuns were walking towards the nunnery, an older mistress and her younger disciple. The disciple said, "Mistress, shall we stay at the Plum Blossom Nunnery ahead of us?" The mistress, the head of the Biyun Nunnery in Shaoyang Prefecture, had been traveling round the country with her disciple. Seeing the flag and the yellow notice and smelling the fragrance of joss sticks, she happily accepted her disciple's suggestion.

When they came to the gate of the nunnery Nun Shi asked them, "Where are you from, nuns?"

The mistress smiled sweetly and said, "We are from Shaoyang Prefecture. Could we please spend the night at the nunnery?"

Nun Shi was pleased to take in the two nuns but the guest room was occupied by Liu Mengmei and she hesitated. "You are welcome to stay in our nunnery. However a young scholar lives in the eastern wing room. He is sick and has not recovered completely. You will have to live in the west wing room."

The mistress thanked her and pointing to the flag and the yellow notice asked, "Are you holding a rite for a dead person tonight? Who is it?"

Nun Shi sighed deeply then replied, "The dead person is Du Liniang, daughter of former Prefect Du. She was an extraordinary beauty."

The mistress, who was keen to repay Nun Shi's hospitality, said, "Oh, what a pity. If we can do anything to help with the rite, we shall be very pleased."

第八章
情魂自献

眼看杜丽娘三年忌辰已到,守坟庵的石道姑选择了吉日,替她开设道场,超度亡灵。今早起来,就请人帮忙,在观门外竖起招魂旗幡,出了黄榜,观内又搭起祭坛,诸事准备就绪,正准备做法事,远处走来一对道姑,原来是师徒二人。将近观前,徒弟对师父说:"师父,我们在梅花观歇下吧。"师父乃是韶阳郡碧云庵主,携带着徒儿各处游方。听到徒弟的话语,见到旗幡黄榜,闻到阵阵炉香,便欣然同意在此借宿。

师徒说话之间,已来到观门前,石道姑问道:"小姑姑从何而来?"

碧云庵主笑着回答道:"从韶阳郡来,特向姑姑借宝庵宝地暂宿。"

彼此都是四方游处的道姑,岂能不借房供宿?但客房已被柳梦梅所占,石道姑略加思索后便应承道:"东头客房有一书生在此养病,只有委屈二位住下厢房了。"

"多谢了。"碧云庵主答谢后,指着旗幡、黄榜问道:"敢问今天道场,为何人而做?"

石道姑长叹一声:"亡灵是一绝色女子,她就是此处前任太守的闺女杜丽娘。"

碧云庵主心想借宿于此,无以回报,现逢着梅花观建坛做道场,正好效力:"是这种事啊!道姑不才,当尽力相助。"

"That's good." Nun Shi was pleased with the offer.

While they were talking bells were rung and drums beaten urging Nun Shi to go up the altar and offer a sacrifice. Nun Shi, who knew of Miss Liniang's fondness for plum blossoms, plucked a branch from Du Liniang's tomb, put it into a vase and placed it on the sacrificial table. Then she led the two traveling nuns in bowing to Du Liniang's tablet again and again. The rite continued all day and at dusk a whirlwind blew from behind the sacrificial altar. Nun Shi, frightened, said nothing about it and, allowed the others to have their supper, then they cleaned up the alter.

After the whirlwind the soul of Du Liniang appeared. How could her soul travel so freely? It was not usual. As it happened, after she died, she went to the hell where Judge Hu who acted under the King of Hell received her. When he saw that she was such a beauty, not like the other ghosts in the hell, he showed concern for her. He asked her if she had been a dancer or a prostitute, whether she had died of sickness and who were her parents. Du Liniang's soul replied politely, "I never married and have not been a dancer or a prostitute. One day I paid a visit to the Back Garden of my residence and had a dream under a plum tree. In my dream, a young man came, broke off a twig of a willow tree, and asked me to compose a poem. We fell in love with each other. After I woke, I missed him very much. From that day on, I became weaker and weaker and finally I died."

"You're telling a lie. No one in the world would die because of a dream." Judge Hu did not believe her. He sent for the God of Flowers from the Back Garden of Du Liniang's residence who proved it was true. Judge Hu wanted to turn Du Liniang into a swallow because she died only for love. The God of Flowers begged him to show her mercy. "I wish say to Your Highness that the girl made a mistake in her dream. What she dreamt did not really happen, so you should not punish her. Also her father is an honest and upright official. He has only one daughter. Please set her free."

"Who is her father?" Judge Hu asked.

"My father is Prefect Du Bao. Now he is the Pacification Commissioner of Huaiyang," Du Liniang's soul replied.

"Oh, you are a young lady from a wealthy family. As your father is an upright official and has done much good work, I'll report the case to the Heavenly Court and let it to make a decision."

"I beg Your Highness to investigate my case. It's such a sad story," Du Liniang's soul appealed.

"这等却好。"石道姑自然欢迎。

正当她们交谈时,钟鼓已奏鸣,催请石道姑登坛拈香祭拜。石道姑倒也尽心,她知道杜小姐因爱花而亡,事先便在她坟头上折得半枝梅花,拿来安置在净瓶中,放在祭台上供养。她率领着众道姑一拜再拜。这道场做了整整一天。到天将黑时,忽见祭坛后面阵阵旋风滚滚而来。石道姑心头一惊,十分诧异,但也不好说什么,吩咐大家先吃了晚斋,再来收拾道场。

旋风过处,杜丽娘的魂灵儿由隐而现——怪了,她的魂灵儿怎能自由自在任意游走呢?原来她亡故之初,去到阴间,由阎罗王殿下胡判官发落。胡判官见她姿色过人,容颜艳丽,不像是阴间鬼魂所有,不免多几分关注,问她是否唱过歌、伴过舞、陪过酒,因患何病而亡,是谁家儿女。杜丽娘魂灵儿回答道:"女囚不曾许嫁人家,也不曾饮酒伴舞,只因为在南安知府衙门后花园中梅树之下得了一个梦,梦见一个书生,折柳一枝,要奴题诗,彼此留连,甚是多情,梦醒以后为此伤感,坏了性命。"

"你真会说谎,世上哪有一梦而亡的道理?"胡判官不信,立即传南安府后花园花神前来询问,花神证实确有其事。胡判官便罚因慕色而亡的杜丽娘变作莺燕,倒是花神替她求情:"禀告老判,此女乃梦中犯罪,不好就发判的,何况她父亲为官清正,只生此女,请开开恩,赦了她吧!"

"她父亲是何人?"

杜丽娘魂灵儿抢先答道:"父亲杜宝知府,今升淮扬安抚使。"

"哦,倒是一个千金小姐。也罢,看在杜老先生分上,当奏过天庭,再行议处。"

"就烦请恩官便中替女犯查查,怎么会有这种伤感之事?"

"这事儿一定注在断肠簿上。"胡判官说道。

"Your case must be in the Broken Hearts Records," Judge Hu replied.

Du Liniang's soul insisted on appealing to the judge. "Could you please check if my husband's surname is Liu or Mei?"

Judge Hu, who could hardly decline her request, opened Marriage Records and began to go through them. "Oh, it is here. Your husband is Liu Mengmei, the latest Number One Scholar. Soon you will meet him at the Plum Blossom Nunnery. You two are fated to marry. If this is so, let me set you free. You may go out of the city of the ghosts of wronged people. You may go anywhere with the wind to look for your lover." Then Judge Hu ordered the God of Flowers to take good care of Du Liniang's dead body in preparation for the day when she would return to the world. After Judge Hu had finished, Du Liniang's soul expressed heartfelt thanks to him and flew away with the wind.

Du Liniang's soul arrived at Nan'an City when Nun Shi and the other nuns were performing the rite for her. Dusk was deepening and the Back Garden was quiet. She went through the bamboo door, passed the Peony Pavilion and the railing, then stood in the center of the garden. Looking around she saw a scene of desolation. It had been three years since her parents had left and no one had taken care of the pavilions or towers in the garden. No one remembered her, Du Liniang. She was so sad that her tears ran down her face.

Suddenly she heard a sound, smelt burning joss sticks and saw candles in the hall. She was so curious that she went over to look and found a tablet on the table inscribed with her own name. All of this told her that Nun Shi, who came to her room three years ago to drive away ghosts, was holding a rite for her. A vase with a plum blossoms branch stood on the table. "Oh, plum blossoms. They're my favorite!" she said to herself. "Since I have come here, I should make them aware of my presence." She waved her sleeve and made all the plum blossom petals fall to the table.

When she was about to leave, she heard a voice saying, "Oh, my lover, my beauty!" It surprised her and she listened attentively. She heard a young man's voice, saying, "I love you so much and call you day and night but you never answer. Why didn't you write your name on the portrait? I don't even know who you are."

The passionate voice stopped Du Liniang and after a pause the young man went on to say, "My lover, my beauty, I love you with all of my

杜丽娘魂灵执着得很，仍无休无止地求情道："有劳恩官再替女犯查查，女犯丈夫到底姓柳还是姓梅？"

胡判官被纠缠得不能脱身，只得取过婚姻簿来查阅，自言自语地说道："是呀，有个柳梦梅，乃新科状元，妻杜丽娘，前系幽会，后成明配。不日相会在梅花观中——此人和你有姻缘之分。罢了，我今放你出枉死城，随风游戏，跟寻此人。"又吩咐花神，好好看护她的肉身，等她还阳。处置完毕，杜丽娘魂灵儿拜谢了，便飞将出去，寻找柳梦梅去了。

正当石道姑等人为杜丽娘祭拜时，她的魂灵儿飘飘忽忽地转到生前住的南安城来了。只见夜色深沉，故园静寂。她越过篱门，转过牡丹亭，又到芍药栏，放眼四望，一片荒凉。父母离此而去已整整三年，有谁来修葺亭台楼阁，有谁还记得昔日的杜丽娘！思念及此，不禁伤心万端，泪水止不住地淌了下来。

忽然间，她听得丁东之声，原来是台上的弄风铃在风中作响；又嗅得阵阵沉香，只见殿中灯火荧荧，不由得发怔，上前偷觑，原来供着神灵，再细看用青藤纸写的祈祷词，方才知道是替她赶过邪的石道姑在此住持，大作道场，为的是超度她。青花瓷净瓶中供养的梅花，又闪入她的眼帘。呀，这不是自己的心爱之物么？既然到了此地，不显点儿灵迹留给人们，也枉了我杜丽娘来到故地一游了。想罢，她把袖儿挥舞，瓣瓣梅花飞满在经台上。

正当她准备离去时，耳畔听得"我的姐姐呵，我的美人啊"，声声不断。她惊讶万分，是谁在此呼叫呢？又仔细聆听，只听到："唉，有情人叫不出情人答应，为什么不写明你这个可爱人的名字呢？此事不分明，就难以了结啊！"

这呼声倒拖住她的脚步，隔了一阵，又重复呼叫"姐姐"、"美人"。她猜想：这大约是个书生，睡着了在说胡话吧。继而又思忖：

heart." Du Liniang thought that the young man was probably talking in his sleep but an idea formed in her mind. Was he Master Liu or Master Mei who appeared in her dream?

Dawn was almost breaking and Du Liniang's soul, afraid of sunshine, had to return to her tomb right away. As she hurried away her garment knocked down the embroidered silk flag making a loud noise and startling the nuns. The young nun ran out shouting at the top of her voice, "Come quickly, mistresses!"

Nun Shi and the mistress of the Biyun Nunnery hurried in and asked together, "What's the matter? What has happened?"

"I saw a goddess leaving, waving her sleeves elegantly. She disappeared in a twinkle. I am so frightened," the young nun said.

"What does she look like?" Nun Shi asked.

After the young nun had described what she had seen, she asked Nun Shi, "What goddess could she be to come down to earth?"

"Well, it seems she looks just like Du Liniang, the dead daughter of Prefect Du. She must have come to the rite to make her presence known," Nun Shi sighed.

Just then the mistress of the Biyun Nunnery found the scripture table covered with flower petals. Surprised, all the nuns began to pray again, wishing Du Liniang's soul would soon go to heaven.

After Liu Mengmei found the portrait in the Back Garden, he fell in love with the beauty in the picture. From then on he hung it up every day and often looked at it with great interest, wondering who she was.

Late one night Liu Mengmei look at the portrait again, read the poems and gazed appreciatively at the beautiful girl. She looked back at him with soft eyes and he could not help asking himself who she was. Why did she always look at him with love but say nothing? How he wished he could meet her in his dream!

Suddenly there was a blast of cold wind which lifted the portrait. Liu Mengmei hurried over to hold it with both hands, fearing that the wind would damage it. He thought to himself that he should take great care of this hard won portrait; it would be a great pity if the wind spoiled it. He had considered looking for a master painter to have it copied but thought again and gave the idea up; there was no such beauty on earth and it would be pointless. He went to lie down in his bed. It was possible that he might meet her in his dreams.

会不会是我梦见的梅相公或柳相公?

东方渐次发白,她有心想探究个明白,但却不敢久停,赶紧回到坟墓中去。飘行之际,带倒绣幡,发出响声,惊动了众道姑。先是碧云庵的小道姑跑进殿来,蓦然见到她的魂灵儿,大吃一惊,高呼道:"师父们,快来,快来!"

石道姑和碧云庵住持一齐赶进殿来,异口同声道:"什么事,怎么大惊小怪的?"

"我看见一位女神仙,挥袖拂花,一闪而去。好不怕人也!"

石道姑忙问道:"怎么一个模样?"

小道姑绘声绘影地形容了神仙的身段、穿戴,又惊惊诧诧地问道:"这是什么真仙下凡?"

"咳,这便是杜小姐生前的模样,定是她的魂灵儿活现!"石道姑叹道。

碧云庵住持忽然发现经台之上,铺撒着一地梅花,连声称异。大家又一再祝赞一番,愿杜小姐早升天堂。

柳梦梅自从拾得画像以后,日思夜想,此事堪奇,此为何人?

此时已夜深人静,他又将画像悬挂起来,吟诵上面的题诗,欣赏像中的人物,只见画中的美人,含情欲语,不禁顿发奇想:这如花似玉的美人,是依照谁的容颜描画出来的呢?为什么又对我偏偏含情不语呢?唉,若是能与她梦中一会,也可稍慰寂聊。

忽然一阵冷风,吹动了这幅观世音菩萨美人图。他赶紧走上前去,轻轻捺住挂勾。由此又想到:此图真是难得,不要被风吹破,当寻个画图高手再临摹一幅。继而,他对自家的幻想又觉得可笑,不免自言自语道:"人世间像这样的天仙多半是假的,哪里能寻到?唉,算了,算了,还是躺上榻去,梦中也许能与她相聚。"

There was a gust of cold wind but Liu Mengmei had already fallen into a sound sleep and did not feel it. Du Liniang's soul came with the wind. A few days earlier, when her soul had gone to the Plum Blossom Nunnery, she heard a young man's voice calling, "My sister! My beauty!" The pitiful sound had attracted her and this time she made a special trip to the eastern wing room. Peeping through a window into the room, she was astonished. Her own portrait hung on the wall and on it was the poem that she had written. Beside her own poem was another with the signature of Liu Mengmei.

While Du Liniang was lost in thought, the young man muttered in his dream, "One year she met a handsome young man from the moon / By a weeping willow rather than a plum tree. My love, the man you mentioned in your poem was me, Liu Mengmei. But you're only a beauty on paper and how can I be close to you and touch you?" Amazed, Du Liniang thought, "I wrote that poem. The scholar calls himself Liu Mengmei. Is he the man I met in my dream?" She was overjoyed and, galvanized into action, knocked at the door.

Liu Mengmei woke up and said, "The bamboo is being blown about by the wind. Is there anyone knocking at the door or is it the sound of the wind?"

"It's me," Du Liniang replied.

Liu Mengmei thought to himself that it was very late and no one would be visiting him at this hour. It must be Nun Shi coming with some tea. He called out, "I don't need tea, Nun Shi. Thank you very much."

"No, I'm not Nun Shi."

"Are you the young nun from the Biyun Nunnery?"

"No, I'm not her either."

"That's very strange. Who is it then? Let me open the door and take a look," Liu Mengmei murmured to himself.

He rose from his bed, draped a robe over his shoulder, unlatched the bolt, opened the door and found an extraordinary beauty standing there. Before he knew who she was, the young lady had passed him by and entered the room, smiling sweetly. Liu Mengmei closed the door in a hurry.

The lady tidied herself up, bowed to Liu Mengmei and said, "Young master, all blessings."

"May I ask where are you from? Why do you come here so late at night?" Liu Mengmei was suspicious.

又是一阵冷风袭来,但他已经入睡,并无知觉。而杜丽娘的魂灵儿,却趁着这阵冷风,飘然而至。原来她在前几天魂游梅花观之际,就听见东厢房中一个书生高呼"我的姐姐,我的美人",声音哀楚,震魂撼魄。今夜杜丽娘悄悄到了东厢房门外,伏窗窥望。不看则已,一看顿时愕然怔住!只见那墙壁上悬挂着一幅画像,上面分明是自己的春容,后面还有和诗一首,落款是岭南柳梦梅。

杜丽娘正自出神,忽然听见那书生口中喃喃低语:"他年得傍蟾宫客,不在梅边在柳边。我的姐姐呀,你指的梅和柳,我柳梦梅虽然有份儿,但你是个纸上的人儿,叫我怎生亲近你呢!"杜丽娘听了大吃一惊,暗想:那两句诗是自己写的,这书生自称柳梦梅,难道就是梦中人么?想到这里,欣喜万分,忍不住连忙上前敲门。

柳梦梅惊醒:"呀,房外竹声和鸣,是风吹的还是人敲的?"

"有人。"杜丽娘随即应答道。

"这是什么时辰了,还会有人——敢是老姑姑送茶来?免劳了。"

"不是。"

"那么是不是借宿于此的碧云庵小姑姑?"

"不是。"

"又不是小姑姑,好怪好怪。还有谁人呢?——待我开门看了再说。"

想罢,柳梦梅披衣而起,拔了门栓,打开房门,惊奇不已,哪里来的这样一位艳丽非凡的少女?当他尚未回过神儿来,这少女微笑着掩身而进,柳梦梅急急把门掩好。

杜丽娘理理鬓角,整整衣袖,深深一拜:"公子万福。"

"小姐到来,敢问府上何处?为何深夜至此?"柳梦梅不无猜疑

"Can you guess, young master?" Du Liniang said with a smile.

Liu Mengmei was very curious and guessed that she was a goddess from heaven, a concubine who had escaped from her husband's residence, or someone who had eloped but lost her way in the night.

As Liu Mengmei could not answer her question, Du Liniang had to introduce herself. "I'm not a goddess from heaven, nor a concubine, nor an eloper. Young master, have you ever met a young lady under a plum tree in your dream?"

"Yes, I once had such a dream."

"During your dream, you came to my home on the eastern side of the nunnery."

Liu Mengmei suddenly realized and said excitedly, "You're the beautiful girl who once appeared in my dream. I thought a dream was not real. It really surprises me that we can meet with each other today."

Du Liniang was also pleasantly surprised and said, "How happy I am to meet you here. I was born into a good family. Since childhood my parents have subjected me to strict discipline and I have never met a young man before. As for our meeting in front of the rockery by the Peony Pavilion in our dream, you know what happened later." Du Liniang lowered her head and was too shy to continue.

"Oh, you're really the beauty in the picture? My lover, my darling, I have missed you very much." Delighted, Liu Mengmei grasped Du Liniang's hand, went to the portrait and said, "God blesses me, and lets you come to life." Like two familiar friends they sat down and spoke to each other earnestly expressing their love for one another. Afraid that it would frighten him, Du Liniang did not tell him that she was dead. Du Liniang left at about four o'clock in the morning and before she went she said, "I have a few words to say to you. I hope you will understand me."

"Say anything you want," Liu Mengmei said, smiling broadly.

"I'm a young lady from a wealthy family. Once I give myself to you, I hope you will never betray me. My only hope is that we shall be an affectionate couple forever." These things worried Du Liniang.

Liu Mengmei promised seriously. "How dare I forget you since you sincerely love me?"

"In addition, please let me leave every morning before the cock crows. You don't need to see me off. It is chilly in the morning and you would be cold."

地问道。

杜丽娘毕竟是少女心性，微笑着说："公子，你猜呢？"

柳梦梅倒也颇有兴趣，一会儿猜她是天上神仙下凡，一会儿猜她是侍妾出逃，一会儿猜她是与人夜奔走错了路。

杜丽娘见他猜不出，只得自报家门，说道："我既不是天上仙女，也不是有污的侍妾，更不是私奔的女子——公子啊！你有没有梦在梅花之下？"

柳梦梅扶头想了半晌："对呀，当初做过这个梦来。"

"正是这一梦，你曾到了我家——我的家你也不必再问，就在东邻。"

经这么一提示，柳梦梅似觉有悟，猛然记起梦中的女郎，喜出望外地说道："原来你就是梦中的美人吗？我还当是梦境无凭，不想真的见面了！"

杜丽娘也喜出望外地说道："听公子如此说，我倒真是盼到你了。我生于好人家，平素管教甚严，从未与男子接触，牡丹亭畔湖山石前，这其中的事儿，你当然知道。"说到这里，杜丽娘再也说不下去了。

"这样说来，想必这画像上的美人也是你了？美人！美人！可想煞我了！"柳梦梅狂喜地一把拉住杜丽娘走到画像前。"小姐，果然将你盼活了！"当下两人故友重逢一般，各自倾吐相思之苦。杜丽娘只怕柳梦梅惊异，不敢直言自己已死。到了四更时辰，方才告辞。临行对柳梦梅说道："妾有一言相恳，望郎君恕罪。"

柳梦梅却笑吟吟地说："小姐有话，但说无妨。"

"妾千金之躯，一旦付与郎君，勿负奴心。每夜得荐枕席，平生之愿足矣。"杜丽娘毕竟有些担心。

柳梦梅信誓旦旦地说："小姐有心眷恋小生，小生怎敢忘了小姐。"

"Please don't worry, I'll do what you say. May I ask you, what is your name?"

Du Liniang could not avoid a deep sigh. As a dead person she dared not tell him her name. She had to equivocate. "I'm from a good family, Master Liu, don't worry about it. For the time being, I can't tell you my name as it might cause trouble. I'll tell you later."

"That's all right," Liu Mengmei said. "I hope you will come to see me every night."

"还有,鸡鸣之前,就要放奴回去。公子也不要送,免得晓风侵袭,受了寒凉。"

柳梦梅答应道:"这些,小生一一照办——敢问小姐贵姓芳名?"

杜丽娘不禁长叹,身为鬼魂,尚未获具人身,如何能亮出姓名?只能含糊地说道:"我是有根有芽的。公子,请放心。一时不能说出姓名,免得风声传漏出去。"

柳梦梅只说得一句:"今后但盼小姐夜夜来此。"

CHAPTER NINE

Du Liniang Tells the Truth

Head over heels in love, Du Liniang and Liu Mengmei stuck to each other like glue every night. They did not expect others to spread exaggerated stories and malicious gossip. Nun Shi, the head of the nunnery, was suspicious and kept an eye on Liu Mengmei's room.

For several nights in succession she heard Liu Mengmei talking to somebody with a woman's voice. She could not help suspecting that there was a woman living in his room. She thought to herself that Prefect Du had built the Plum Blossom Nunnery for his dead daughter. In the past three years nothing had happened and the nunnery had been peaceful. However, since Chen Zuiliang had introduced Liu Mengmei, a young man who called himself a scholar from Guangzhou, to the nunnery, it had not been peaceful. When Master Liu came, he had been sick and weak. But after he recovered, he took a walk in the Back Garden rather than leave. Since then he had been absent-minded, restless and in low spirits. The day before yesterday two nuns from Shaoyang had come to the nunnery. According to Taoist rules, nuns should not marry, nor give birth to children; they should devote their lives to Taoism and worship the three Taoist founders. However the young nun was only 16 years old, a pretty girl with a flirtatious manner. Her Taoist dress did not hide her beautiful face and features. With this in mind, Nun Shi could not help suspecting that the young nun was having an affair with Liu Mengmei.

"Aunt Shi," someone was calling her. Nun Shi looked up and saw that it was none other than the young nun. She said without thinking, "Young nun, you go out every night. Did you visit Master Liu last night?"

"Alas! Why do you ask me this? Who saw me entering his room?" the young nun replied angrily, blushing and knitting her brows.

"I saw for myself. Why do you dress up beautifully every day? Don't you go with a young man?"

"Aunt Shi, that is even more objectionable to my ears. Please point

第九章
沟通生死

杜丽娘与柳梦梅这一对炽热相恋的青年男女,只贪你欢我爱,哪管他人飞短流长。别人尚不打紧,惟有看管梅花观的石道姑却不断窥视刺探。

几夜来,她老是觉得柳梦梅住的客房中有人声,唧唧哝哝的似是女儿声腔,便不能不疑虑丛生。心想:杜老爷为小姐创建这座梅花观,到如今已有三年。三年来,观内凡事清清白白,没有半点儿差错。自从陈最良这个老不死的,引来一个什么柳梦梅,自称是岭南柳秀才,住在东客房养什么病,病好了又不走,要去游什么后花园;自从游园之后,终日像着了魔似的,到处悠悠晃晃,无精打采,真是令人疑惑。这也罢了,岂知前天又来了韶阳的一对道姑。论起道姑来,原本就不能婚嫁生子女,只应一心守着元始天尊、太上道君、太上老君三尊清像,换水添香,一心修道。哪知那个小道姑,芳龄正值二八,虽然仍着道妆,但透出一片淡雅,不但长得出众,而且还颇有风情……这,这,这怎不令人生疑呢?

“姑姑。”一声清脆的招呼声,惊破了石道姑的沉思,抬起头来一看,原来正是她放心不下的韶阳小道姑,便脱口而出地问道:“小姑姑,你昨夜游来游去,游到柳公子房里去了吧?”

“唉呀呀,姑姑这话儿怎的说起?谁看见的?”小道姑脸儿挣得

out who I'm going out with? Though I'm young and like to dress myself simply and elegantly, I have always preserved my purity. How could you suggest that I would do such a thing? Though you're over 50, you're still charming. Maybe it's you who wants to find a boyfriend."

"You, you.... How can you falsely accuse me?" Nun Shi was so angry that she did not know what to say.

"You may think what you want. Why do you allow a young scholar to live in a nunnery? That is simple evidence." The young nun did not let Nun Shi off easily.

"Alas! Don't you accuse me of having an affair with the young scholar? You're traveling nuns and he is a traveling scholar. The two of you can stay here, why can't he? Before you came the young scholar's room was quiet after he went to bed. But in the past two days the young man has opened the door late at the night and talked to a woman all night. Who does he talk to if it is not you? I'll take you to the official government and let the local official decide on it." Nun Shi reached out trying to seize the young nun.

The young nun, who was not at all frightened, grasped Nun Shi's robe and said, "All right! Let's go right now. As the head of a nunnery, you let a local ruffian live here. I don't believe the local official will let you off so easily."

While the nuns were quarreling, Chen Zuiliang walked in, saw them and made fun of them. "What are you doing? Fighting for the right to win over believers?"

Nun Shi said, "Mr. Chen, let me tell you, I heard Master Liu open his door and talk with a woman at midnight. Then I asked the young nun if she visited Master Liu at night. Instead of giving me a proper answer, she falsely accused me by asking why I let a young man live in my nunnery. Please tell her who brought the young man here and I'll take her to the local government and let the prefect decide who is right and who is wrong."

The two nuns were really angry and Chen Zuiliang tried his best to calm them. He told them to stop quarreling and consider Master Liu who should not be put in a position where he would lose face.

"All right, I'll listen to you." Nun Shi let go of the young nun.

"Let's work together to find who talks with the young scholar at midnight," the young nun suggested and the two nuns finally reached agreement.

通红通红,柳眉倒竖,气忿忿地诘问道。

"我见到的!你这么着意打扮,不是与那书生去欢会又是为啥?"

"唉呀,姑姑这话越发不中听了!请问我与哪个书生相会?我虽然年青,喜欢淡雅,但一向冰心玉洁,你怎为此诋诬!——像你这半老佳人,怕还不如我妥当哩!"

这回是石道姑难以开口了:"你,你怎倒打一耙,栽赃给我了?"

小道姑倒不依不饶继续追问道:"你不仔细想想,这个女尼观里,怎地住了一个书生?这不是明明白白的大证据么?"

"哎呀呀,难道我与这书生有什么关涉!这梅花观,你是云游道婆,他是云游书生,你能住,偏偏他不能住?往常东客房中,书生一睡觉,就寂静无声,自从你来到观中,那书生又是半夜开门,又是通宵唧唧哝哝的,不是与你说话,又与何人说话?我将你扯到衙门告你去!"说着就动手将小道姑拽住。

小道姑并不惊恐,更不省事,反而扯住石道姑的道袍,说道:"去便去。你这女尼道观,让地痞流氓停宿。衙门难道会放过你!"

正当这两个道姑你争我吵之际,陈最良慢慢地踱将进来,见到这种情况,不免调侃起来:"你们这两个道姑是争施主还是咋的?"

"先生你不知。我听见柳公子半夜开门,与人说话,我好意问这小姑'是不是你与柳公子说话',这小妮子不好好回答反倒说我养个书生在观里。先生,你评说评说,谁引了这个书生来的?我要扯她去衙门说个明白。"

陈最良见这一老一小两个道姑动了真气,也不便再调侃了,劝她们照顾柳梦梅体面,不要再吵闹,闹得大家都无趣。

石道姑倒先罢手,说:"便依你说。"

小道姑也说道:"我与你再细细打听究竟是谁与书生说话的。"一老一小终于在这个问题上达成共识,一致行动。

The lovers had no idea that the two nuns were watching them and, as usual, they met that night.

Liu Mengmei prepared everything after dark and sat by the table waiting for his lover to come. Soon he dozed off, one hand supporting his head.

Du Liniang arrived and saw him sleeping soundly on a chilly spring night without any cover over his body. She felt tender affection towards him and went up and called him gently, "Master Liu! Master Liu!"

Liu Mengmei woke up and seeing his lover he stood up and bowed to her. "I should have come out to greet you but I fell asleep while waiting for you. Your footsteps were so light that I didn't hear you coming. Darling, you are late tonight."

"I wanted to come earlier, but I had to wait for my parents to go to bed. I put the needles and threads for my needlework into order and dressed myself up before coming. That's why I'm late," Du Liniang explained.

"I appreciate your deep feelings and love for me," Liu Mengmei said. He paused then continued, "It's a wonderful night, but it's a pity we don't have wine or cakes."

"Oh, I forgot to tell you that I brought a pot of wine and two boxes of cakes and snacks with me. I left them outside. I'll bring them in. We shall have a good time tonight." Du Liniang had prepared for everything.

They sat down to drink wine and chat but soon they both blushed revealing their thoughts of love. Liu Mengmei urged Du Liniang to make love but Du Liniang, who was shy, tried to say no. Happily engaged in their conversation the two young people were unaware of the eavesdroppers. Nun Shi and the young nun from the Biyun Nunnery had been standing by the window of Liu Mengmei's room for quite a while. The young nun said to Nun Shi, "Listen, the young man is talking to somebody now. But I'm standing by you so there is no reason to suspect me."

Nun Shi put her ear close to the window and said, "It's a woman's voice. Knock on the door." The young nun did as was told.

"Who is it?" Liu Mengmei asked.

"It's Nun Shi. I'm bringing you some tea," Nun Shi replied.

"It's very late at night. I don't want tea, thank you, Nun Shi." Liu Mengmei was unnerved.

"Do you have a guest in your room?" Nun Shi asked.

"No, no, there is no one here." Liu Mengmei was flustered.

柳梦梅与杜丽娘哪里知道有人猜疑？今宵依然约好相聚。

柳梦梅早早做好准备，坐等杜丽娘前来赴约。坐了很久，未免有些疲乏，支着头，歪在椅子上睡着了。

岂知杜丽娘刚好在他酣睡时飘然而至，见他倚椅而眠，春寒时节，连床单儿也未加，心想大约是候着我睡着的，爱怜之心更增几分，便轻步上前，低低叫道："柳郎，柳郎！"

柳梦梅蓦然惊醒，连连作揖："小姐，失敬，失敬。——我正准备远远相迎，哪知居然睡着了，你的脚步声真轻，我一点儿也未觉得。小姐，你今夜来的迟了些。"

杜丽娘解释说："我也不是故意拖延，慢待你，一要等双亲上床安睡，二要收拾好绣妆活计，三要稍稍修饰修饰，因此迟来。"

"真多谢你的深情厚谊了，值此良宵，没有酒点，未免煞风景。"

"我都忘了。我倒携酒一壶，花果二盒，放在门外，可取来消夜。"杜丽娘却有准备。

他们对饮闲话，几杯酒下肚，彼此春意盎然。柳梦梅急着催杜丽娘早早上床安歇。杜丽娘仍然有些羞怯，半迎半拒，你一言我一语，却忘了隔墙有人。观主石道姑与碧云庵小道姑早就相约前来探听究竟。她们在窗外潜立多时，小道姑对石道姑说道："老姑姑，你听，书生房里有人哩。这总不会是我小道姑吧。"

石道姑又贴在窗框上听个仔细："是女人声，快去敲门！"小道姑遵命敲门。

"是谁？"柳梦梅大吃一惊。

石道姑厉声回答："姑姑送茶。"

"夜深了，免劳。"柳梦梅惊魂未定。

"公子房里有客哩！"石道姑依然不走。

"没有。"柳梦梅口气慌张了。

"I heard a woman's voice," Nun Shi said.

When they heard this, Liu Mengmei and Du Liniang knew that they had been found out and were so frightened that they did not know what to do. Liu Mengmei's face turned white and in a low voice he asked Du Liniang what to do.

Nun Shi urged him again to open the door and warned that if their voices were heard by the local people they would all come.

Panic-stricken, Liu Mengmei rubbed his hands and said once more, "What shall we do?"

Du Liniang appeared calm, smiled and said to her lover, "Don't worry. I'm only a girl from a neighboring family. If Nun Shi will not forgive me, I'll accuse her by saying it is her who seduces me. Master Liu, don't be frightened. Open the door. I'll hide myself behind the portrait."

When Liu Mengmei opened the door, Nun Shi and the young nun competed with each other to enter the room while congratulating him.

"Why do you congratulate me?" Liu Mengmei asked holding his arms wide and trying to stop them from entering.

The nuns shouted, "In the dead of night when the nunnery is locked you are sporting with a girl."

Du Liniang was invisible and Liu Mengmei said firmly, "What are you talking about? Where is the girl? How can a girl hide herself in my room?"

The nuns pushed Liu Mengmei aside and came to the center of the room. Suddenly the candle became dim. Nun Shi was very surprised and said, "We saw a shadow of a woman with our own eyes. In a twinkle, she disappeared and there is only a portrait of beauty. Has this ancient portrait turned into a spirit, Master Liu? What is this portrait?"

"Every night I burn joss sticks and candles in front of it. Late at night I pray for her. But you think I have a woman in my room. How rude you are!"

"So, that's how it is! I heard you talking with someone the night before last. I suspected it was the young nun. Now all is clear, Master Liu, you're lonely by yourself. Let the young nun stay behind and keep you company." Nun Shi was trying to get into Liu Mengmei's good graces.

"It's unnecessary. Please don't bother me from now on. I am an honest scholar and someone you can bully. Nun Shi, you woke me up from my dream." The two nuns went away, depressed. Liu Mengmei felt angry and out of sorts. He said to himself, "Those nuns spoilt my

126

石道姑并不放松:"是女客哩!"

柳梦梅、杜丽娘闻言,知道事已败露,尤其是柳梦梅手足无措,满脸惊惶,低低对杜丽娘说:"这怎么好,这怎么好!"

石道姑更是步步紧逼:"柳公子,快开门,免得咱们张扬起来,地方上可有巡查呢!"

柳梦梅更加惊恐,搓着双手:"怎么得了,怎么得了!"

杜丽娘却镇定自若,微笑道:"不要紧。俺是邻家女子,道姑若不罢手,就说是她勾引的。柳郎,不要慌,你去开门,我去美人图像后面躲一躲。"

柳梦梅开了门,两个道姑一老一小挤着门框儿赶将进来,口中嘈嘈杂杂地说着:"恭喜,恭喜。"

"有何喜事?"柳梦梅一边反问,一边拦着她们。

两个道姑你一句我一句地嚷道:"夜深人静,观门下锁,哪处来的女子,正好引燃你这堆干柴?"

"你说什么女子,藏在哪里?"柳梦梅眼见小姐已经隐逝,倒也硬朗起来。

这两个道姑硬是朝里闯去,柳梦梅一时抵挡不住,被她们闯到画前,只见灯光忽然一暗,继而复明,石道姑也不免诧异:"刚刚分明见一个影儿,怎么只见一轴美人图在这儿?古画成精了么?柳公子,这是什么画?"

"这是我供奉的香火,每每寂静时,我就向她祈祷。你也太莽撞了。"

"对了,不说不知道么。我前天晚上听见公子房里啾啾唧唧,怀疑是这小道姑。如今明白了。柳公子,留下这小道姑陪你说说话。"石道姑又讨好地说。

"不必了。你专门欺负我这个安分守己的书生!"两个道姑也

enjoyment. How disappointing!"

Leaning on the door of his room Liu Mengmei looked out and saw the shadows of dusk lengthening. Flags fluttered in the wind and the sound of bells and drums subsided. The young man became excited when the sun set. When he recalled how the two nuns spoilt his happy reunion with Du Liniang the night before he was quite upset. He had looked forward to the arrival of his lover the whole of the previous day, but the irritating nuns had frightened her away. He thought to himself, "It's nighttime. My darling will come at any moment. I hope the clouds will make it darker when she is comes, otherwise the nuns will find her and cause a disturbance again. Why don't I go to the main hall and have a chat with Nun Shi so that she won't be suspicious before my lover comes?" He went into his room to light an oil lamp leaving the door open for Du Liniang. Then he walked towards the main hall.

Du Liniang's soul soon appeared. Fearful, she flew slowly towards Liu Mengmei's room. On the way she was startled by a sound and the shadow of a tree which looked like a man. She kept looking around fearing that there was someone hidden in the dark. Finally she came to the east wing room.

"Oh, Master Liu is not in the room. Where has he gone?" She took a risk and entered to find that the oil lamp that he had lit had become dim. She added some oil and soon the room was brightly lit with two parallel strands of wick — a good omen for a marriage. Du Liniang sighed and said, "How I wish that Master Liu and I will become a happy couple! All ghosts know that I come here to meet my lover, but none of the people on earth know what is going on. Though I belong to the hell, my body is well preserved. I died for Master Liu three years ago and now I will return to the world for him. I should tell my lover the truth and end all the secrecy." Though she was worried that Liu Mengmei would be frightened when she told him that she was actually a ghost, she had made up her mind to tell him the truth.

After exchanging a few casual remarks with Nun Shi, Liu Mengmei took his leave and headed for his room. He passed the winding corridor shaded by bamboo and his footsteps woke up several sleeping birds, which flew into the dark sky causing flower petals to drop to the ground. The door opened automatically before he stepped into his room and Du Liniang's soul walked out to greet him. "Oh, you're back," she said.

觉无趣,便灰溜溜地退了出去。柳梦梅既好气又好笑地叹道:"一天好事,被这两个歹货扰乱,真令人扫兴。"

柳梦梅依在客房门边,但见暮云四起,风幡摇动,云堂上钟鼓之声渐歇,一颗激动的心却渐热。想到昨晚之事,既有几分懊恼,又怀几分热望。难得美人下临,却未料到被一对令人嫌、叫人厌的道姑扰乱。眼见夜色渐浓,美人也许会再度来会,但愿美人来时有花影遮掩,免得又被两个道姑发现,前来罗唣生事。对了,趁美人尚未到,何不先上云堂去找石道姑闲话,借此消除她的疑惑?主意一定,便将灯光剔亮,房门半掩,以便美人儿进房歇息。

此际,杜丽娘魂灵儿又姗姗而来,一路上担惊受怕,微风吹得环佩丁东作响,乍一听来蓦然一惊;月亮穿云出云,猛一见到地面,以为是人影儿,心中难免一跳。好不容易,飘行至东客房。

"呀,柳郎不在,何处去了?"杜丽娘不顾一切,掩身而入,只见柳梦梅先前剔过的油灯此刻又明灭不定,便趋步案前,再续上一些灯油,剔出一节灯草,灯光渐渐明亮,不一会儿,灯草居然结出并头结。见此景象,杜丽娘不由不长叹一声:"唉,但愿奴家与柳郎也能并头相结。唉呀,奴家与柳郎的欢会,是鬼都知晓,偏偏人间不得知!奴家虽入鬼域,但人身未捐,复生有望。前日为柳郎而死,近日将为柳郎而生。夫妇之缘,去来根由都要说个明白,今晚再不坦诚,人鬼交会到何时?"又想到,只怕说出真情,要惊煞柳郎。顾不得他怕不怕了,再也不能拖延,她下决心,今晚定要说个清楚。

柳梦梅怎肯与石道姑多唠叨,稍稍敷衍就离座告辞,沿着走廊回客房,只见两廊竹影横斜,步履之声惊起二三睡鸦,扑刷刷飞起,残花闪落一地。此时已近客房,房门自动打开,杜丽娘魂灵儿已迎出门外:"柳郎来了。"

Liu Mengmei bowed low at the sight of his beautiful goddess and said happily, "How are you, Miss?"

Du Liniang said that she had been making the oil lamp brighter while waiting for him.

"Thank you for your kindness." Liu Mengmei held her hand and entered the room.

"Master Liu, I thought of a Tang poem while I was waiting for you." Du Liniang was determined to tell him the truth through a poem.

"That's fine. I'll listen to it with my full attention," Liu Mengmei said.

Du Liniang walked to the young scholar slowly and recited a Tang poem in a low voice:

I feel sad when planning to find a go-between;
Cold is the moon and grey is the mountain.
I wonder who is singing a love song now,
Trying to seduce my lover on earth.

"It's a wonderful poem," Liu Mengmei said. The last sentence hinted at Du Liniang herself, but unfortunately, Liu Mengmei did not understand. He was intent on enjoying time with his beauty and Du Liniang had to try again. "Master Liu, where have you been at such a late hour?"

"Last night I was most annoyed by the two nuns who disturbed us and I went to Nun Shi's room to see if there was anything suspicious before you came. I didn't expect that you would arrive so much earlier than last night," Liu Mengmei answered.

"I was longing to see you so much that I came earlier than usual."

When he heard this, Liu Mengmei felt most grateful to Du Liniang and said, "As a poor scholar, I am very lucky to have you. You're as beautiful as a goddess and love me with all of your heart. I'm the happiest person in the world. Oh, I felt so outraged when the nuns disturbed us last night and I am so sorry for it. You must have been very frightened. Let's enjoy every minute tonight and make up for last night. What do you think, my dear?" Liu Mengmei looked eagerly at her.

"Yes, I was very frightened last night. I didn't expect them to be so rude. Fortunately, I hid behind the portrait and when they entered the room, I sneaked out under the cover of the black clouds so that they didn't see me. However, I slipped and fell on the stairs and have never suffered

柳梦梅顿觉仙女下凡,深深一揖:"小姐来了。"

"我在房中剔亮灯花,专等柳郎。"

"哎呀呀,小生真的感激小姐如此诚意。"说着,携着杜丽娘纤手,一同走进房内。

"柳郎,等你不来,我集唐人诗作一首。"杜丽娘魂灵儿决心表白,先行用唐诗试探。

"洗耳恭听。"

杜丽娘魂灵儿便慢慢走近柳梦梅身边,低低念出所集唐诗一首,诗云:

拟托良媒亦自伤,月寒山色两苍苍。

不知谁唱春归曲,又向人间魅阮郎。

"小姐高才。"最后一句分明是说杜丽娘并非人身,但柳梦梅全然未识得诗中含意,一心只思念两人欢合。杜丽娘魂灵儿只能再作试探:"柳郎,这般夜深人静,你从何处归来?"

"小姐,想起昨夜被两个道姑败兴,令人十分恼伤。今晚我趁你尚未来时,先去道姑房内看看她们动静,便好回来迎接你。不曾想到,今晚小姐来得倒比昨晚早。"

"我也盼望早些见到柳郎,所以早早就来了。"

柳梦梅听了这般话语,更是感激不尽:"唉,我这个小小书生,如此幸运,得到仙女般的小姐眷顾,对我如此志诚,如此温存……,呀,昨晚正是欢情浓烈时,被那两个该死的道姑无端地冲破!小姐呵,让你受了半夜罪,担了几回惊。如果不嫌弃小生,咱们今晚再好好接续昨晚欢会,如何?"柳梦梅热巴巴地等着小姐回答。

"是呀,想不到这两个道姑恁般厉害,气势汹汹,把我吓得魂灵儿都收不拢。幸亏一帧画像遮掩,又赖一阵乌云挡住月色,我才悄悄走出客房,不料又在台阶上闪了一跤。我从小也未遭到这样

so much in my life. I'm very worried that my parents will hear about our relationship. If my mother finds out, she will punish me severely." After what had happened the previous night she had became really scared.

Liu Mengmei said nothing, but stood up and bowed to his lover saying that he was very sorry for what had happened that night. Then he said, "May I ask why you love me so much? I am a poor scholar but you seem to be concerned about me all the time."

"That is obvious. I love your outstanding character and morals."

Then Liu Mengmei asked frankly, "Have you been promised to any man?"

"No, I haven't," Du Liniang replied.

"What kind of man do you want to marry?"

"I want to marry a young scholar who genuinely loves me."

"I love you from the bottom of my heart and will love you forever."

"I believe you. That's why I risked my life to come to see you every night."

Then Liu Mengmei came straight to the point and said, "Would you please be my wife?"

"Your home is far away from here and I fear that you already have a wife and want me to be your concubine."

"I've never married. Why would I make you my concubine? You'll be my formal wife."

This made Du Liniang happy and she asked with a smile, "Are there anyone in your family?"

"My father and mother. My father used to be a court official."

"Oh, you're from an official family. If you are from a good family why haven't you married much earlier?"

The question made Liu Mengmei sad and he said, "My parents died when I was a child and as an orphan I lived a poor life roaming about. That's why I haven't married before. You're such a beautiful and intelligent lady and from a good family. I'm really no match for you. If you are willing to be my wife, I'll love you all my life and will never abandon you."

Liu Mengmei's frankness set Du Liniang's mind at rest. She said to him, "Why don't you ask a go-between to make an offer of marriage since you're so determined to marry me? After we marry we could be together all the time."

Liu Mengmei thought that this was a good idea and said that he

的磨折。差点儿风声传到我家,果真如此,我倒先要被老母痛痛责罚呢!"杜丽娘魂灵儿一气说了昨夜感受,显然还有些后怕哩。

柳梦梅听了小姐的陈述,还能说什么呢? 只能是连连作揖表示歉意和感激:"只不知,小姐因何错爱小生,甚至为小生担惊受怕?"

"自然是因爱你一等的人品。"

柳梦梅听了此话后, 不及再问其它,只是直截了当地追问:"请问小姐有没有许配人家?"

"并不曾。"

"不知小姐喜欢什么样人家?"

"只望有个秀才诚心诚意地喜欢我。"

"小生倒是个有情的人。"

"正是呀,正因为你有一片真情,才引得我深夜闯来。"

说到此时,柳梦梅便单刀直入地提出:"小姐,你就嫁给小生吧。"

"我担心你家乡路远山遥,万一嫁给你却成了二房之妾!"

"呀,小生并未曾娶妻,怎会将小姐做妾!"

杜丽娘魂灵儿听到此处,渐露笑容,又探问道:"请问柳郎,家中还有何人?"

"先父曾为官朝散大夫,先母也曾受封为县君。"

"这样说来,你是官家子弟,又为何这般年纪,还未婚娶?"

说到此处,柳梦梅不觉有些伤感:"总因父母过世,小生孤单一人,四处飘零,所以至今未婚。但只要小姐爱上我,我是绝不会轻易丢弃小姐的!"

柳梦梅自诉胸臆,终于使杜丽娘魂灵儿放下心来,自允婚事:"柳郎果有此心,何不请媒人前来聘定? 也免得奴家担惊受怕。"

"好呀,明日清早就去尊府拜见令尊令堂,便好求亲。"柳梦梅立刻说道。

would visit her parents the following day to ask for her hand.

This went further than Du Liniang expected and she was startled. She said, "Tomorrow you see me, not my parents."

"Does that mean you're really a goddess from heaven?" the young man asked. Du Liniang smiled and gave no answer. "It's no wonder you're extraordinarily beautiful, totally different from the girls on earth," Liu Mengmei added.

"I'm not a goddess."

"If you're from a good family why doesn't a maid accompany you when you walk at midnight? And what is your name? You have never given it to me." Liu Mengmei raised question after question and Du Liniang who had difficulty answering lowered her head and sighed. The longer it took her to answer, the more Liu Mengmei suspected and said that she must be a fairy maiden. He urged her to tell the truth and said, "If you're from heaven, I would not dare have you as my wife. Even if you love me wholeheartedly, you'll never escape heavenly punishment. Let's put an end to our personal relationship."

Du Liniang denied that she was a fairy maiden and Liu Mengmei said that if she was not from heaven or earth, she must be a flower or moon spirit.

"All right, let me tell you everything."

"That's good! I'll listen to every word," Liu Mengmei encouraged her. Du Liniang thought about it but still did not know how to start. "My darling, who can you tell your story to if not me?" Liu Mengmei persuaded gently.

Du Liniang was moved by his sincerity and love. She sighed and said, "Where shall I start? Master Liu, I'm so worried that if I tell you the truth, you won't marry me and will take me as your concubine instead. You must swear on this before I tell you everything about myself."

"Oh, that's easy," Liu Mengmei said without hesitation. "Since you want me to promise to marry you, I'll do it." Then he lit some joss sticks, held them high, knelt on the ground and said, "I shall live with you in the same room while I'm alive and I shall be buried with you in the same grave after I'm dead. If I can't keep this promise, I'll die right away."

This oath so moved Du Liniang that her eyes filled with tears. She was determined to tell the truth. She warned him first not to be frightened to her story. Then she described in detail how she died after a dream in the Back Garden and how Judge Hu in the hell allowed her to be free and

　　杜娘魂灵儿倒未料到这一步,慌忙说道:"到我家来,只好见奴家,要见我爹娘,为时还早。"

　　"如此说,小姐当真是仙女下凡!"杜丽娘魂灵儿笑而不语。柳梦梅继续说道:"难怪小姐这般神情,与人间女子迥然有别。"

　　"呀,不是人间,难道是天上? "

　　"你说是人间闺秀,我倒要问你,你怎敢不带一个婢女深夜独行? 你说说你的芳名!"柳梦梅倒也毫无顾忌地追问。杜丽娘魂灵儿一时也难以说清楚,只是低头叹气而已。她越是不说,柳梦梅越是疑虑,索性反激一番,开口便道:"小姐不肯说出姓名,定是天上仙女了。小生福薄,不敢再陪小姐欢宴,虽然仙女眷顾小生,但怕逃不过上天责罚。"

　　杜丽娘魂灵儿自然不能谎说自己是仙女。柳梦梅又追问:"既不是天上仙女,又不是人间闺秀,必是花月之妖了! "

　　"哎呀呀,奴家正要你掘草寻根哩! "

　　"怎么说? "柳梦梅不明不白,迫不及待地问道。杜丽娘那张樱桃小口开了又合,合了又开,欲说还休,不说难受。柳梦梅见这般情景,便鼓励她说:"小姐,小姐,你不与小生说清楚,又与谁人去说? "

　　柳梦梅的痴情与鼓励,倒感动了杜丽娘:"唉,我是要说的,一时不知从何说起。——柳郎,我怕说了,你却不愿娶我为妻,将我当作小妾看了,你立盟誓我再说。"

　　柳梦梅此时却十分爽快:"你既要我发誓娶你为正妻,可以,我与你拈香作誓。"说罢,就发出"生同室、死同穴,口不心齐,寿随香灭"的誓言。

　　这番真挚的话语感动得杜丽娘魂灵儿热泪直流,决意说出真情。但又事先告诫柳梦梅听了她的话语,不要被吓倒。待柳梦梅有了一些精神准备后, 她便缓缓说出自己的身世,因后花园一梦而

look for her lover. "Tomorrow night is the time for me to be brought back from death. I hope you will help dig up my grave tomorrow, then I can come back to life," she said excitedly.

Liu Mengmei was not at all frightened, but he did not know how to help her. "You're my wife and I'm not afraid. I just have no idea how to help you out of the tomb. I fear that my efforts may be in vain."

"My body has been well preserved and looks as if I were asleep."

"Oh, that's wonderful. But where is your grave?"

"Please learn it by heart. Beside the big Taihu rock in the Back Garden there is a plum tree. My tomb is under the tree."

Just then there was a gust of cold wind, and Liu Mengmei trembled all over with cold. "What can I do if I frighten your soul while digging the grave?"

"Don't worry about it. Though my grave is surrounded by twisted roots and gnarled branches, there is an air hole leading to the world. Also, my cold body has already been warmed up by your body so my soul won't be frightened...."

The subject had been broached after they had chatted for several hours and they both realized that they could talk the whole night through. Liu Mengmei suggested that they should discuss the most important things right away. He said, "I believe every word that you have said. However I'm only a scholar, not a laborer. I am afraid that I'm not strong enough to dig your grave by myself."

"You could let Nun Shi to help you."

Liu Mengmei thought that this was a good idea and asked how deep the grave was. He feared that it might be too deep to be dug out.

"My coffin is buried only one meter under the ground. You will certainly need to dig it out with all of your might. My darling, I rely on you to save me." At this moment a cock crowed in the distance startling Du Liniang's soul. It was the time for her to go back to the grave. Before leaving, she entreated him over and again, "My darling, I died for you. I love you with all of my heart. Now I place all of my hope in you. Whether or not I come back to life all depends on you. You must try everything to save me. Please remember your promise. Otherwise I'll hate you forever." Du Liniang disappeared with a gust of cold wind.

Standing in the middle of the room, Liu Mengmei pinched his arm to make sure that he was not dreaming. Then he said to himself, "It's strange. I, Liu Mengmei, became the son-in-law of Prefect Du overnight.

为情死,以及判官令其回阳寻他的经过。"今宵是我还魂之期,望你助我一臂之力,明日掘开我的坟墓,那时我就可以复活了!"杜丽娘兴奋地说。

柳梦梅怕倒不怕了,只是不知如何助她复生,说道:"你是我妻,我也不怕了。只是如何让你从墓穴中起来? 此事怕如水中捞月哩!"

"我人身未坏,虽死犹生呀。"

"既然如此,你的坟墓在何处?"

"柳郎记住,在那后花园中太湖石边,有一株梅树,我的坟就在那梅树之下。"

说到此际,忽然阵阵冷风,吹人发寒,柳梦梅虽觉冷不可当,但依然追问道:"掘坟起棺,万一惊了小姐的魂如何是好?"

"这,这你可放心,虽然是花根树枝盘结,但仍有通向人间的小孔穴。我的冰冷肢体,不是已被你偎倚得半冷半热了么! 你不要怕惊了我……"

说了大半夜话,至此才逐步说到正题,两个人都感到:"一夜夫妻百日恩,整宿闲话无尽休。"还是拣重要的事儿说:"你的话,我都相信,不烦小姐再三叮嘱,我只怕掘坟开棺之事,我一介书生独力难以完成。"

"可与石道姑商议,请她协助。"

柳梦梅觉得此计可行,但又问道:"不知棺木埋葬得深浅如何,万一太深了,一时掘不到底如何是好?"

"唉,你真是! 我的棺木埋了不过三尺,你用一把好的铁锹,尽力去掘,哪有掘不开的? 柳郎呀柳郎,你救人要救彻底啊。"说到此处,远处已传来鸡鸣,杜丽娘魂灵儿骤然一惊,眼见残夜即将过去,要迅速返回冥府,便叮嘱柳梦梅:"柳郎呀,我的幽情一时也说不尽。你记住,我之能否复活,全在你了! 请你千万实践诺言,不

Am I just indulging in wishful thinking? She told me she was 18 years old. After she died she was buried under a plum tree in the Back Garden and looks just like living person but insists she is a ghost. It's strange. Since she told me everything in detail, I have no reason to suspect her and should do as she asks. I'll have to discuss the matter with Nun Shi." Dawn had broken and Liu Mengmei walked out of the room to see Nun Shi.

然,我必怨恨你的薄情负义!"说罢,随着阵阵寒风,刹时不见了。

柳梦梅神情木然地停立在书房中,掐掐手指,分明不是做梦,自言自语地说道:"奇哉,怪哉!我柳梦梅一夜之间做了杜太守的女婿,这不是做梦吧?待我回过神儿来好好想一想:她名叫杜丽娘,年华二八,死后葬在花园梅树之下。啐,分明是有精有血的可人儿,怎么她反颠倒说自己是个鬼,奇怪,奇怪。——不过,她说得这般分明,这般凄切,不论有无,只得依她说的办,且和石道姑商量去。"此时,天已放亮,他便急不可待地走出书房。

CHAPTER TEN

Du Liniang Is Saved

When Prefect Du built the Plum Blossom Nunnery for his dead daughter, he also bought sacrificial fields. Chen Zuiliang was instructed to collect rent and Nun Shi took care of the nunnery. Chen Zuiliang was able to earn some income from rents but Nun Shi who cleaned the nunnery every day had no chance of earning anything extra. Not long before, Chen Zuiliang had proposed that the local people build a temple to Prefect Du. His proposal had been accepted and he benefited from its construction. The more Nun Shi thought about it, the angrier she became. Early one morning, when she was sitting and cursing Chen Zuiliang, she heard someone calling her. "Good morning, Aunt Shi." She looked up and saw that it was Liu Mengmei.

"Young Master Liu, what can I do for you?"

As it happened Liu Mengmei had been pacing up and down outside the hall for a while. After he decided how to explain things to Nun Shi, he entered the hall and said, "Aunt Shi, since I came to the nunnery, I have never been to the hall. Today I want to take a look at it."

Nun Shi went over to greet him, delighted to find him so reverent and respectful; she volunteered to show him around and introduced him to every statue of Buddha. However Liu Mengmei's mind was elsewhere and, while pretending to listen attentively, he searched for something he needed. Suddenly he saw Du Liniang's tablet and said, "Aunt Shi, the inscription on the tablet reads, 'The sacred tablet of Miss Du.' Who is Miss Du? Is she a queen?" Liu Mengmei pretended to know nothing about her.

"No, she is not a queen. Don't you know why the nunnery was built? Former Prefect Du constructed it for his beloved daughter Du Liniang. Miss Liniang died when she was 18 years old. Just after she had died Prefect Du was promoted and, before leaving for his new post, decided to build this nunnery for his daughter."

第十章
掘坟救人

　　话说当年杜宝太守初建梅花观时，设置了祭田，收租之权被陈最良谋得，石道姑只落得个在杜小姐神位前添香换水的苦差事。这陈最良只管收取祭租，却不管梅花观一应杂事，近日又诱使县中众人共同出资为杜老爷盖了一座生祠，也捞到不少好处。这就更使石道姑忿忿不平，整日坐在观中怨天尤人。今日一早又在那里自言自语地诅咒陈最良，忽然一声"姑姑"将她从怨艾中招唤回来，抬头一看竟是柳梦梅。

　　"柳公子，清早来此有何贵干？"

　　其实柳梦梅已在堂外徘徊多时，考虑如何开口向石道姑求助，此刻想出了主意方才上堂来："姑姑，小生自从借住仙居以来，不曾到宝殿上礼拜过，今天很想上殿瞻礼一番。"

　　石道姑见柳梦梅毕恭毕敬的模样，颇为高兴，满口答允，立即在前引导，上得殿来，指着座座佛像向柳梦梅逐一介绍。其实柳梦梅之意哪在此，他一边竖起耳朵装作仔细听讲，一边瞪大眼睛四处寻找，有了，他终于找到他要找的东西。"姑姑，左边这牌位上写着'杜小姐神王'，是哪位女王？"柳梦梅故作不懂地问道。

　　"啊呀呀，你真的不知道？你不知道这座道观为何人所建？这是此地前任太守杜宝杜老爷为他的爱女所建造的。杜老爷独女杜

When Liu Mengmei heard this, he covered his face with his sleeve and cried, "Actually Miss Du Liniang is my charming wife."

"Master Liu, is it true?" Nun Shi was surprised.

"Absolutely true," Liu Mengmei said firmly.

Thinking it very odd, Nun Shi began asking Liu Mengmei all about Du Liniang, when she was born, when she died, how Liu Mengmei met her, and how they were married. Liu Mengmei did not know how to reply but suddenly had an idea. He said, "Let me show you. If I add a character to her tablet, the table will move and prove that my words are true."

Nun Shi did not believe him but she was curious. She brought a brush from the inner room and gave it to Liu Mengmei who began to add the character to the tablet. As it turned out, Liu Mengmei had not been sure himself, but as he had made the claim, he had to do it. How strange it was when the table actually began to move! Dumbfounded, Nun Shi bowed to Du Liniang's tablet and said, "Oh, Master Liu is really your husband. I did not know. Please forgive me." Then she turned to Liu Mengmei and said, "Since Miss Liniang is your beloved wife, you should guard her tomb."

After seeing the tablet move by itself, Liu Mengmei asserted that he would help her revive and return to the world. Then he told Nun Shi of his plan to dig up Du Liniang's tomb.

"Do you have magic power? Are you the king of the Hell?" Nun Shi still did not believe him.

"Don't argue with me. You just find a laborer and you could give me a hand too," Liu Mengmei said.

"According to the law, anyone involved in opening a dead person's coffin is liable to be executed. It does not matter whether they are the culprit or an accomplice. I dare not help you."

"Don't' worry about it. It was suggested by Miss Liniang herself. She also told me that your help is indispensable."

"If Miss Liniang wants me to, I'll take the risk. Let me find an auspicious day for her."

"I have looked for it in the almanac and tomorrow will be an auspicious day. We shall dig the tomb tomorrow." Liu Mengmei did not want any further delay and Nun Shi agreed. Then Liu Mengmei sent Nun Shi to Chen Zuiliang's drug store to buy soul-saving medicines. On the way there she called on her nephew to ask him to come to the Back Garden of Plum Blossom Nunnery to help dig up the coffin.

丽娘,十八岁上就亡故,葬在此处。杜老爷因急于奔赴新任,来不及题主,所以牌位空至今日。"

柳梦梅问得明白后,掩面哭泣道:"啊呀,这样说起来,杜小姐正是我的娇妻呵。"

"公子,此事当真么?"石道姑乍闻此言,十分吃惊。

柳梦梅斩钉截铁地表示:"千真万确。"

石道姑觉得此事太蹊跷,不断盘问柳梦梅:杜小姐生于何年、死于何夕,你们如何会面、又怎样成婚。柳梦梅被问得窘然不知所措,突然想到一个主意:"你要不信,我让小姐显个神通给你看——取笔来,我来为她题主,她的牌位会动的。"

石道姑不相信会有此事,拿了一枝笔来递给柳梦梅。其实柳梦梅哪曾有把握,此时话已说出口,只能硬着头皮在牌位上加了点。不曾料到杜小姐的神主牌位儿真的动了起来,石道姑惊得目瞪口呆,好一会儿才回过神来,对着神主牌又作揖又诉说:"小姐呵,哪里想到这个柳公子倒真的是你的娇客。"说罢,又侧过头来对柳梦梅说:"柳公子,小姐既是你的娇妻,你要替她守墓。"

"我还要请她立起来,让她还阳回生哩。"柳梦梅见神主牌居然动起来,也有了胆子敢说出掘坟开棺的话来。

石道姑依然不信:"你当真有如此神通?难道你是阎罗王?"

"不必争论,你替我找个出力气的人就成,你也帮帮忙。"

"律令规定,开棺见尸,不论主犯、从犯,一律斩首,我可不敢!"

"是小姐自己的主见,姑姑,小姐说此事一定得你帮忙。"

"既然是小姐吩咐,不得不冒这个风险了,待我选个吉日动土。"

"不用选,明日就是吉日,正可破土。"柳梦梅见石道姑已答允帮忙,不想拖延,便趁热打铁地订下日子,石道姑也同意了。柳梦梅又吩咐石道姑先去陈最良药铺中赎点安魂药,石道姑即时去

Early in morning the following day Nun Shi's nephew came to the Back Garden by himself carrying a string of paper money. He hung it up by the Taihu rock, burnt some joss sticks and prayed to all the heavenly gods. "We shall be digging up Du Liniang's tomb today and I am doing what I have been told to do. If it is not right, please don't blame me."

When he had finished praying and burning the paper money, he saw Nun Shi and Liu Mengmei arrive. On the way there the nun talked incessantly, but Liu Mengmei, who was smoldering with impatience, was not in the mood to chat. He walked straight to the Taihu rock to look for the tomb, but found only a pavilion full of broken tiles and bricks and a garden covered with thick grass. He said anxiously to Nun Shi, "Aunt Shi, I remember picking up the portrait by the Taihu rock. However, now I cannot find the place. What can we do?"

"Master Liu, don't worry. Look, the mound under the plum tree is Miss Du Liniang's tomb." Nun Shi pointed to the mound ahead of them.

Liu Mengmei sped to the tomb and threw himself onto it crying bitterly, "Alas, my darling, I'm so sad to find you lying here by yourself in a desolate garden. You must be very lonely." Nun Shi followed closely behind and her nephew limped along. Nun Shi said, "It's not the time for crying. Let's make the best use of our time and dig up the tomb."

Nun Shi's nephew began burning another string of paper money while Liu Mengmei knelt on the ground to pay homage to the local god of the land. Nun Shi's nephew was very experienced. He walked around the tomb and said to the other two, "Let's start digging here. It's the end of the tomb." Nun Shi and her nephew dug with all of their might and soon their spades touched the coffin. "You two must be very careful. Please don't frighten Miss Liniang." Liu Mengmei was worried.

"Alas!" A sound from the coffin startled them. "Oh, it's the voice of Miss Liniang!" Nun Shi said after she had calmed down. Her nephew was very brave. He jumped into the pit, pulled the snails off the coffin, brushed the dust off the lid and prised it open. Du Liniang lay there peacefully. She looked as if she were sleeping and a pleasant smell rose from the coffin. At the sight of the sleeping beauty, Liu Mengmei lost his fear. He jumped into the pit, gently raised Du Liniang in his arms and lifted her out of the coffin. Just then Du Liniang's eye-lids moved. Nun Shi, who had sharp eyes, shouted in surprise, "Miss Liniang is opening her eyes."

"Oh, my darling, open your eyes and look at me," Liu Mengmei

了,顺便通知侄儿癫头鼋明日清晨早早来后花园中帮忙掘坟。

　　次日清晨,癫头鼋拎了一串纸钱,独自一人进了园门,来到太湖石边,将纸钱挂起来,又烧起香来,向上天诸神祷告一番,又向土地爷祈求,今日动土,自己是奉命行事,请不要怪罪。

　　癫头鼋焚纸烧香,向天地祈祷刚刚完毕,石道姑便与柳梦梅一边说话一边走了进来。柳梦梅心急如焚,没有心思听石道姑絮絮叨叨的诉说,忙于寻找杜丽娘的坟地,只见半亭瓦砾,满园荒草,一时寻它不得,急得对石道姑说:"姑姑,我依稀记得,太湖石边是我拾着画像之处,但如今却认不清,怎生是好?"

　　"柳公子,你急啥? 梅树下面那个土堆儿不就是!"

　　柳梦梅闻言急步上前、扑倒在坟堆上,放声哭道:"哎呀呀,小姐呀,你独自一个眠在这里,令人好不伤感呀!"石道姑一摇一摆、癫头鼋一颠一跛地先后来到坟前,劝止柳梦梅说:"哭什么? 还不抓紧时间挖坟!"

　　癫头鼋又烧起一串纸钱,柳梦梅急忙忙拜告土地老爷保佑。祷告完毕,便动起手来。癫头鼋不愧为盗墓能手,左右度量一番,便招呼石道姑和他一起从坟脚头下锹,不一会儿,就挖到棺木,柳梦梅赶紧叮嘱:"小心,要十分小心,不要惊着小姐!"

　　"哎哟!"棺木中忽地传来一声,倒把这三个男女吓了一跳。石道姑转过神来说:"活鬼做声了。"癫头鼋到底胆子壮,拔起已经锈断了的棺材钉,抹去棺材板上的积土,推开棺材板,只见杜丽娘端然而卧,异香袭人,幽姿如故。柳梦梅此时再无惧怕之心,而有千种万种怜惜之情,一步跳下坑去,伸出一双手臂,轻轻托起杜丽娘。经这番折腾,杜丽娘一双星眼,半闭似开,石道姑眼尖,惊呼道:"小姐开眼哩。"

　　柳梦梅跟着也看到了:"小姐呵! 这是天开眼哩。"

said with emotion.

Gradually Du Liniang came to. She opened her eyes and asked, "Is it real or false?" There was a gust of wind and Du Liniang closed her eyes hurriedly. Liu Mengmei hastened to carry her to the Peony Pavilion to shelter from the wind. He asked Nun Shi to put the soul-saving medicine that she bought the previous day from Chen Zuiliang's drug store into warm wine and gently poured the medicine into Miss Liniang's mouth. Soon Du Liniang's cheeks turned red and the three around her exclaimed, "She's come back to life. It's wonderful!"

With the help of the medicine and wine, Du Liniang gradually recovered consciousness. When she opened her eyes and saw the people around her, she was startled and said, "Who are you? Have you robbed my tomb?"

"Miss Liniang," Liu Mengmei called out happily and astonished, "I'm Liu Mengmei."

Excited Nun Shi said, "It's a miracle that has never happened since ancient times. Today you came back to life after you had been dead for three years." Then she went to Du Liniang and asked, "Do you remember me, Miss Liniang? I'm Nun Shi." Du Liniang stared at her for a while, but could not remember who she was.

Liu Mengmei was anxious and said, "Do you remember the Back Garden?" Du Liniang was silent and but after a pause asked, "Who is Liu Mengmei?"

"It's me," Liu Mengmei answered. Du Liniang looked at him with tenderness and love. "You've kept your promise. Your great love has moved heaven and earth. That's why you could save me from death. Your love for me is utterly honest. I'm so grateful to you."

Liu Mengmei put his palms together and said: "Amitabha!"

After Du Liniang awoke from death, she felt very weak and lacked the strength to do anything. Her body felt like jelly, but with a few days rest and the care of Nun Shi and Liu Mengmei, who prepared various kinds of nutritious food and fresh fruit for her, her energy gradually improved and her health recovered. One day when she was with Nun Shi, she thanked her. "Aunt Shi, I died three years ago for love. Now that I am back from Hell and restored to life, I'm very grateful to you and Master Liu. Without your help, I would still be in the tomb. I owe my life to you and I'll remember your help and kindness forever."

杜丽娘渐渐清醒了,听到人声,自言自语地说道:"此情此景不知是真的还是假的?"一阵风过,她又赶紧闭上双眼。柳梦梅见状,急忙将她扶到牡丹亭中去避风,同时吩咐石道姑快快用温酒将还魂散调匀,轻轻给杜丽娘灌下去。只见她的脸色渐渐红润起来,三人一齐高兴地说道:"好了,好了!"

杜丽娘借着酒力、药力,慢慢恢复了知觉,睁开眼睛,看见几个男女站在周围,不禁有些吓怕,问道:"你们都是些什么人?该不是前来掘我坟的无赖歹徒吧!"

"小姐,小姐!"柳梦梅惊喜地叫道,"我是柳梦梅。"

石道姑也高兴地叫着:"这真是千古没有的奇事,小姐死去三年,居然又能复活!"说着上前问道:"小姐可认得我石道姑么?"杜丽娘看了一会儿,不肯应承。

柳梦梅急了:"小姐,你可记得这后花园?"杜丽娘仍然不语,停了半晌,突然问道:"哪个是柳郎?"

柳梦梅高兴得上前一步:"小姐,我便是。"杜丽娘又仔细看觑一番,含情脉脉地指着柳梦梅道:"咳,柳郎真是讲信用之人!真情感天地,生者可以死,死者可以复生;情之所至,生死不移呢!"

柳梦梅合掌念了声:"阿弥陀佛!"

杜丽娘回生之初,全身软绵无力,在石道姑与柳梦梅悉心调护之下,天天以美酒香酥、时鲜嘉果供养。经过几天的养息,精神渐渐旺盛,体力日逐增强。她见了石道姑,再三称谢,说:"姑姑,奴家死去三年,为一点儿衷情,死而复生,全靠姑姑和柳郎救护,奴家终身不忘大恩。"

石道姑对她的感激倒不十分在意,见她今日提起"柳郎"二

"Don't mention it. It's the least I could do," Nun Shi said. "I have something to tell you. Master Liu has urged me many times recently to speak to you of marriage."

"I think it's too early to discuss. First of all I have to ask for my parents' approval. They are in Huaiyang. Then they must find a go-between for us," Du Liniang said.

Nun Shi was not pleased with her answer and said, "How can you say that? Isn't it something for you to decide? Do you remember what happened before your death?"

"Yes, it is still fresh in my mind. I fell ill because I missed Liu Mengmei who I met in a dream. Then I drew a self-portrait which was buried under the Taihu rock. Master Liu found the portrait and from that day on he burnt joss sticks before it, bowed to it and called for me day and night. Although I was buried, I'll never forget his sincerity."

Nun Shi saw Liu Mengmei coming and said, "Look, Master Liu returns."

Liu Mengmei visited Du Liniang several times a day. He saw Du Liniang's face glowing with health and was overjoyed. After a deep breath, he exclaimed, "My dear wife Liniang, how are you today?" Du Liniang blushed a deep red.

Liu Mengmei was pleased with himself and said, "I retrieved a goddess from a tomb."

"Thank you very much, Master Liu. It is you who gave me another life. I can never thank you enough for what you've done," Du Liniang said.

"Let's get married tonight," Liu Mengmei said eagerly.

"According to Chinese tradition, a marriage between a man and a woman should be approved by their parents and arranged by a go-between," Du Liniang replied.

"Oh, Miss, now you want to act according to tradition. Do you remember when you visited me every night? We had many happy times together."

"Master Liu, things have changed. Before I was a ghost. A ghost needn't follow human rules. Now that I have returned to life, and as a lady from a good family, I must follow traditions." Then she bowed low to Liu Mengmei and said, "I'm very grateful to you for granting me a second life. But as far as marriage is concerned, we must have my parents' consent and it must be arranged by a go-between."

字，便开口说道："好了，我也不要你谢，只是柳公子这几日来，已
三番五次，不断求我为你作成亲事哩。"

"哎呀，今日谈论此事，尚嫌过早，得有人去淮扬问过老爷、夫
人，还要有个媒人才成。"

"你倒说得好自在！这也由你一个作主？我要问你，你可记得
前生之事？"石道姑倒有些不满了。

"奴家记得。那时因伤春而病，病中自画春容，埋在太湖石
下。柳郎拾到此画，殷勤叩拜，热忱呼唤，我虽埋在土下，但柳郎的
一片衷情，令奴家难以忘怀……"

不待杜丽娘把话说完，石道姑眼尖，远远望见柳梦梅迤逦走
来，便打断杜丽娘的话头，说："你看，柳公子又来了。"

柳梦梅近来几乎一日数次前来探视，但从未见到杜丽娘今日
这般容颜焕发，更显出天生艳质，不觉手舞足蹈地大步向前，长长
一揖，兴高采烈地叫道："丽娘贤妻。"这一声不打紧，直把个杜丽
娘羞得红了半边脸。

"小姐，我是从地窟中抉出一个天仙哩。"柳梦梅得意非凡。

"谢谢柳郎，使奴家得以重生，恩同爹娘。"

"今晚，我和你，就成婚吧。"柳梦梅急不可耐地脱口而
出。

杜丽娘说："书上不是说，男女婚配，必待父母之命，媒妁之言
么？"

"小姐，你怎么倒引经据典起来！你不记得前日欢会？"

"柳郎呀，今日比不得以前了！以前是鬼，今日是人，鬼可虚
情，人要实礼——柳郎呀，"叫了一声，她深深下拜，又说道："我得
以重生，要感激柳郎，只是匹配婚姻，必得有父母之命，还要有作
伐媒人呀。"

"That's not a problem. After we marry, we can visit your parents. They will be very glad to see their dead daughter has returned to life. As for a go-between, Nun Shi is qualified," Liu Mengmei said firmly.

Du Liniang was about to say something when someone knocked on the door. "Is anyone home?"

All the people in the room were alarmed. "Who is it?" Liu Mengmei asked.

"It's me, Chen Zuiliang. I come to pay you a visit, Master Liu."

The three people were panic stricken. "What shall we do now, Nun Shi? Mr. Chen is knocking at the door." Liu Mengmei did not know what to do.

Du Liniang was startled, but calmed down and said to Nun Shi, "Aunt Shi, I'll hide myself first."

Chen Zuiliang was surprised at hearing a woman's voice in the room. He had no doubt about it and kept on knocking.

"It's very nice to see you," Liu Mengmei said after opening the door. "I was not properly dressed so I didn't come to the door straight away. I hope you will forgive me."

"It's very strange," Chen Zuiliang said.

"What's strange?"

"I heard a woman's voice."

When she heard this, Nun Shi walked out from the inner room to greet Chen Zuiliang. "Oh, Mr. Chen is here. How are you?"

"Aunt Shi was in my room. That's why you heard a woman's voice," Liu Mengmei explained.

Chen Zuiliang did not know what was happening and said to Liu Mengmei, "Tomorrow will be the Mid-Autumn Festival. It is also the anniversary of the death of Miss Du Liniang. I have prepared some sacrificial offerings for her and came to invite you to go with me to pay our respects to Prefect Du's daughter tomorrow."

"Yes, I'll wait for you tomorrow," Liu Mengmei said.

"Well, I'll take my leave now." Chen Zuiliang left.

After he had gone, Liu Mengmei closed the door and Du Liniang came out of the inner room. Nun Shi said to the two young people, "What shall we do then? Tomorrow Chen Zuiliang will go to the Back Garden to sweep the tomb. If he finds that the tomb is empty, he will report it to the local officials. They will think that Miss Liniang is a spirit and criticize Mr. and Mrs. Du for not educating their daughter. Master Liu will be suspected

"这不难，成了婚，再去拜见令尊、令堂，女儿复生，老人家自会高兴，哪能说三道四；媒人也现成，石道姑就是。"柳梦梅此刻倒颇有主意。

杜丽娘正想说什么，一阵扣门声，打断了他们的谈话，"有人么？"

大家不觉一惊，问道："谁人？"

"是陈先生探望柳公子。"

三人更是大惊失色，柳梦梅问石道姑："陈先生来了，怎么办？"

杜丽娘也有些惊惶，但还有主意，对石道姑说："姑姑，我暂且避过。"

陈最良立在门外，见房门久扣不开，房内似有女儿声音，不禁有些诧异，又再三扣门。

柳梦梅打开房门，抱歉地说："承先生光临。因我衣冠未整，迎接有迟，请谅。"

"奇怪！奇怪！"陈最良意有所指。

"有何奇怪？"

"怎么听到女客声音？"

石道姑闻言迎了出来，招呼道："原来是陈先生到来。"

柳梦梅趁机解释道："陈先生说房中有妇人声音，正是姑姑。"

陈最良没有抓着什么把柄，便对柳梦梅说："明日中秋节是小姐的忌辰，我准备了祭奠礼品，去杜小姐坟上，特来约柳公子同去。今日无事，我就告辞了。"

柳梦梅见陈最良走远了，掩上房门，将杜丽娘从内房请了出来。石道姑首先说道："这怎么办？明日陈最良要到后花园祭坟扫墓，他若看出破绽，如何得了！这桩事非同小可，一旦败露，一来小

of luring Miss Liniang. I will be punished for digging up the tomb. We have to find a way out."

As it happened, Nun Shi had already thought of something but she used the opportunity to urge Du Liniang to marry Liu Mengmei. Du Liniang was so worried that she begged Nun Shi for a solution. "Aunt Shi, what shall we do then? You must find a way for us to cover our tracks."

Du Liniang was very anxious and Nun Shi said calmly, "Miss, don't be alarmed. I have an idea, but I'm not sure if you agree with it."

"I'll agree with you. Please tell me, Aunt Shi," Du Liniang said keenly.

"Master Liu is going to Lin'an to take the highest imperial examination. I suggest that you marry him right away, then the two of you leave for Lin'an by boat tomorrow morning. You'll be gone without a trace. What do you think of it?"

"Yes, that's a good idea!" Liu Mengmei exclaimed looking anxiously at Du Liniang.

After some time, Du Liniang nodded her head; she had no choice. Nun Shi took out a wine jar and two cups then presided over the wedding ceremony. The bride and bridegroom kowtowed to Heaven and Earth, to each other and then drank wine from nuptial cups. They were thus married.

Early next morning Nun Shi's nephew, who had already hired a boat, waited for Nun Shi, Liu Mengmei and Du Liniang at the wharf. He saw them coming and the boatman urged them to hurry. After Liu Mengmei had helped his wife board the boat, Nun Shi took her leave saying, "Master Liu, and Miss Liniang, you must take great care during the trip."

Liu Mengmei invited Nun Shi to go with them. "There is no one to attend to my wife on the way. Could you please do me a favor and go with us? If I pass the imperial examination and become an official, I'll repay you for everything you've done."

After while Nun Shi agreed. She thought that it would be better for her to leave as there could be trouble if she stayed. She said, "All right, I'll go with you but, Master Liu, could you please give something to my nephew and let him go home?"

Liu Mengmei, who had not much money, took off an article of clothing and gave it to Nun Shi's nephew. After thanking him Nun Shi's nephew asked, "What shall I do if they ask me about it?"

姐有妖冶之名,二来老爷夫人无闺阃之教,三来柳公子有诱骗之嫌,四来我也有发掘之罪,如何是好?"

　　其实,石道姑已有了主意,故意以此相逼。杜丽娘闻言,急得搓着双手,向石道姑求救:"姑姑,这怎生是好? 请姑姑务必想法遮盖。"

　　石道姑见小姐情急了,方才慢吞吞地说出计谋:"小姐,你也不要先慌起来。我倒有个办法,不知小姐是允还是不允?"

　　"哪有不允之理! 姑姑快快说出。"

　　"小姐,这柳公子正准备去临安应考。不如你委屈一下,先和他成了亲事。然后叫一只江西船,连夜离开此地,踪迹全无,就全没事了。不知小姐意下如何?"

　　"是呀,姑姑想得周到,小姐,就这样吧!"柳梦梅正中下怀,用恳求的眼神望着杜丽娘。

　　杜丽娘沉吟半晌,事已至此,确也别无它法,只得应允。于是石道姑取出酒来,为他们两个主持婚事,拜告天地后又相互对拜,饮了合卺酒,匆匆成就了夫妻。

　　次日凌晨,癞头鼋已在码头雇好船,等着石道姑一众人等前来。不一会儿,果然见石道姑与柳公子、小姐三人行来。船家已在催发船,柳梦梅先行扶着小姐上船,石道姑告辞说:"柳公子,小姐,一路小心。"

　　柳梦梅却不让石道姑回去,邀约道:"娘子无人服侍,烦姑姑一路同行,小生若是考试得官,一定重重相报。"

　　石道姑沉吟了一会儿,也觉得万一事发必然牵连自家,三十六计,走为上策,便答允道:"也罢,老身与你们同行——公子,你赏侄儿点东西,让他回去吧。"

　　柳梦梅囊中并不充盈,便脱下一身衣服赏给癞头鼋,癞头鼋谢过之后,问道:"事发了怎么办?"

"You just tell them that you know nothing about it." Liu Mengmei boarded the boat, the boatman untied the rope and it floated down the river.

Du Liniang looked at the scenery on both sides of the river and shed tears. Liu Mengmei said, "Why are you weeping, my darling?"

Du Liniang said nothing for a while then in low spirits replied, "I'm thinking that I once lived in this city for many years, then was buried here. But after I returned from death, I have to leave. I don't know when I shall come back again."

Liu Mengmei and Nun Shi tried their best to comfort her and Du Liniang overcame her sadness. Liu Mengmei went to her and whispered, "How nice it is to enjoy a honeymoon in a small boat!"

Du Liniang blushed and said in a low voice, "Master, I did not realize until today that life on earth is so full of happiness. After so much trouble, the love between us is as deep as the sea!"

Now let's turn to Chen Zuiliang in Nan'an Prefecture. Mr. Chen got up early the following morning, put some joss sticks, candles, wine, cakes and fruit in a basket and carried them to the Plum Blossom Nunnery. When he arrived, he found the door of the nunnery open and no sign of Liu Mengmei and Nun Shi. Miss Du's tablet had disappeared too. He was astonished and thought that they must have paired up and run away. He had never come across such a callous nun and immoral scholar.

He had to go to the Back Garden by himself and, when he approached Du Liniang's grave, he was stunned to find the coffin open and Miss Liniang's body gone. The scene made him call to mind that the people to the south of Mount Meiling were good at robbing tombs. Liu Mengmei came from there. He was sure that he had robbed the tomb and escaped with Nun Shi. Chen Zuiliang lost no time in reporting the case to the local government of Nan'an Prefecture and asked the prefect to have Liu Mengmei arrested. Then he packed up his things, and started his journey to Huaiyang to report it to Mr. Du Bao.

"你只一推二不知。"柳梦梅说罢,也上了船,船工解了缆绳,船沿江而下。

杜丽娘坐在舱中,见两岸风物渐渐后退、消失,不禁落下泪来,柳梦梅不知何故,问道:"又因何落泪?"

"唉……"杜丽娘长长叹了一口气,情绪低沉地回答道:"想我住在此地、埋在此地,重生之后,却远走天涯,何年何月,才能重返!"

听得此言,柳梦梅与石道姑二人好言劝慰,杜丽娘渐消愁怀,柳梦梅又悄悄附耳问道:"风月舟中,新婚佳趣,其乐如何?"

杜丽娘羞红了脸,也悄悄应和道:"相公,我今日方知有人间之乐呀。我和你生生死死,情深似海哩。"

且不说柳梦梅、杜丽娘、石道姑三人离别南安府前往京师临安。再说那南安府的陈最良,那天也是很早起床,将香烛酒点装了一只提盒,拎了去梅花观,邀约柳梦梅去杜丽娘坟上看望。走近梅花观,只见观门洞开,寂无人迹,柳梦梅不见,石道姑不见,连杜丽娘的神主牌位也没了影儿,不禁大骇。他想:必定是柳梦梅勾搭了石道姑潜逃他方,真是没人伦的道姑、没品德的秀才!

他只得独自一人去了后花园。走近杜丽娘坟山,更令他大惊失色,坟堆平了,棺木开了,连小姐的骨殖也不见了。他推想:岭南人惯于劫坟,柳梦梅既是岭南人,必是劫坟贼无疑。随即抽身而出,向南安府禀报,请府尊大人缉拿劫坟贼柳梦梅。随后,又收拾行李,连夜赶往淮阳,要将此事报告杜宝老先生知道。

CHAPTER ELEVEN

Liu Takes the Imperial
Examination

On the day that his beloved daughter died Du Bao, the prefect of Nan'an, had been designated by the court as the Pacification Commissioner of Huaiyang. Since then three years had elapsed.

When Du Bao assumed his post, the Kin minority in the north were a serious menace to the Song Dynasty. After Wanyan Aguda annihilated the State of Liao and established the Kin Dynasty, the Kin people controled all the northern area and challenged the Song Dynasty. Emperor Zhao Gou of the Song Dynasty crossed the Yangtze River in panic, fled to Lin'an (now Hangzhou, Zhejiang Province). This period was known in history as the Southern Song Dynasty. Time flew swiftly and 30 years later Wanyan Liang distinguished himself as Emperor of the Kin Dynasty, while Zhao Gou, the lotus-eating emperor, never thought about reclaiming the central plain but concentrated on building up Lin'an city. In this man-made paradise the emperor and ministers enjoyed themselves to their hearts' content, celebrating peace with song and dance.

At that time many poets composed works depicting the green hills and water of West Lake and the splendor of Lin'an. One of the best known poems was called "Viewing Sea Waves." It described the beautiful scenery of Hangzhou city and boasted of "three seasons of laurel and 10 miles of lotus flowers." The image so tempted Emperor Wanyan Liang of the Kin Dynasty that he could not restrain his desire to invade it.

After he came to the throne, Wanyan Liang secretly sent a painter with the envoy to the Song kingdom to paint a panoramic picture of the West Lake. The painting was made into a screen for his room. Painted on the screen was a portrait of him standing beside a horse on the top of the Mount Wu by West Lake. There was also a poem inscribed on the screen:

I want to rule the whole country,

第十一章
临安应试

　　南安太守杜宝在掌上明珠杜丽娘亡故之日，被朝廷任命为淮扬安抚使，匆匆走马上任至今先后已历三年。

　　他接受此职时，金人南侵形势十分严重。自从完颜阿骨打灭了辽国，建立金王朝后，金人便与赵宋王朝形成直接对抗的局面，整个北方全在金人控制之下。宋朝康王赵构仓皇渡江南逃，一直逃到临安(今浙江杭州)，史称南宋高宗。

　　岁月悠悠，三十余年后完颜亮成了大金皇帝，他听说宋高宗赵构是个贪图享受的皇帝老儿，不思收复中原大地，一味妆点临安风景，在他经营之下，临安的繁华早已胜过北宋都城汴梁(今日河南开封)。南宋君臣就在这"天堂"中朝欢暮乐、歌舞升平。

　　当时不少诗人词客纷纷写诗填词，描摹西湖的山青水秀、临安的富丽堂皇，其中数词人柳永的《望海潮》一词最是脍炙人口，词中说到杭州"有三秋桂子，十里荷花"，直把大金国当今皇帝完颜亮引诱得蠢蠢欲动，要起兵百万，直下江南。

　　完颜亮做皇帝后，曾派遣画工混在出使宋朝的人员中，偷偷地画了一幅西湖全景图，制成屏风，置于堂上。在西湖吴山之顶，又加画了自家立于马侧的形象，并亲自题诗一首于其上：

What difference is there between the Kin's land and the south?
Millions of troops will head to the West Lake,
I'll ride a horse and stand on the Mount Wu.

The screen allowed him to enjoy the scenery of West Lake and at same time reminded him of his plan of annexing the Southern Song Dynasty.

Wanyan Liang never ceased in his attempts at conquering the Southern Song Dynasty. He thought that in war it was a good strategy to mix falsehood with the truth, nothing could be too deceitful. Hence he decided that a Han would lay the ground for his invasion by sowing dissent. After careful selection, Wanyan Liang finally picked a robber named Li Quan from Huaiyang area. Li Quan was brave enough to defeat 10,000 men and the local Song official could do nothing to stop his attacks. So Wanyan Liang decided to use him to pave the way to Lin'an. Li Quan always fawned on Wanyan Liang who called him "sweet mouth king."

Li Quan had been a hooligan in Huai'an, Jiangsu Province, and had gathered round him a group of local ruffians called the Five Hundred Gangsters. They incessantly harassed local people and the Southern Song court neither offered them amnesty nor could it wipe them out. It had to allow them to wreak havoc on local people at their pleasure. Nevertheless, Li Quan was not content with being a robber; he had ambitions of taking up a post in the court. The Southern Song court would not accept him and the Kin beckoned him to the other side so he fell into their arms and called himself "a Han who knows the Kin language and teaches the Kin to curse the Han."

Although Li Quan was brave enough to defeat 10,000 men, he was in fact a lout, bold but not crafty. Fortunately, his wife, Lady Yang who used an invincible spear, was resourceful and good at strategy. All of Li Quan's soldiers were in awe of her. This husband-and-wife duo colluded in evil acts, causing anger and discontent in the Huaiyang area.

After Du Bao had been made Pacification Commissioner of Huaiyang, he first of all reassured the people but his priority was to eliminate the gangsters. However, the gangsters outnumbered imperial soldiers and it was not easy to do this in the short term. Therefore he focused for the time being on keeping the enemy at bay. After careful investigation Du Bao decided to build Yangzhou as strong as iron. Led by Pacification Commissioner Du, the soldiers and the people of Yangzhou

万里车书盍混同,江南岂有别疆封?

提兵百万西湖上,立马吴山第一峰。

既为欣赏西湖景致,又以此时时提醒自己不忘南下吞并赵宋王朝之计。

完颜亮灭宋之心有增无减,他想到兵法虚虚实实,兵不厌诈,离间分化,可兼而行之。于是决定启用南方汉族人,为他进兵先导。几经物色,终于在淮扬一带找到一个叫李全的贼人。此人有万夫不当之勇,当地宋朝官员对他的骚扰束手无策,完颜亮决心利用这个家伙,为自己开辟进军临安的道途。又因这李全一直拍马顺溜自己,就封他一个虚衔"溜金王"。

李全原是江苏淮安的一个无赖,他聚集了一批地痞流氓,号称五百之众。这伙人不断骚扰百姓,南宋朝廷既不肯招抚,又无力剿灭,任由他们践踏地方、蹂躏百姓。而这个李全并不甘心为寇为贼,一心想为官当宰,南朝既不受,金人又招手,便一头栽进金人怀抱,自谓"汉儿学得胡儿语,又替胡儿骂汉人。"

其实,李全虽有万夫不当之勇,却是个有勇无谋的莽夫,幸亏有他的婆娘杨氏相助,这杨氏不但使一条梨花枪,万人无敌,而且颇有计谋,善于权变,帐下军士都畏惧她。这对强人夫唱妇随,狼狈为奸,直扰得淮扬一带天怒人怨。

杜宝自南安府任来此做安抚使后,安民自然是第一要着。而要安民又首先要剿灭贼人,只因 贼人势众,官军力弱,一时尚不能进剿奏功,只得着重防贼。杜宝经过全面考察,认为淮扬一带尤数扬州为重镇,必须加意经营,使之固若金汤。于是率领扬州军士民众,在城外又加筑了一座罗城,环绕旧城四周,以外城防内城。这座罗城修筑得高大厚实,城上建有瞭望楼,城墙上修有女墙,女墙上留有箭眼,可以射杀城外贼众。

built a new wall around the old city wall. This provided strong protection to the inside wall. The new wall was high and solid with watchtowers on top. On the wall were several short walls with arrow holes from which the soldiers could shoot the enemy outside. On the day that they finished building it, Du Bao, civil and military officials and soldiers and civilians of Yangzhou held a riverside ceremony to celebrate. Followed by a couple of high-ranking officials Du Bao inspected the wall's quality and defense capability. He also invited local wealthy merchants to walk along the new wall with him. With a big enough army, sufficient provisions and fodder, Pacification Commissioner Du would not be afraid if Li Quan attacked.

However, Du Bao had not taken everything into account. Although, for the time being, Li Quan could not take Yangzhou City, he never gave up the idea. Emperor Wanyan Liang of the Kin Dynasty kept on pushing him to clear the way for an invasion of Hangzhou. It was three years since Li Quan had established himself and his men in Huaiyang. Although under orders of the Kin, he continued harassing the local people and provoking riots. He achieved nothing by taking over the city or occupying the land. As time went on, Li Quan found it harder to justify himself to his Kin masters, which placed him in a dilemma.

One day Li Quan received further urgent instructions from the Kin court which left him with no choice. He went to consult his wife, Lady Yang, who had not slept well the night before. Her face was gloomy and Li Quan, had who had no time to offer greetings, came straight to the point. "My lady, our Kin master is about to head south. I was supposed to pave the way by attacking Huaiyang, but the new Pacification Commissioner Du Bao of Huaiyang has accumulated funds and provisions in the city of Yangzhou and has improved the city defences making it difficult to take. I am desperate. Do you have any good ideas?"

Lady Yang was really capable. For her this was no problem and she said straight away, "In my opinion, we should first of all besiege another city, Huai'an, which is also in the Huaiyang area; Du Bao will definitely send for troops. Then we can deploy our elite men to cut off his reinforcements. In that way we will be assured of victory."

"You are really smart! My love, you have persuaded me! Let's attack Huai'an city right now!"

With the help of Nun Shi, Liu Mengmei disinterred Du Liniang's coffin and brought her back to life. To avoid detection Du and Liu,

此城完工之日，扬州的文武官僚，军兵士民，无不倚为抗击贼众的长城，临江酾酒，以为庆贺。杜宝亲率几名要员，检视工程质量和防御能力，又邀请盐商富绅一同登楼，借此动员他们踊跃输纳钱粮，支持军需。有兵有粮，杜宝也就不怕李全贼人前来攻城掠地了。

但杜宝对敌情估计不足，这李全虽然一时难以攻占扬州，但也并未放弃这一念头。因为金主完颜亮不断催逼，要他为发兵南下，进军杭州扫清道路。他率众盘踞在淮扬也已三年之久，虽然奉金主之命不断骚扰地方，挑起事端，但攻城掠地，尚未奏功。迁延日久，也不好向金主交代。如何是好，着实委决不下。

这一天，金主又下令催促，不得已，他只得硬着头皮，请压寨夫人出来商量。压寨夫人一夜未曾睡稳，满腹不高兴地被请了出来。

李全也顾不得什么夫妇相见之礼，开门见山地说：

"娘娘，金主就要南下，叫我做前锋攻打淮扬，为他征进开路。近来扬州有个安抚使杜宝，广积钱粮，加筑城墙，急切之下，难以攻占，如何是好？"

李全夫人颇有能耐，在她看来，这事有何为难之处，便不假思索地回答道：

"依奴家所见，先围攻淮安，那时杜宝定然分兵去救，我们则率领精兵，断他的援军，再设法取胜。"

"高，高！娘娘这计谋儿真高！我们即刻起兵攻打淮安去！"

自从柳梦梅在石道姑等人帮助下，挖坟开棺，救活了杜丽娘之后，为怕事情败露，柳、杜这对情侣，在石道姑相伴下，凌晨即乘江西船离开南安，辗转到了浙江，在京都临安租了一所空房暂时

accompanied by Nun Shi, boarded a boat at daybreak, left Nan'an and after a journey through many places finally arrived at Zhejiang. They rented an empty house in the capital city, Lin'an, and settled down. Liu Mengmei returned to his books and started preparing for the imperial examination.

As Liu Mengmei's wife, Du Liniang decided to help her husband achieve honor as a scholar and official rank. However, recently she noticed that her husband was downcast and lost in thought. So one morning Du Liniang asked Nun Shi to go to the market to buy wine which she hoped would help drive his gloom away.

The house in which they lived was beyond the urban area, because Liu Mengmei was short of money and they had to find a place with low rent. Thus, although Nun Shi left early in the morning, she would not be back for several hours. The young couple stayed in their room chatting about how they met in the dream and their reunion in the garden. Both of them felt love swell in their breasts.

Nun Shi bought the wine at the market and was about to return when she saw scholars from all over the country rush one after the other to the examination hall. It surprised her and she hurried back. As soon as she entered the room she shouted, "Master, Mistress, do you know what is happening?"

Liu Mengmei and Du Liniang had no idea and seeing Nun Shi in such a hurry asked her what the matter was. Catching her breath Nun Shi said, "When I bought wine at the market, I heard that the examination begins today. I saw all the scholars going to the examination hall. Master, you will have to be quick or you will miss this golden opportunity. Let's drink a cup of wine to the Number One Scholar. Drink your success!"

When they heard the news, the young couple did not dare waste a moment. Liu Mengmei prepared to go immediately and Du Liniang said to him, "My love, you have to concentrate in the examination. We will look for your parents-in-law the day you win."

Liu Mengmei arrived at the examination hall only to find that it had finished. The only person there was the chief examiner, Miao Shunbin, who was going over the papers recommended by the sub-examiners. The question asked in this examination was, "Which of the following deserves the most attention: suing for peace, fighting, or defending?" Obviously the question applied to the serious situation in the north which was threatened by the Kin and asked the scholars for their opinions. His Excellency Miao read some of the papers. Some of them wished to sue

住下。柳梦梅温习经史,准备应试。

　　杜丽娘已成为柳梦梅的妻室,自然竭力助夫成就一段功名。近日见柳郎不时掩卷长思,郁郁不乐,今日早起便吩咐石道姑去市曹沽酒,以解夫君之闷。

　　这座房舍离市面较远,因柳梦梅囊中羞涩,只能在房价较低的偏僻之处租屋而居。因此,石道姑虽一早出门,去了已有好一晌,还未能回来,夫妇二人就坐在房中闲话,回忆梦中之会、园中之聚,彼此感情更趋浓烈。

　　此际,石道姑在江头沽了酒,正准备返回,忽见各路云集临安的秀才们,纷纷赶赴考场,未免一惊,急急忙忙回到住处,进门便大声喧嚷道:

　　"呀,公子、小姐,你们还不知道哩……"

　　柳梦梅、杜丽娘见石道姑这般张皇,不知出了何事,连连询问,石道姑喘息方定,才从容说出:

　　"我在江头沽酒,听说已经开考,各路秀才们一簇簇地赶往考场去了。公子,你快快去吧,不要错过这大好机会——这杯酒,就权当做状元红,祝公子春风得意。"

　　听见考场已开,小夫妇俩也不敢急慢,柳梦梅立即准备出门,杜丽娘反复叮嘱道:

　　"相公,你要打起精神来对付金殿对策,高中了,我和你同去寻访你的丈人、丈母啊!"

　　柳梦梅紧一阵、慢一阵,待他赶到考场时,已散了场。只有主试大人苗舜宾在院里审阅各分房考官举荐的试卷。这次试题为《和、战、守三者孰便?》显然是针对当前金人南侵的局势而出,以听取天下秀才的意见。苗大人读了几份,有主张和的,有主张战的,有主张守的,各说各的,都没有说到点子上。苗大人颇费踌躇,

for peace, some were for fighting and others were for defending, but none got to the point, which bewildered him; how could these scholars be so pedantic? However, the imperial examination was held once every three years and he had to enrol somebody. Reluctantly, he picked out three papers and went through the motions of ranking them.

He was pondering over his last choice when he heard a commotion outside the examination hall. The noise was getting louder and louder. He was very surprised and wondered who would be so barbaric as to make a disturbance here and he ordered the doorkeeper to bring the offender inside for investigation.

The offender was non other than Liu Mengmei. When he found that the examination had ended, he took it for granted that the same rules applied as for local examinations in which those who missed the test would be allowed to sit it. Liu Mengmei had pleaded to be allowed to, but the doorkeeper just would not let him in and they had quarreled.

As soon as the doorkeeper hauled him in, Liu Mengmei said to the chief examiner, "Your Excellency, I must sit the examination. Please allow me to."

"Good Heavens! How can you be so stupid! This is the imperial examination! It is against regulations to take in one more paper after the Imperial Academy has sealed them."

"I came 10,000 *li* from the south of Mount Meiling with my family to take part in the imperial examination. If there is no hope, I'd rather kill myself right here and now!" Liu Mengmei was desperate and would have bumped his head on the stone steps.

Fortunately the doorkeeper pulled him back in time. The phrase, "south of Mount Meiling," rang a bell in Miao Shunbin's mind. He took a good look at the young man; wasn't he the Liu Mengmei whom he had helped financially? He had given him the money to come to the capital to take the imperial examination and he had to make an exception. He said, "Come here, young man. Do you have the examination paper?"

"Yes, I do."

"In that case, you can take the examination and will be enroled according to your performance, just like other scholars."

Liu Mengmei was ecstatic. He kowtowed in gratitude and asked the chief examiner for the question. Miao Shunbin read it out. "It is known that the Kin in the north are about to invade our country. Now here are three strategies: suing for peace, fighting, and defending. Which one in

这些秀才们怎的如此迂腐！但三年一科的考试，也不能一个不录取呀！只得免强检出三份考卷，取出一、二、三名，应付一下。

正当他尚未做出最后决定时，忽然听到场外喧哗之声，越来越高，不绝于耳，颇为诧异：何人大胆敢来此吵闹！随即吩咐掌门的将吵闹之人拿进来问话。

吵闹喧嚷之人正是柳梦梅，原来他赶到考场时，已过了考试时间，他以为京城殿试也和地方考试那样，误了考期可以参加叫作录遗的补考，一再请求让他进场补考，掌门的不允，因此争吵起来。

他被掌门的一把揪了进来，当即朝坐在上面的主试大人声称："小生是要求录遗的，望老大人准予补考。"

"哎呀呀，你真不晓事！京城殿试，翰林院封进考卷后，谁人敢再收卷？"

柳梦梅眼见无望，口称："生员从岭南不远万里携家拖口来京应试，如今走投无路，不如一头撞死金阶。"说罢，就作势向石阶撞去。

掌门的人手脚十分麻利，赶紧上前拽住。主考苗舜宾听说"岭南"，心中一动，留心看了一眼，这不是柳梦梅么？是自己曾经资助他路费进京来考的，倒也不能不网开一面："秀才上来，你可有卷子？"

"卷子早已备有。"

"既然有了卷子，姑且准考，与其它考生一视同仁，凭才录取。"

柳梦梅喜出望外，跪下叩谢，请主考赐题。苗大人随即念出题目：《问汝多士，近闻金兵犯境，惟有和、战、守三策，其便何如？》柳梦梅再次叩头致谢。领了题目到左近考舍去做文章了。

your opinion is the best?" After thanking him, Liu Mengmei went to compose his answer in a nearby examination hall.

His Excellency Miao then brought out another three papers to mark. He had hardly decided on them when Liu Mengmei handed in his paper. Miao Shunbin gasped in admiration at his speed and said, "Oh, good for you! You finished your work in such a short time! I'll read it later. Now, just tell me, what do you think of the three proposals?"

Liu Mengmei expressed his views calmly and frankly. "I have no particular preference for any one of the three choices. However, it is advisable to act according to the situation and any changes in it. Our first step should be to fight and defend and then peace will come. It is like the doctor curing disease with medicine. Fighting cures something outside, guarding is the inside cure and making peace is something in between." Liu Mengmei stepped back and stood to one side.

Miao Shunbin found Liu's analysis fresh and penetrating, entirely different from the perfunctory and pedantic arguments put forward by other scholars. He could not help praising him. "Excellent! Brilliant! Now, what shall we do about the current situation?"

Gaining confidence from the chief examiner's praise, Liu Mengmei approached and declared, "As to the current situation, His Majesty should not sequester south of the Yangtze River and officials should not indulge themselves in the waters and mountains of the West Lake. If they do so, when will the northern land be reclaimed? If they kneel down and sue for peace, how could we overcome the disgrace? If they intend waging war against the enemy, His Majesty should head north and direct the frontline battles."

Miao Shunbin slapped the table saying, "Superb! How reasonable and convincing your speech is! Of the 1,000 scholars who took the examination, none showed a real understanding of the current situation. They don't deserve the title of scholar. You have a rare talent and arrive at the crucial point with only a few remarks. Now please wait for the news outside."

Although chief examiner Miao had recognized Liu Mengmei as the scholar he met before, it was not appropriate to acknowledge each other or talk about the old days on such an occasion. Nevertheless, Miao Shunbin had made up his mind to grant Liu first place in the examination. Collecting the papers, Miao ordered his attendants to go to the palace with him to have an audience with His Majesty.

苗大人又取出三份卷子衡量，尚未决定时，柳梦梅已前来交卷。苗大人见他作文敏捷，不禁赞叹道："呀，片刻之间，立扫千言，可敬可敬——我即刻阅卷。只说和、战、守三种意见，你的主张怎样？"

柳梦梅见到主考大人问及，从容不迫地坦陈自己意见："生员对这三种策略，并无偏主，总以形势变化相机而行方宜。可战、可守而后能和，就如同医生用药治病一样，战为表，守为里，和么则在表、里之间。"说罢，垂手立在一边。

苗大人听了他这般分析，觉得十分精辟，耳目为之一新，全然不同于众多秀才考卷只是一片敷衍、迂腐之论，连声赞扬："高见，高见。——如今形势下，又当如何措置？"

柳梦梅得到主考大人称赞，更有信心，又上前半步，慷慨陈辞："当今之世，圣驾不宜逗留江南一隅，君臣不能醉心于西湖山水。果如此，燕云之地何日方能收复？若是屈膝求和，岂不难洗羞耻？如果真心抗战，则请将京师向北迁移，便于指挥前方军事。"说罢，又退了下去。

苗大人拍案称赞："秀才言之有理！应试对策的秀才不下千余人，都是些不晓时务的人，怎配得上是读书人！像你这样的秀才，几句话就说到紧要之处，难得，难得——你且出去，午门外候旨。"

苗大人已认出这个秀才就是岭南柳梦梅，但在这种场合不便相认叙旧。不过，心中已决定拔他为头筹，收拢了试卷，吩咐左右随从跟他去殿上进呈。

苗大人缓步行至殿前，忽闻枢密府人声马嘶，接着又鼓声不断，他心头一惊，知道边疆必有重要军情，派员前来报警。回头一望，果见枢密大人急步上朝。他知道枢密院主管全国军情，有事可

While he was walking slowly to the palace he heard noises and neighing from the Bureau of Military Affairs. A drum was being beaten. His heart sank; the situation must be serious in the frontier area and someone had raised the alarm. He looked back and saw the Minister of the Bureau of Military Affairs hurrying. Miao Shunbin knew that the bureau was in charge of the military affairs for the whole country and had priority in reporting so he stepped back to allow the minister meet the emperor first.

The palace messenger heard the drum and came out. When he saw the minister in a panicky state, he said, "What do you have to report so urgently?"

"The Kin have invaded...."

"Who leads the vanguard?"

" 'Sweet mouth king' Li Quan, Li Quan...."

"Where are the enemy now?"

"In the Huaiyang area."

So that he could give a clear message to the emperor, the palace messenger asked, "Which official is there now?"

"Du Bao, the ex-prefect of Nan'an, is the Pacification Commissioner of Huaiyang. He has strengthened the defense work and accumulated funds and fodder. But I am afraid the real battle will start sooner or later. We'd better arrange for reinforcements."

Noticing the presence of the chief examiner Miao Shunbin, the palace messenger asked about his report. Miao said that he had the result of the imperial examination and he would like to ask for the emperor's instructions on the right day to release it and when to hold the banquet for the successful candidate.

The palace messenger asked them to wait and went into the palace. A moment later he came out and announced the emperor's instructions: "In administering the country I have to take into account the urgency of a case while paying equal attention to civil and military affairs. Now that the Huaiyang area is in imminent danger, I order the Pacification Commissioner Du Bao to fight the enemy without delay. As to publishing the imperial examination result and holding the banquet, this must be postponed until the war ends. Make my order known to all the candidates." The two officials kowtowed and went to do their own business.

以优先禀报,便退处一边,让枢密大人先行朝见皇上奏事。

内使已闻鼓而出,见枢密大人神色慌张,乃问道:"有何紧急之事启奏?"

"风闻金人入寇……"

"谁人打头阵?"

"那个被称为溜金王的李全,李全……"

"现敌军到达何处?"

"已到淮扬地方。"

内使索性问清楚,以便启奏皇上:"现今有何人可以调度?"

"已派原南安太守杜宝为淮扬安抚使,修筑工事,广积钱粮,怕早晚要大战一番,须早早安排后续人马。"

内使又见主考大臣苗舜宾,问他启奏何事,他说殿试名次已定,呈请皇上批示,选定黄道吉日,好唱名揭晓,宴请新进士。

内使吩咐他们先在午门外伺候,自己即刻进入,不一会儿,又领出旨意来,高呼道:"听旨:朕治理天下,有缓有急,文武并重。如今淮扬危急,便着安抚使杜宝前去迎敌,不可迟误。至于殿试揭晓,琼林设宴诸事,可稍缓延,待干戈平息,再予施行,可谕知诸士子。"两位大臣叩头山呼万岁后,各自分头办事去了。

Chapter Twelve

Huai'an Rescued

The Pacification Commissioner Du Bao had guarded Yangzhou for three years. Although Li Quan's gangsters had not been exterminated, their power and ability to bully society had been curbed. Generally it was peaceful. But the Kin in the north were always ready to act and recently they seemed prepared to invade which made Du Bao extremely worried.

However, Madam Du was not very concerned about the emergent military situation. She only had one daughter and she had died at a young age in Nan'an where she was buried. In her spare time Madam Du missed her dead daughter and felt most miserable and resentful. One morning seeing her husband alone in a tent meditating she approached slowly and said, "Hello, my dear."

"Hello, my lady."

"Master, we have been away from Nan'an for three years. You see, time flies...."

Du Bao knew that his wife missed their dead daughter and realized what she implied. He intentionally tried to divert her. "Yangzhou is prosperous and almost as good as Nan'an."

"Master, whenever I mention our late daughter you have nothing to say. You don't know how depressed I am!" Madam Du's words revealed her unhappiness.

"Well, it is not true that I don't miss our daughter. But the country is in such danger that I cannot always think about our personal misfortune!"

"Master, we are now both old and feeble. If we have no children, who will take care of us and attend to us on our death bed? I am thinking of finding a girl in Yangzhou to bear children and carry the family name for you. What do you think of the idea?"

"That is just not possible. I am an official in Yangzhou, which makes me the parent of the people. How can I behave like that!"

"Then how about finding a girl on the other side of the Yangtze

第十二章
移师救淮

安抚使杜宝镇守扬州，三年以来，虽未能尽剿贼人李全之众，但也抑制了这伙歹徒的横行社会，大势尚称平安。不过，金兵蠢蠢欲动，近日颇有南下迹象，令他忧虑万分。

杜夫人却不管营帐中紧急缓慢之事，因膝下无儿，只有独女，又青春凋谢，且远葬南安，闲常无事，思念亡女，愁恨无限。这天清晨，见杜宝独自一人坐在营帐中沉思，便缓步前来："相公万福。"

"夫人免礼。"

"相公呀，我们离开南安已三个年头了，你看，春去秋来……"

杜宝听话听音，知道夫人又在眷念亡女，便有意岔开话题："扬州繁华不差似南安哩。"

"相公，我一提起亡女，你便一言不发，我心中好不愁闷哩。"杜夫人不悦之情已溢于言表。

"唉，夫人呀，不是我不念女儿，如今王事匆匆，何能念及家门不幸！"

"相公呀，我俩年老力衰，全无子女，有谁养老送终呢？不如在扬州寻一女子，为相公传后？不知相公意下如何？"

"此事不可办，我在扬州为官，民之父母，怎能如此！"

"那么，江对面金陵（今江苏南京）女儿可好？"

171

River?"

"The enemy in the north is threatening and could invade at any time; the situation at the frontier is so critical that I have no time to consider other things." Du Bao would not agree and Madam Du, who did not know what to do, shed tears.

"Master!" A messenger rushed into the tent distracting the old couple from their discussion.

"What's the matter?"

The messenger approached and handed over a memoir. Du Bao took it and read out: "The Bureau of Military Affairs has reported an invasion in Huai'an. His Majesty orders Du Bao, the Pacification Commissioner of Huaiyang, to go to Huai'an immediately." Du Bao said to his wife, "My lady, there is a crisis in the military situation. Imperial orders must be obeyed without delay. We must go to Huai'an right now. Go to pack quickly." Madam Du hurried to prepare and Du Bao ordered his subordinates to get ready to start.

After a while an attendant came into the tent and reported that the ships had been assembled at the dock and were waiting for deployment."

"Start!" Du Bao ordered.

When they heard the news, all the officials in Yangzhou came to farewell Du Bao who thanked them and boarded the flagship with Madam Du. Subordinates and attendants embarked on the other large ships and they left for Huai'an.

Not long after they sailed, they noticed a man on a horse galloping alone along the embankment. He waved and shouted. A moment later he was close to the flagship. It was the messenger and Du Bao shouted, "What's happened?"

"Li Quan is assaulting Huai'an city and the situation is most critical! The city could be lost at any time!"

"Aren't there soldiers defending it?"

"The small armed force cannot hold on too long. The Bureau of Military Affairs is worried that travel by boat will take too long and, if precious time is lost, Huai'an will be in real danger. So it orders you to leave the ship and make haste to rescue Hui'an by horse as fast as you can!"

Madam Du was unaccustomed to such things and was so scared that her whole body trembled. Du Bao was quick to reassure her. "My lady, don't be afraid. I will go on land to Huai'an. You can go back to

"寇兵入侵,边事紧急,何暇顾及。"杜宝只是不允,杜夫人无奈,掩泣而已。

"禀老爷,有朝报。"报子此际急步踏入帐中,一声招呼,将这对老夫妇从愁闷中唤过神来。

"何事?"

报子趋前,双手捧上朝报,杜宝伸手接过,不觉念出声来:"枢密院一本,为边兵寇淮事。奉圣旨:便着淮扬安抚使杜宝,刻日渡淮,不许延误。钦此。"读至此处,杜宝抬头对夫人说:"呀,兵机紧急,圣旨不可违。夫人,我同你移镇淮安,现时就起程,快去稍作收拾。"夫人闻言,急忙退去。杜宝立即召聚属下文武,宣布此事,并吩咐有关人员速速准备开拔。

驿丞最早得到通知,不到一遍茶时间,便进帐禀道:"老爷,船只已齐聚码头,听候调遣。"

"上船。"

一声令下,扬州属官齐来送别,杜宝拱手称谢,与夫人登上帅船,帐下幕僚众人分乘几艘大船离扬而去。

船行不久,便见沿河大道上,一人骑马飞奔而来,一路举手高呼。刹时已近帅船前,方才看清,原来是帐前报子,杜宝高声问道:"赶来何事?"

"李全攻打淮安甚急,旦夕之间怕城池不保。"

"不是有守兵么?"

"那点儿兵力怎支撑得住——上司有文书,恐怕大人水路行船缓慢,耽延时日,淮安有危,要大人弃船登岸,从陆路星夜急驰,以解淮安之警。"

杜夫人哪曾见过这种阵势,惊惶得全身颤抖不停,杜宝连忙劝慰道:"夫人,不要惊怕。我登岸去淮安,你转船回扬州。"

Yangzhou by ship."

In the distance Madam Du saw a horse galloping at full speed. She sighed and said, "Oh, here comes another messenger." The messenger shouted from the bank, "Master, Kin soldiers are pushing into our country and will cut off our retreat. The soldiers defending Huai'an cannot hold on for too long. Master, the Bureau of Military Affairs orders you to move without delay!" The messenger wheeled his horse and galloped back along the way he came.

Madam Du could not help weeping. She said to her husband, "What shall we do? You are old and weak, where will you find the strength to resist the Kin invaders? Alas! Battle flames rage everywhere and we have to part!"

"My lady, the situation has changed suddenly and unexpectably. I was afraid that the way to Yangzhou would be cut off. Now it has happened. Oh, where can we meet again?" He thought and then said, "My dear, I cannot stay long. I have military affairs to take care of and must leave for Huai'an now. It seems that Yangzhou is in danger too. Don't return to Yangzhou. Go directly to Lin'an and wait there for me to return."

"Oh, my God! What kind of life is this! In such dangerous circumstances we cannot stay together but have to spend the days separately!"

Du Bao felt sad too and said with regret, "It is because I am a local military officer." Then he left without looking back. Left behind, Madam Du called out to her husband to take care of himself but did not know whether he could hear her or not. When Du Bao was out of sight, Madam Du sighed deeply. She said to Chunxiang, "Yangzhou must be full of battles and fires. We have no choice but to go directly to Lin'an." Thus they left for Lin'an together.

After Du Bao had transferred from Nan'an to the Huaiyang area, he had been stationed in Yangzhou city most of the time. He was not familiar with Huai'an city and after riding his horse non-stop he asked a soldier where they were.

"We are not far from the Huai'an City."

Seeing the weeds spread over the land and hearing the distant sound of the Kin's music, Du Bao could not help shedding tears which fell like raindrops wetting his robes. He announced loudly, "Look everybody! Huai'an can be seen in the distance and it is in great danger. Let's not

"咳,后面又有报马人啦。"杜夫人看到岸上自远而近飞奔前来的一骑,不禁发出深深叹息。那报子却不管杜夫人忧愁,在岸上高声呼道:"老爷,老爷! 金兵已长驱直入,要断我后路;淮安守兵,眼看抵挡不住,老爷快行,上司有令,不得迟误!"传达完毕,立即勒转马头,由原路飞奔而去。

杜夫人闻言泣下数行,扶着杜宝臂膀说道:"怎么办? 你年老力衰,如何抵挡金兵? 唉,这般烽火连天、兵刃满地,我们却要各自天涯了!"

"夫人啊! 局势骤变至此地步,真出人意料,也令人发愁啊! 我就担心扬州被隔,路途不通,果然如此! 唉,我和你又在何处相逢呢?"沉思一会儿,开口叮嘱道:"夫人,军务在身,不能久留,我就要赴淮安去了。看来扬州定然有警,夫人也不必回扬州了,可直接去京师临安安身,待我归来。"

"唉,老爷,这是什么日子啊! 我们老俩口不能相濡以沫,却要各自了此残生!"

杜宝也无可奈何,自怨地说道:"谁让我做了这个地方的军务长官!"头也不回,怅怅离去,杜夫人也不管他听得见听不见,一味叫他善自珍重。眼见杜宝走远了,杜夫人长叹一声,对春香说:"天呵,扬州看来也是兵火满道了。春香,我们只有直接去临安了。"说罢,两人相扶而去。

杜宝一直在南安做守,调来淮扬,却长驻扬州,对淮安地面并不熟悉,此刻,他马不停蹄,行军至此,不禁问军士道:"前面何处?"

"淮安城不远了。"

"唉,天啊!"眼见城外尽是荒草,耳中又传来阵阵胡笳,杜宝感慨万千,泪如雨下,湿透战袍。他大声宣告:"众军士,你们看,淮

spare ourselves and charge into it! I'll ask the court for more reinforcements. All soldiers and officials, listen to my order! March on!"

Enemies blocked the way. Nevertheless, encouraged by their chief commander, the soldiers dashed on without stopping. Li Quan had so many soldiers that they surrounded the city in seven circles and were so close that not a drop of water should have been able to trickle through. But, to the enemy's great surprise, Du Bao's troops rushed into the city at the first attempt. Li Quan's soldiers called in astonishment, "Du's army has broken into the city!" But Li Quan did not seem very concerned and said to his attendants, "Let them be. When they run out of provisions and fodder, they will surrender."

Du Bao galloped into the city at the head of his force. As the relieving force arrived in the city, all the civil and military officials came to express their thanks but Du Bao had no time for such trivial formalities. He first asked about the deployment of the armed forces and their provisions. There were still 13,000 soldiers in the city and the provisions could last for another six months. Feeling assured he said to his attendants, "From today, civil officials will guard the city, and military officials will go out to fight the enemy. Working together and acting according to circumstances we can hold on till reinforcements arrive."

A subordinate said with concern, "One thing that I fear is the Kin's troops making a massive invasion to the south."

Du Bao said, "We will not fear the Kin's troops. Their attack will depend on the general situation and that is not settled yet. Don't give comfort to the enemy and dampen our own morale. At worst, even if they did come, we will risk our lives fighting them."

"Master!" A messenger entered interrupting Du Bao.

"What's happened?"

"M-m-master, Li Quan is attacking again."

"What an unreasonable hooligan! I know that he must have thought that it was a dirty trick letting me into the city. Let him be. Guarding the city is more important."

After entering Huai'an city, Du Bao stressed strengthening of the defenses, improving military discipline, and improving the morale of soldiers and civilians. Therefore, although they could not end Li Quan's siege, the situation of Huai'an had been made safe for the time being and the inhabitants waited for the relieving troops and for further developments.

安近在咫尺,形势危急万分,我们一边拼死冲进城去,一边奏请朝廷添兵救助。三军听我号令,鼓勇前进!"

前面虽有寇兵阻路,但众军士在统帅安抚使杜宝的激励之下,一鼓作气地冲杀过去。李全实在兵多势众。将一座淮安城围了七遭,真个是水泄不通。但杜宝众军士居然一冲便进了城。李全贼众大惊,高声呐喊:"杜家兵冲进围城去了。"

李全并不在意,对左右身边亲信说:"由他去,待他们吃尽粮草,自然投降。"

杜宝一马当先,抢先进城,淮安文武官员见救兵入城,纷纷前来拜见,致谢。杜宝却无暇与他们假虚文,直截了当地询问兵力粮草。知道城中尚有一万三千士卒,粮草也可支持半年,心中便有了底,乃对左右说:"从今日起,文官守城,武官出城,文武同心,随机策应,可以等到救兵之至。"

有一属官不无担忧,说道:"只怕金兵大举南下。"

杜宝说道:"金兵也不怕。他们来不来攻打淮扬,也要看看大势,并无定向。不要长他人志气,灭自己威风。就是金兵到来,大不了拼一死战而已!"

"禀老爷!"报子一声呼唤,打断杜宝话头。

"有何事?"

"报,报,报老爷得知,李全兵又紧围上来了。"

"这贼好无理——他放我进城,我就料他必有奸计。由他去,防城要紧。"

杜宝率众突入淮安,着意加强防备,整肃军伍,鼓舞士民,虽然一时打不破李全的包围,但淮安城也初步转危为安,专等援军开来,再做计较。

Although Li Quan commanded a large army and surrounded the city he was frustrated because he could not take it without waiting. A great amount of provisions and fodder were consumed everyday and he became really worried. On one hand, he was afraid that he could not hold out for long if the Song's reinforcements arrived; on the other, he was worried that his Kin masters would accuse him of being incapable if he achieved nothing. The dilemma caused him to make one unwise decision after another which disheartened the troops. Moreover, recently it was said that the Kin court had sent an envoy to parley with the Song imperial court. Li Quan wondered what they had conspired at and thought that if the Kin betrayed him he would be doomed.

One day Li Quan asked his wife for advice. "You see, my love, a rather long time has passed since we laid siege to Huai'an, but we just can't take the city. What can we do? I want someone to take a message to Huai'an and find out Pacification Commissioner Du's intentions so that we can decide what next to do."

"You are right. It's time to consider our options."

"But at the moment we don't have a suitable person to send."

His wife agreed, "Yes, those under our command are not suitable. We must find someone who enjoys Du Bao's confidence."

Just then they received a godsend in the form of Chen Zuiliang, the teacher who worked for Du Bao when Du was the prefect in Nan'an. Chen Zuiliang had arrived in Huai'an. He had made a special trip just to report to Du Bao that someone had dug up Du Liniang's grave. Chen heard first of all that Du Bao was in Yangzhou and he went all the way there only to be told that Du Bao had moved to Huai'an so he hurried there.

He had not anticipated the difficulties of leaving home, particularly during the tumult of a raging war. Robbers and invading soldiers frequented the road from Nan'an to the Huaiyang area making walking almost impossible. What's more, Chen Zuiliang was not familiar with the road. He was fearful and rushed into bushes and down paths whenever he saw someone. One day he rashly plunged into the tent of some of Li Quan's men and was caught. He was brought immediately to Li Quan's tent.

Li Quan learned from the interrogation that the man named Chen Zuiliang used to work for Du Bao. He also extracted from him the fact that Du Bao had a wife and a maid. With his wife's help Li Quan arrived at a plan. Two soldiers brought in a pair of women's heads and claimed

聚集城外的溜金王李全所部，虽然人众势大，但急切里也未能攻占城池，围城之众每日消耗粮草不计其数。贼首李全心中也着实焦急：既怕宋朝援军不断开来，自家抵挡不住；又怕金人见他久战无功，责其无能。有此两难，心中乃颇为疑虑，因而用兵失当，举措欠周，斗志渐衰，情绪消沉。近日又听说金人派使臣去临安，与赵宋朝廷对话，不知宋金两家又有何勾结？心想：不要被金人所卖，果如此，就死无退路了。

今日升帐议事，李全便讨计于夫人，说道："娘娘，我和你围了淮安城，已有多日，只是攻打不下，如何是好？我想派几个人去淮安传话，兼且看看杜宝的动静，再计议我们今后如何活动。"

"对呀，是要考虑考虑咱们的进退了。"

"只是眼下没有适当的人可派遣。"

娘娘也表同意地说："帐前这些人众，都不可使唤，必须找个杜老儿亲信的人，才可行得。"

也真是天假其便，正当其时，杜宝任南安太守时的西席陈最良来到此地。他是因为杜丽娘的坟山被掘一事，专程前来给杜大人报信的，他听说杜大人镇守扬州，便一路寻到扬州；到了扬州，方知杜大人已去了淮安，又行色匆匆地赶来淮安。

他哪知道出门之难，尤其是兵荒马乱之日。从扬州到淮安，一路上满是贼兵，不能行走；他又不识途径，一见小路就朝里钻，冒冒失失一头撞进贼兵营中，当即被贼众拿住，解往李全帐中去。

李全从审问中知道被拿的人叫陈最良，是杜宝的西席；又从他口中套出杜宝家眷的情况，便与娘娘计谋，让手下人拣了两颗抢掠来的妇女头颅，前来报捷，故意说成是杜宝夫人和使女春香之头。陈最良听此报，未暇细看，便以为真，一时伤心，放声大哭。

falsely that they had killed Madam Du and her maid, Chunxiang. Chen did not look closely and assumed that what they said was true. He could not stop himself from wailing and Li Quan who was bluffing said, "Hey, stop crying, you pedantic old scholar! Very soon I will break into the city and kill old Du Bao!"

Chen Zuiliang did not know the truth and pleaded with him again and again not to kill Du Bao.

"I can spare his life, but he must give up the city of Huai'an." This was Li Quan's real intent but Chen did not know it. And he said, "That is easy. Let me see him and tell him about your overwhelming power and he will do what you say."

Li Quan's wife then pretended to do Chen Zuiliang a favor. She said, "Since that is the case, the king will not kill you today. Tell Du Bao about this quickly." Chen Zuiliang ran off as fast as he could.

The Pacification Commissioner Du Bao stayed on the city tower day and night, observing every movement of the enemy. He guessed that Li Quan had 10,000 soldiers but was hesitant. He had not acted and there must be a reason for it. After an ill-considered movement by the enemy, Du Bao worked out a plan to frustrate them but there was no suitable person to carry it out. While he was thinking about it, an attendant reported to him, "Your Excellency, an old friend of yours has arrived. He calls himself Chen Zuiliang from Nan'an."

Du Bao was really surprised. "How did the old scholar get into the city? Ask him in immediately."

Chen Zuiliang rushed into the tent, crying out, "Where is Master Du?"

Du Bao stepped forward and said, "How unusual it is that an old friend arrives from afar."

Chen Zuiliang immediately saw Du Bao and his white hair and could not stop himself saying, "It is only three years since we parted, and your hair is all white." They saluted each other formally and a servant brought in two cups of tea. When they were seated Chen Zuiliang said, "Master, poor Madam Du was killed on her way to Lin'an."

Du Bao stood up astonished and said, "How did you know that?"

"On my way to Huaiyang I was captured by the enemy and I saw it with my own eyes! And Chunxiang was killed too!"

"Oh, my god! My lady...." Du Bao cried and was about to faint

李全更是虚张声势,呵斥陈最良:"嗤,你这腐儒啼哭什么! 我还要打破淮安,杀杜老儿去!"

陈最良哪知真假,连声恳求:"大王,大王,饶了吧。"

"要饶他也不难,除非他献了淮安城!"这才是李全的真实意图。陈最良自然不明白:"这事好办,让我去告知他大王的虎威,杜宝自然照办。"

李全婆娘作好作歹:"既然如此,大王饶你一刀,快去通报杜宝杜老头儿。"陈最良得了赦免,抱头而去。

且说杜宝坐卧不离城楼, 时刻观察城外贼情动态, 分析敌情。他在猜测,李全有数万之众,为何进退迟疑,其中必有缘故。针对贼众这般举措失当,他已考虑了一条破敌之计,只是一时找不到恰当人员为之施行。正在前前后后思考这一计策时,忽然有随从禀报:"有个故人来访——他自称是南安府陈最良。"

杜宝十分意外:"这迂儒怎能插翅飞进城来? 快快请见。"

陈最良扑进堂来:"杜老爷在哪里?"

"难得故人千里来此!"杜宝迎上前来。

陈最良骤然见到满头白发的杜大人。惊呼:"别后三年,如今老爷头发全白了。"说罢,重新行礼相见。彼此坐定,从人捧上茶来。陈最良迫不及待地禀报道:"老爷,可怜夫人在去临安的路上,被贼兵害了!"

杜宝大惊失色,立起身来:"您先生怎么知道有这等事!"

"生员来淮时,被掠进贼营,亲眼所见,连春香也被杀了。"

"啊呀,天呀,痛杀我了……"杜宝大哭,向后便倒,从人赶紧上前扶住。帐前众人也无不悲痛异常。此时,杜宝反倒镇静下来,擦去眼泪,向众人挥手:"啊呀,我怎能如此! 夫人是朝廷命妇,骂

181

when a servant rushed over to support him. Those who were present and heard it were all extremely grieved. But Du Bao calmed down, wiped away his tears and said to them, "Alas, how can I behave like this? My wife was killed because she denounced the enemy. It was a worthy death. I cannot lose control and lower morale because of this. Please stop crying. We have more important military affairs to discuss!"

The others stopped one after another and Du Bao said, "Mr. Chen, as the enemy released you, did 'sweet mouth king' ask you to bring a message?" Du Bao was a truly capable officer and he knew Li Quan must have required Chen Zuiliang to bring information, otherwise, how could this feeble old scholar, who was not strong enough to tie a chicken, escape from the fiend?"

"Yes, there is a message, but a bad one. He is going to kill you!"

Du Bao was not angry. He sighed and said, "Why does he want to kill me? I'd kill him for the sake of the country."

Chen Zuiliang stepped forward and said, "What the 'sweet mouth king' asks for is just Huai'an city."

"Shut up!" Du Bao shouted angrily. After he had calmed down a little he said, "Mr. Chen, how many tiger-skin armchairs did you see in Li Quan's tent? One or two?"

Chen Zuiliang did not understand why Du Bao asked such a question and he answered honestly, " 'sweet mouth king' sat beside his wife."

Du Bao laughed and smacked the table. "If that is so, I can free Huai'an from the siege." The others did not understand what he meant and when they were about to ask he said, "Mr. Chen, why did you hurry to this chaotic battlefield from faraway Nan'an?"

Chen Zuiliang slapped his forehead and said, "What a dotard I am! I might have forgotten if you had not asked. I came to tell you that Miss Du Liniang's grave has been robbed!"

Du Bao was taken aback again and said in a pained voice, "Oh, my God! Why has my daughter's grave been robbed? It must be the funeral objects that tempted the robbers. Who robbed the grave?"

Chen Zuiliang had resented Nun Shi for a long time and he gave a detailed account implicating her. "It is Nun Shi's fault! After you left, she brought back a companion named Liu Mengmei, an idler from the south of Mount Meiling. When they saw the valuables, they were covetous, robbed the grave and fled the same night. What's more, they abandoned Miss Du's remains in the pond." He did not mention that it was him who

贼而死,理所当然。我怎能为她乱了方寸,灰了军心?诸位止哭,军
情大事要紧。"

众人陆续止住了哭声,杜宝问道:"陈先生,贼众既然放了你,
溜金王有什么话儿交代你?"杜宝毕竟是干员,知道溜金王必然有
信息要陈最良传递,否则双手无缚鸡之力的老秀才怎能逃脱这杀
人魔王的手心!

"是有话儿,他要杀老爷哩。"

杜宝听了这话也不以为忤,说道:"咳,他杀我为了什么?我杀
他却是为了国家。"

陈最良上前半步说道:"那溜金王只是要这座淮安城。"

"住口!"杜宝厉声喝住,断然拒绝。继而,又稍稍和缓下来,问
道:"陈先生,你看贼营中是一个虎皮交椅,还是两个虎皮交椅?"

陈最良想不出杜宝提出这一问题的用意,只能如实回答:"那
溜金王和他浑家连席而坐。"

杜宝手拍几案,笑道:"果真是这样,我可以解淮城之围了。"
众人也不知他有何计策,正待发问,杜宝又问道:"陈先生为何千
里迢迢从南安赶来这战乱之地?"

陈最良以手拍额,连声说道:"啊呀呀,该死,该死!我老糊涂
了。老爷不问,我都忘了,只为小姐坟山被盗,所以才不辞万里,前
来相告的呀!"

杜宝又是一惊,悲痛万分地说:"天呵!坟中枯骨,与贼何仇!
大概都是陪葬之物惹动歹人了——那劫坟贼又是何人?"

陈最良原就对石道姑不满,一五一十地诉说道:"全是那石道
姑坏的事!自老爷走后,石道姑招来一个岭南的游棍叫柳梦梅的
作伴,他们见财起意,夜中劫坟逃去,还把小姐的尸骨乱丢在水池
之中。"他就不提柳梦梅原是他引来的。

first brought Liu Mengmei to the nunnery.

Du Bao sighed. He had no choice but to be philosophical. "My daughter's grave was robbed, my wife was killed. It fits the proverb, 'A death without a burial is not a perfect death; even after you are buried the grave cannot be perfect.' Well, under the circumstances I cannot do anything at the moment. However, I humbly thank you for your kindness."

Hearing the phrase, "humbly thank," Chen Zuiliang promptly complained that he had become much poorer after Du Bao left.

Du Bao nodded and said, "I understand. But as I am on the battlefield I cannot repay you right now. But I have a great opportunity at hand which will guarantee a meritorious service. It's yours if you want it."

"I would love to do it," Chen Zuiliang said without hesitating.

As Chen had volunteered, Du Bao explained the task. "I have written a letter to Li Quan and hope to persuade him to dismiss his troops. However, there is no suitable messenger in my tent. Since you are here, I am asking you to carry the letter. If you succeed in talking Li Quan into surrendering I will ask the court to record your meritorious deed. I promise that you will have your day." Du Bao then ordered the attendant to bring Chen some traveling expenses.

Chen Zuiliang humbly accepted the money. Nevertheless, he was very frightened at the prospect of returning to the enemy's tent. Du Bao assured him saying, "Don't be afraid. Although Li Quan is a ruthless man, he must act according to circumstances. Since he let you walk safely through the siege, he must regard you as a messenger. Please accept my reassurances and go. If you succeed, the court will surely reward you!"

Chen Zuiliang had to take the risk if he was to win glory and rank. Holding Du Bao's letter above his head and trembling with fear he approached the enemy's tents and asked to see 'sweet mouth king'. The guard recognized him as the scholar that they had released two days earlier and went inside to report. "Respected king, the scholar has come back on his own from Huai'an and asks to see you about something urgent."

Li Quan had hardly begun to speak when his wife said, "Great! Bring him in!" Chen Zuiliang trembled as he walked through two rows of soldiers holding weapons. He entered the tent, saw "sweet mouth king" and his wife sitting on raised chairs and said hastily, "Chen Zuiliang comes humbly to see the respected king and his lady."

Paying no attention to his flattery Li Quan asked directly, "Did Du Bao agree to surrender?"

杜宝长叹一声，无可奈何地自我宽慰道："女坟被劫，夫人遭难，正如俗话所说：'未归三尺土，难得百年身；既归三尺土，难得百年坟。'事到如此，也只得罢了。只是要拜谢先生一片好心。"

听见"拜谢"二字，陈最良慌不迭地自叹苦经："生员自从拜别老爷后，更加贫寒难耐了。"

杜宝点头叹息："我也知道，只是身在军营，一时难以报答——罢了，俺有一件大功劳，就托付先生去干。"

"生员愿意效力。"陈最良急急忙忙应承。

杜宝见他愿意出力，方才说出是何功劳来："我早就写了一封书信，要李全解散众军。只是帐前一时无恰当人员可为信使，先生此来，正好劳烦一行。倘若说降李全，即可奏知朝廷，先生自有出身之处——来人，取些盘缠银两来。"

陈最良笑纳了盘缠银子，但对再入贼营送信一事，却恐惧万分。杜宝安抚他说："先生，你去不妨。他虽然凶残，但也相机而动。只看他开围放你前来，就是借你做个信使传书递信，先生只管放心前往。事成之日，朝廷自会给你恩宠。"

陈最良为了将来的荣华富贵，也只得再冒一次险了。当他战战兢兢地走近贼营时，双手高举杜宝的书信，高声求见溜金王。把守营门的兵丁见他确实是前日放出去的秀才，就转身进了大帐禀报："大王，大王，那个秀才从淮安城中单人前来，说有紧急之事，求见大王。"

李全尚未开口，他的婆娘却答道："正好，叫他进来！"于是陈最良从两排手执干戈的卫兵中抖抖索索地进了大帐，见到溜金王夫妇高高坐在上面，连忙口呼："万死一生生员陈最良，百拜大王殿下、娘娘殿下。"

溜金王不答理他的这份阿谀奉承，开口就问："那杜宝献了城

Chen Zuiliang did not answer the question and said, "Who cares about a city? A city is nothing! I came to present a throne to you!"

Li Quan laughed and said, "I have a throne already."

However, Chen Zuiliang continued, "This is a higher official rank — a promotion! Respected king, the Pacification Commissioner Du Bao has a letter for you. Please read it."

Li Quan opened the letter but found that it only tried to persuade him not serve the Kin Dynasty and pledge loyalty to the Song Dynasty. In doing so he could win glory and be loyal at same time, etc. At the end of the letter there was a line that read, "There is another secret letter for your lady." Li Quan chuckled. "This Du Bao is really funny, he knows how to revere my wife too." He passed the letter to her although he knew that she could not read.

"Read it to me. Read carefully," his wife said.

So Li Quan read the letter and explained the contents to her. The letter said it was quite unreasonable for the Kin court to offer an official post only to Li Quan and neglect his lady. In addition, Du Bao said that he had requested the Song court to guarantee her the title of the Lady of Fighting Kin.

Li Quan's wife thought for a while and said to him, "I have made up my mind. Let's do as the letter asks. We'll write a letter of surrender tonight and ask the scholar to take it back."

"But I am afraid that if we pledge loyalty to the Song, the Kin won't let us off lightly," Li Quan said much concerned.

Ignoring Li Quan, she turned to Chen Zuiliang and said, "Scholar, you must guarantee that all your promises are realized."

Right away Chen Zuiliang answered, "Of course."

Li Quan knew that his wife would talk to him alone later, so he stopped questioning the scholar and spoke politely to him. "Would you like to come to our house, have a meal and take a rest. We will write the letter tonight so that you can leave tomorrow morning."

After Chen Zuiliang left, Li Quan's wife said to him that they had been attacking Huai'an city for a long time but had achieved nothing. The Kin would resent this. However, if they sought refuge with the Song court, the consequences would be unimaginable. Without the backing of the Kin, the Song court could punish them any time they wished. His wife's insights weakened Li Quan and he immediately asked her what they should do.

池么？"

陈最良却不正面回答，转弯抹角地说："一座淮安城有什么稀罕！我前来敬献一座王位给大王。"

李全哈哈大笑："寡人早为王了。"

陈最良倒也不感为难："这正是官上加官、职上添职——大王，杜宝有书信一封给大王，谨呈上一阅。"李全身边兵丁接过信递给溜金王。

李全拆开来信，无非是杜宝劝他勿事金朝，还是回归大宋，可得富贵，以全忠孝云云。看完信后，又见底层还有一小札，上面写着："外密启一封，奉呈大王娘子。"看罢，莞尔一笑，道："这个杜宝倒有趣得紧，也晓得敬畏娘娘。"随手将小札递给安坐身边的娘娘，虽然他也明白浑家不识字。

"念给我听。念仔细点儿。"

李全倒也听话，一边细念还一边解说。原来信中说，金朝只封李全为溜金王，却未封娘娘，真是非礼。又说，他已向大宋朝廷保奏夫人为讨金娘娘之职云云。

娘娘听罢，略作思索，便对李全说："我的主意定了，就照来信所说——我们写下降表，打发秀才去回奏。"

"我们投顺宋朝，只怕金人放不过！"李全不无顾忌地对娘子说道。

娘娘却不答话，只对陈最良说："秀才，你说的话要负责兑现！"

陈最良连忙应承："自然，自然。"

李全知道浑家当别有说话，也不再询问她的主张，顺势说了几句客套话："秀才，请到公馆用饭歇息，我们连夜写表送行。"

陈最良退下后，娘娘方才对丈夫李全说明原委：一座淮安城

"Let's be the Fan Li and Xi Shi."*

Li Quan thought for a while then clapped his hands and said, "Yes! Fan Li and Xi Shi wandered far and wide by rivers and lakes! But today all the rivers and lakes are under the control of the Song troops. It seems that the only choice left to us is to go to sea and be pirates!"

"That's right!" Once they had made up their mind, the couple ordered the soldiers to lift the siege of Huai'an. That very night they boarded boats and sailed off to sea.

---

*Fan Li was a politician from the Spring and Autumn Period, and Xi Shi, a favorite concubine of King Fu Chai of the State of Wu in the Spring and Autumn Period. They loved each other. Wandering by Rivers and Lakes is a famous love story about them in China.

久攻不下，金人已有不满，难免有后患；投降宋朝，后果也不堪，失去金人支持，大宋朝随时可将我们治罪。这婆娘颇有见识，一席话说得李全恍然醒悟。赶紧向娘娘讨个决策："那我们怎么办？"

"学个范蠡载西施。"

李全思索半晌，双手一拍道："范蠡伴同西施，放浪五湖——而今五湖又在何处？还不是在宋朝范围！看来，我们只有出海去做海盗了！"

"这就对了！"这一对儿拿定主意，立即吩咐军众解开淮安之围，准备船只，连夜泛海而去。

CHAPTER THIRTEEN

Reunion of Mother and Daughter

After Liu Mengmei hurried off to sit his examination, Du Liniang waited patiently at home for the good news. She thought to herself that with all his talent her husband would surely become a first-rate scholar and obtain official rank.

When she saw Liu Mengmei stumbling into the yard, she immediately stood up and greeted him. "How are you, my darling? I expected to see you come back in official robes and in a splendid chariot. How is it that you have returned by yourself on foot?"

After drinking some tea, Liu Mengmei related the whole story in detail: he was late for the examination but was allowed to take it; he won the favor of the chief examiner, but publication of the result was postponed because the court had to discuss the military situation in the Huaiyang area which was said to be serious. Liu Mengmei sighed and said, "My darling, I'm so sorry that I delayed the confirmation of your honorable title."

Du Liniang did not seem very concerned about her status, but the words "Huaiyang" and "serious" attracted her interest. Straight away she asked, "My darling, is Huaiyang the area that my father administers?"

"Yes, that's it."

When she heard this she burst into tears. "Oh, my God! I wonder what has happened to my parents?" Liu Mengmei hurried to comfort his wife and after she had calmed down, she thought a while and said, "Darling, I have something to say, but I find it difficult to speak out."

"Please speak, don't hesitate." Liu Mengmei always listened to his wife.

"As the examination result will not be published for a long time, could you go to Huaiyang and ask about my parents for me?" Du Liniang asked.

"Your wish is my bounden duty." Liu Mengmei said straight away

第十三章
母女相遇

　　柳梦梅急急忙忙前去应试后,杜丽娘在家中专等好消息,她一心想:以柳郎才华,必然高中,功名如握。岂知事与愿违,出人意料。

　　当她见到柳梦梅步履蹒跚地迈进院门时,不禁起身迎上前去,问道:"相公,你回来了。我望你乘车衣锦归来,如今怎地自己走回？"

　　柳梦梅坐定后,咽了一口石道姑送上的茶水,方细言慢语地将自己如何迟到、如何求得补考、如何得到主考大人青睐,正准备上奏朝廷放榜时,淮扬一带军情紧急,朝廷商议军国大事,便将考试发榜之事暂时搁置,"娘子呀,延误了你的夫人花诰。"

　　杜丽娘倒不在意夫荣妻贵,而是听到"淮扬"、"紧急"等字眼时,却十分留意,忙问道:"相公,我问你,淮扬地方,是不是我爹爹管辖之处？""正是呀。"

　　杜丽娘闻知,放声痛哭:"天呀,我的爹娘不知怎样了？"柳梦梅再三劝慰,杜丽娘方才止住哭泣,沉思半晌,她又对柳梦梅说道:"相公,奴家有一句话,就是说不出口。"

　　"尽管说。"柳梦梅对娇妻一向言听计从的。

　　"相公,发榜日期还远,奴家想请你去淮扬打听一下爹娘消息,不知能否应允？"杜丽娘迟迟疑疑地说出心愿。

　　"娘子即有此意,我是义不容辞。"柳梦梅不加思索地答允,但

191

and added with concern, "I am just worried about leaving you alone at home."

"You don't need to worry about me. I'll be fine and have the companionship of Nun Shi. But you must take care of yourself in the turmoil and chaos of war."

"I will."

Then Du Liniang and Nun Shi prepared Liu Mengmei for the journey making up a bundle and fetching an umbrella. Suddenly, Liu Mengmei remembered something. "My love, when I meet my parents-in-law face to face, they will wonder where this new son-in-law came from. How can I explain your coming back to life?"

Du Liniang knew her father was very difficult to convince and might not believe what Liu Mengmei said. She thought for a while and said, "I know what to do. You take my picture with you. When my father sees it he will ask what happened to us."

"Then what should I say?"

Du Liniang could not think of anything more convincing and exclaimed, "Just say that our marriage was predestined by God and, when you walked on my grave, the tomb suddenly opened!"

Liu Mengmei could not think of a better idea and had to agree with his wife. He picked up the bundle, said farewell and asked her to take care of herself. Du Liniang hated to see him go and walked part of the way with him. The pair were in tears when they said good-bye.

After Liu Mengmei left for the north, Du Liniang spent her days with Nun Shi waiting for him to come back. One day at dusk they sat in the room chatting about the time that they opened the grave and helped Du Liniang return life. They could not help sighing with emotion. Gradually it got dark, but Du Liniang still did not want to go to bed and she asked Nun Shi to light the oil lamp. Seeing the oil had run out, Nun Shi told Du Liniang to wait in the yard while she went to the owner of the house to borrow some.

After farewelling Du Bao, Madam Du and her maid Chunxiang traveled towards Lin'an. In the chaos and turmoil of war they had to stop from time to time; sometimes they took a boat and sometimes they walked. Finally they crossed the Yangtze River and sailed smoothly along the Grand Canal to Lin'an.

After the boat arrived at the dock outside the city proper, the boatman told everyone to get off and Madam Du and Chunxiang had to go ashore.

又不无担心地说：“只是撇下你一人在这里，我有些不放心。”

“不碍事，有姑姑陪伴，不必挂念。倒是你在兵荒马乱之中，要特别谨慎才好。”

“这个我自然知晓。”

杜丽娘见柳梦梅已应允，立即吩咐石道姑准备衣物，打成一个包袱，再备上一把雨伞。临行之际，柳梦梅忽然想起：“娘子，鄙人拜见岳父岳母时，他们必定问：哪里跑出来这个女婿——你这回生之事如何交代？”

杜丽娘自然知道她的父亲十分固执。未必肯相信柳梦梅所说，思索半晌：“有了，相公可将奴家画像带去。只要老父见到这幅画像，自然会问到我两人之间的事。”

“问起来，又如何回答？”

杜丽娘说不出令人信服的理由，脱口而出：“相公，你就说俺两人姻缘是上天注定的，你走到我坟前，坟山蓦然就开启了！”

柳梦梅也实在想不出更好的说法，只得依着杜丽娘了。“娘子，我去后还望你多多保重！”柳梦梅拎起包袱向杜丽娘告辞。杜丽娘恋恋不舍地送了他一程，才挥泪而别。

柳梦梅北上后，杜丽娘与石道姑两个相伴，安生度日，等待他归来。一天傍晚，两人闲坐屋里，回忆当日开棺掘坟、回生转世情景，相对叹息不止。谈着谈着，不觉夜色四合，杜丽娘不想早睡，吩咐姑姑上灯。石道姑拿起灯台一看，灯油全用光了，她让小姐在院中月下小坐，自己到房主人家去借灯油。

哪知正当此际，杜夫人和丫头春香在赴淮安途中与夫君相别后，主仆二人陆地乘车、水路行船，在兵荒马乱之际，赶一程，停一程，好不容易渡过大江。自此之后，方才船行无碍，一路沿着运河，到了临安。

It was dusk and smoke from kitchen chimneys rose all around. The two stood on the dock bewildered, not knowing what to do or where to go. They had no relatives or friends in the city to help them and they could not spend the night on the dock. Their only choice was to find an inn where they could stay for the time being. However, they were not familiar with the roads and just walked where their steps took them. Fortunately, Chunxiang had a good eye and noticed a house not far away. The door was unlocked and the pair made hurried steps to the house. Pushing open the half-closed door, Madam Du said in a faltering voice, "Anybody at home?"

"Who is it?" A voice answered.

Chunxiang was very surprised to hear a female voice and cried out, "Hello! Anybody there?" Madam Du called out that they were two woman passengers who were passing by and would like to stop in the house overnight.

Du Liniang listened carefully and decided they were indeed female voices. Nun Shi had not come back, so she cautiously opened the door. As soon as Madam Du, supported by Chunxiang, walked into the yard she thanked her and said, "Sorry to disturb you. We are on our way to Lin'an. Because it is late and we are not familiar with the roads, we came to your place to see if we could stay overnight. Could you provide us with accommodation?" As Madam Du said this, she lifted her head and caught a glimpse of the hostess in the moonlight. The girl's countenance stunned her and she said, "Young lady, do you live alone in this shabby house without any light?"

"This is an empty house and I am admiring the moon here."

When Madam Du heard this she felt doubtful and whispered to Chunxiang, "Look, who does this girl resemble?"

After taking a good look at her, Chunxiang was astonished too. She murmured, "Oh, Madam Du, this girl looks like Miss Liniang!"

"You check whether there is anyone else in the house. If not, I am afraid this girl is a ghost." Chunxiang moved stealthily and peeped into the room.

Du Liniang also was examining the two women. She whispered to herself, "The old lady looks like my mother and the young girl looks like the maid Chunxiang." Tentatively she said, "Excuse me, Madam, could you tell me where you come from?"

Madam Du heaved a deep sigh. "Well, I came from Huai'an to seek

　　船到码头,舟子催客离船。她们主仆二人只得舍舟登岸。此时已是傍晚,只见暮烟渐起,立在码头仓惶四顾,不知何往。她们在京城并无眷属亲友可以投奔,但也不能就在码头过夜。无可奈何,春香傍着夫人只得到处寻找旅舍以便暂时栖身。可是又不熟悉路途市井,只是信着脚步乱走。春香眼尖,忽然发现前面不远处,有一座房舍,大门并未完全闭上,赶紧扶持杜夫人急走两步,推开半掩的大门,杜夫人颤巍巍地问道:"里面有人么?"

　　"谁呀?"

　　春香听出是一个女子声音,也觉意外,不免又呼:"有人么?"倒是杜夫人说得清楚,声明是一对女子,因赶路经过此地,想借宿一宵。

　　杜丽娘凝神细听,果然是妇道人家声音。姑姑借油未回,只得亲自去门前,迟疑地开了门。春香搀扶着杜夫人走了进来。杜夫人忙着道谢,说,"我们是到临安去的,只因天晚路不熟,特来借宿一宵,请行个方便吧!"说着,抬头借着月光偶然瞥见女主人面目,不禁大惊失色,问道:"小娘子啊,这屋子如此破败,灯火又无,你怎么一人在此?"

　　"这是座闲废的屋院,我在此赏月。"

　　杜夫人听了这话,越发疑心,悄悄对春香说:"春香,你看这人像谁?"

　　春香端详一番,也惊异不止,低声说道:"夫人,她好像小姐哩。"

　　"你再瞧瞧内房还有人没有!若是没人,怕不是鬼啊!"春香听从杜夫人吩咐,悄悄移动几步,朝房内窥探。

　　杜丽娘也在审视这一老一少,心中暗自嘀咕,老者像是自己的亲娘,少者颇似丫头春香,不禁也探问起来:"敢问夫人,从何处来此?"

　　杜夫人不禁长叹一声:"唉,我从淮安避难来此。我相公是现

refuge here. My husband is Pacification Commissioner Du Bao." Madam Du was testing Du Liniang too.

Du Liniang recognized the voice and said to herself, "Isn't this my mother? Should I recognize her or not?" While she hesitated, Chunxiang ran panicking to Madam Du. "It is a totally empty house! Not a trace of anyone! She must be a ghost! A ghost!"

At this Madam Du became speechless with fright. Involuntarily she backed away. Du Liniang saw her and approached with the intention of identifying herself and explaining the entire matter. But Madam Du thought Du Liniang's ghost was about to spring on her. She lost no time in trying to escape and cried over and over, "Aren't you the ghost of my dead daughter? I neglected you when you were alive. Now I know that I was wrong. Chunxiang, Hurry up! Throw her some of the ghost money we carry. Be quick!" Muddled, Chunxiang produced a wad of ghost money and threw it to Du Liniang.

"I am not a ghost!" Du Liniang asserted bluntly. At the time she had no better explanation.

"If you are not a ghost, then who are you?" Madam Du asked Du Liniang to answer her call three times. If she were not a ghost, the voice would get louder each time. However, Du Liniang had not fully recovered her life energy and her three answers became fainter. During the hustle and jostle Madam Du touched Du Liniang's hands; they were really cold! Now Madam Du was even more convinced that the girl was a ghost. Chunxiang was so scared that she knelt on the ground and kowtowed again and again pleading, "Miss, please don't punish me!"

"Dear child, we didn't hold the ceremony to release your soul from purgatory. It is your stubborn father's fault," the old lady said desperately as she tried to get away.

Du Liniang heard her and held her mother's sleeve more tightly. "Mother, why are you so frightened? I can't let you go!"

Just then Nun Shi came back with the oil. She had been surprised to hear noisy human voices before going into the yard. She held the oil lamp high and found the ghost money scattered on the ground, which also surprised her. Chunxiang saw Nun Shi and beckoned her. "Look, Madam, isn't the woman coming in the door Nun Shi?"

"Yes, it is her!" The old lady looked at the door and was sure.

Nun Shi saw Madam Du and Chunxiang. She was surprised and said, "Oh! Aren't you Madam Du and Chunxiang? Where do you come

任安抚使杜宝。"杜夫人在答话之中又包含着几分试探之意。

杜丽娘听得分明，暗自思量："这不正是我的娘么？我要不要出面认她呢？"正当她委决不下时，春香慌里慌张地走到杜夫人面前："一所空房子，前前后后没个人影儿。是鬼，是鬼！"

杜夫人听后大惊，吓得说不出话来，身子不由得直向后退缩。杜丽娘见状，只得向前相认，以便说明前因后果。杜夫人见杜丽娘扑向前来，更是吓得闪避不及，口中直呼道："这不是我女儿？老妇平素怠慢你了，你如今现身于此，我知道了。春香，快快取随身纸钱丢给她，快，快！"春香身边原就剩有未曾烧完的纸钱，手忙脚乱地取出一叠来，随手撒去。

"孩儿不是鬼。"杜丽娘无以辩解，只得直通通表白。

"你不是鬼，又是谁人？"杜夫人让她连应三声，要一声比一声高，但杜丽娘毕竟阳气未足，三声应承却是越呼越低。推让之间，杜夫人碰到她的双手，煞是冰凉，便益发相信她是鬼无疑。春香吓得跪在地上不断叩头："小姐，千万不要拿捏春香。"

"儿呀，不曾超度你，只怪你父亲固执。"杜夫人不断解说，力求脱身。

哪知杜丽娘听了这些话儿，更是紧拽住老夫人的衣袖："娘，你怎这般害怕？孩儿更不敢放娘走了。"

石道姑借了灯油，还未进门，就听见堂上人语喧哗，十分诧异。擎起手中的油灯，又照见一地纸钱，更是奇怪。那春香年轻眼尖，早已瞥见石道姑，招呼杜夫人说："夫人，你瞧，门口进来的不是石道姑！"

"正是。"杜夫人向门外望去，确认不疑。

此时石道姑也看见这一老一小了，顿感意外："呀，这不是夫人和春香么？你们从哪里来？怎么这般大惊小怪？"

from? Why are you so frightened?"

Du Liniang shouted, "Aunt Shi, come! Be quick! My mother is scared!"

Hearing them speak fluently, Chunxiang cried out, "Oh, my God! This aunt might be a ghost too!"

As the situation seemed to be getting more and more confusing, Nun Shi walked straight into the house and put the lamp on the table. Then she dragged Madam Du close to the lamp and asked her to look carefully. Gradually Madam Du calmed down, but she was still suspicious. Then Nun Shi and Du Liniang explained in great detail what had happened during the past three years: how Du Liniang had been brought back to life and met Liu Mengmei; how they came to Lin'an and Liu Mengmei's trip to Huaiyang to look for Du Liniang's parents after he had taken the imperial examination. Madam Du could exclaimed that it was all most unusual and the four brought face to face sobbed with emotion. As it was really late, Nun Shi made arrangements for the other three to rest.

It was well into autumn. With a bundle on his back, a scroll in his hand and an umbrella under his arm Liu Mengmei headed for Huaiyang to carry out Du Liniang's request. In the confusion and chaos of war he had to make use of every available means of transport whether it was boat or cart. When there was nothing available, he walked. Having traveled day and night, he finally reached Yangzhou, only to find that his father-in-law had gone to Hai'an. Thus he had to begin another journey and on the way suffered many hardships. He had been cheated out of almost all the money that he had and at the end of the journey all that was left was the bundle and the umbrella. Although often hungry, he had endured.

Finally he arrived at Huai'an city. It was dusk, the city gate was closed and he had to stay at an inn outside the city. However, when he sat down at the table, he found that he had no money for food and he asked the inn owner if he could trade his brush, pen or umbrella for a meal but was refused. In the circumstances his only option appeared to be to reveal his identity.

"Sir, have you heard of Pacification Commissioner Du Bao of Huaiyang?"

"Everybody here has heard of Pacification Commissioner Du! He suppressed the rebellion and repulsed Li Quan's gangsters by strategy. Tomorrow a banquet will be held in a tent to celebrate his victory."

杜丽娘也叫道："姑姑快来,娘害怕哩。"

春香听她们应答自然,竟然大呼:"不好,不好,这姑姑大概也是个鬼!"

石道姑见这么闹鬼下去也不是个了结,干脆把油灯向堂前案上放定,拉住杜夫人到灯前,让她看个仔细。杜夫人方才半信半疑地镇定下来。然后听石道姑和杜丽娘你一句我一句地将三年来如何还魂、如何遇到柳梦梅、如何前来应试、如何命柳相公前去淮扬等等情节,细细诉说一番。杜夫人叹为人间少有的罕事。四人相对,唏嘘不已。

石道姑见夜色深沉,料理一番,让她们母女二人还有丫头春香安歇下来。

柳梦梅奉了杜丽娘之命,背了一个包袱,提了一幅画儿,夹了一把雨伞,在这兵荒马乱之际,深秋叶落之时,见水登舟,逢岸搭车,无车船之便时,便徒步赶路,日夜趱行,终于赶到扬州。岂知岳丈杜宝已移师淮安,又不得不重上旅途。一路上受尽跋涉之苦,身上携带的盘缠银子,沿途被人赚骗了不少;到后来,仅剩下包袱雨伞,少不得忍饥挨饿。

且喜这天傍晚,行来已是淮安城外,但城门早已关闭,只得在城外找了一家小客店歇息。哪知进店坐定后,盘缠已尽,无银钱可以换取酒食,他和店家商量,愿以笔伞换酒吃,店家不答应。无奈之下,只得说出自己的身份。

"店家可知道淮扬安抚使杜宝么?"

"杜宝谁人不识! 他计退了李全,平息了战乱,明日大帐里摆下太平宴哩。"

"这就好了! 店家,我便是他的女婿,特意来探望他的。"

"That is great. You know, I am His Excellency's son-in-law. I came here specially to visit him."

This really surprised the inn owner who looked at the young man again. He examined him from head to foot and from back to front and, although he observed very carefully, he just could not make himself believe that this poor and dull looking young man was the son-in-law of Pacification Commissioner Du. After thinking, he decided what to do and grinned at Liu Mengmei. "Oh, why did not you tell me about this earlier? His Excellency has an invitation for you!"

"Where is it?" In such desperate circumstances Liu Mengmei would have clutched at any straw and was overwhelmed with joy but did not realize what the inn owner intended.

"Come with me and I'll show you."

They left the inn, walked along several streets, turned a few corners and arrived at an open ground. Nearby was a compound, slightly higher than ordinary civilian house, surrounded by a long wall from which the paint had peeled. On the wall hung a piece of white paper and pointing to it the inn owner said to Liu Mengmei, "That is the invitation. Read it carefully."

Liu Mengmei took a few steps forward and saw that it was not an invitation at all, but a notice. The inn owner pointed to it and said, "Look, it reads, 'Stop Being an Idler and Defrauder.' This is a notice issued by Pacification Commissioner Du Bao. It says, 'I have neither nephews in the imperial court nor a son-in-law. Anyone who claims that they are related to me in this way will be arrested.' It not only refers to you, young man, it talks about me. 'Anybody offering help to the defrauder will be punished too.' How dare you intend such a thing! Leave quickly, I will not report you and don't you incriminate me." The inn owner walked off by himself.

Abandoned by the inn owner and without a penny Liu Mengmei faced a dilemma. Du Bao's notice had stated clearly that he had no son-in-law. He did not know what to do; desperation and misery gripped his heart and he burst into tears.

After he had shed tears, he looked around and caught sight of a big house with a notice on which several characters were inscribed. He stepped forward and saw that they were the four golden characters — Mother Piao's Memorial Temple. Mother Piao was the woman who gave Han Xin* financial help. Liu Mengmei walked into the temple. It was empty

---

*Han Xin (?-196 B.C.), a general of the Han Dynasty.

此言一出，倒使店主人吃惊不小，重新打量眼前这书生。从头到脚，从前到后，仔仔细细看了个够，这副穷酸模样说是安抚使大人的女婿，他怎么也不敢相信。略作沉吟，计上心来，便笑嘻嘻地对书生说："唉呀，你怎么不早说？杜老爷早已给你发了请帖了。"

"请帖在哪里？"柳梦梅绝处逢生，喜不自禁，一点儿也未曾看出店主人话中有诈。

"待我和公子去瞧。"

两人出了店门，上了大街，转过小弯，不远处是一块空旷之地。附近有一所较一般民房为高敞的院落，一带长墙，白粉已剥落，上面一张大白纸显得分外耀眼。店主人指着这张白纸，对柳梦梅说：

"公子，那就是请帖。你看看仔细。"

柳梦梅走前几步，这哪是请帖，分明是告示。店主人指着告示说："你瞧，《禁为闲游奸诈》，这是安抚使大人的告示哩。杜老爷是四川人，到此做官，'不教子侄到官衙，从无女婿亲闲杂'，这句话不是单单指你这个公子，'若有假充行骗，地方禀拿'，下面说到小人了，'有扶同歇宿，罪连主家'，……公子，你竟敢打这个主意？趁早走吧，我不报你，你也别连累我。"说罢，扬长而去。

柳梦梅被店主人抛弃在此处，岳丈出的告示上分明不承认有女婿，自家身上又无分文，真是进退不得，不知如何是好，一时悲伤凄惶，穷途痛哭。

哭了一阵，又伸头四望，忽然见前面一座大屋宇，门额上有几个大字，不免上前几步，原来是"漂母之祠"四个大金字——就是当年接济过韩信的漂母了。

他便走进祠堂。漂母祠内一个人也没有，神坛上点了一盏长

and on the altar stood an everlasting oil lamp. Inscribed on the wall were a few lines by Han Xin expressing his gratitude for Mother Piao's meal. When Liu Mengmei saw this, he felt bitter. He bowed to the statue of Mother Piao and said, "When Han Xin was down and out, he met generous Mother Piao and had a meal. Now I am suffering from hunger and cold, but cannot beg even for a cup of cold water!" Full of emotion he stayed the night on the temple porch.

On the morning of the following day Liu Mengmei went into the city and walked straight to Pacification Commissioner Du's office. For a while he paced up and down in front of the door then made up his mind. He said to the doorkeeper, "I am the son-in-law of Pacification Commissioner Du Bao. I have come specially to pay a formal visit."

The doorkeeper had been watching the young man in ragged clothes for a while. He carried a worn-out bundle, a broken umbrella and a torn picture; he could not believe what he claimed and said distainfully, "What a day-dreamer you are! Look at you, shabby dress, wan countenance, how can you be the son-in-law of Pacification Commissioner Du? Hunger must have driven you out of your mind!"

Liu Mengmei saw that the doorkeeper was a snob and rebutted him indignantly, "Bullshit! I am a dignified scholar who has graduated from a regular school. I came from Lin'an to visit my father-in-law, but have spent all my traveling expenses on the way. That's why I am in such an awkward situation. You should not judge a person on appearances alone. Go and report that I am here immediately!" Liu Mengmei spoke so vehemently that the doorkeeper felt uneasy. He thought that if by any chance this man was indeed the son-in-law of Pacification Commissioner Du, and if he did not report him, he would be in trouble himself. He decided to report him, impostor or not.

At the time Du Bao was alone in a room deeply grieved by Madam Du's death. When the doorkeeper reported to him, he thought, "My daughter has been dead for three years. How could there be a son-in-law? He must be an impostor." Nonetheless, he said to the doorkeeper, "What does the man look like?"

"Nothing special. Oh yes, he has a scroll under his arm."

Du Bao concluded that the man must be a poverty-stricken painter seeking financial help. However, today was such a happy occasion that he did not feel inclined to punish such an idler. He said to the doorkeeper,

明灯，墙上有汉朝淮阴侯韩信的题字，意思是感激漂母的一饭之恩。柳梦梅巡视之下，颇有感触，乃向漂母塑像拜了几拜，叹道：

"当初韩信潦倒，尚能遇着一个漂母舍饭给他，我柳梦梅如今饥寒交迫，连碗冷水也没处去讨！"说罢感伤了一回，就栖身在这祠堂侧廊之下。

次日清早出门，一路步行进城，走到安抚使衙门。在衙门前来回走动好几回，方下定决心，向守门的军士说道：

"我是杜老爷女婿，特地前来拜见。"

门子早已注意到这个人，见他破衣破巾、破包袱、破雨伞、破画儿，哪里肯信，轻蔑地说：

"你这人真是白天说梦话，凭你这副衣衫褴褛，形容憔悴的模样，也配称是安抚使大人的乘龙快婿？我看你简直是饿昏了！"

柳梦梅见门子是个势利小人，气忿地辩道：

"胡说！我乃堂堂黉门秀才，只因探望杜老大人，从临安到此，盘缠用尽，才落得这般狼狈。你们不要以貌取人，快快与我禀报去吧！"门子见他口气硬朗，万一是真，不为通报，将来有碍。且不论真假，替他禀报一声。

此时，杜宝正在为夫人被害之事在那儿独自伤心哩。听到门子来报，心想女儿已经死去三年，哪来的女婿？此事必假无疑，但又问门子道：

"那人怎样？"

"也不怎么样。呵，袖着一幅画儿。"

杜宝判断此人大约是个画师，穷愁潦倒，前来打秋风的。在这喜庆之日也不想处治这类闲人，就吩咐门子道：

"Tell him that His Excellency is busy with military affairs and has no time to meet him. Ask him to go on his way."

Although Liu Mengmei had been denied admission, he was eager to try again. He knew that on that very day there would be a celebratory banquet, an occasion attended by all the civil and military officials. He sat on doorstep waiting for a chance to rush in.

After a while civil and military officials arrived one after another. The adjutant ordered the banquet to begin and drums rolled. Sitting at the head of the banquet Du Bao addressed everyone there. "Although Li Quan's gangsters have been repulsed, the Kin still look at us like a covetous tiger. It is too early to sing songs of triumph. However, today, let's celebrate our small victory with a cup of wine."

All the civil and military officials began praising Pacification Commissioner Du's great skill in outwitting the enemy. A messenger arrived and announced that the court had replied to His Excellency's memorandum. His Majesty instructed Pacification Commissioner Du Bao not to retire. He was to return to the court and be designated Joint Manager of Important National Affairs. Madam Du had been conferred a posthumous honor, Grade One Courageous and Virtuous Lady.

At once all the officials congratulated him. The position of Joint Manager of Important National Affairs was in fact that of Prime Minister and those present competed with each other in trying to flatter Du Bao and win his favor. After thanking everyone, Du Bao said modestly, "You are in the prime of your lives and have bright prospects as officials. I return to the court in my old age and am not worthy of praise."

While Du Bao and his subordinates were exchanging toasts and eulogies, Liu Mengmei waited outside, famished and exhausted. He decided to disregard formalities and rushed towards the hall. Of course the doorkeeper tried to stop him and the two began quarreling. The noise carried through to the hall and Du Bao said to the adjutant, "Who is causing that commotion?"

"It is a man calling himself your son-in-law, Your Excellency. He said he was very hungry and wanted food. Our man tried to stop him but he beat him."

Du Bao was enraged at hearing this. "Damn! I announced a prohibition. How dare this poor idler behave as he likes here!" Without listening to his subordinates' conciliatory words, Du Bao ordered the adjutant to arrest Liu Mengmei immediately, place him in jail for the

"你对他说,老爷军务繁忙,无暇接待。请他自在。"

门子回绝了柳梦梅,但他怎肯离去?听说今日开太平宴,文武官员都将前来赴席,他索性坐在门房等待机会闯进去。

说话之间,只见所属文武官员陆续入内,中军见文武将相都到齐了,便吩咐开宴,一时鼓乐齐鸣。杜宝坐在主席,对大众拱手为礼,招呼道:

"退了李全这伙贼人,金兵尚虎视眈眈,还不能大奏凯歌,不过借此一杯水酒,大家一抒怀抱。"

文武官员却纷纷赞扬安抚使大人计退贼人的功劳。正当其时,偏偏报子也来凑趣,报道老爷奏本已经朝廷批复,有圣旨下:安抚使杜宝不得退休,令其回朝任同平章军国大事。夫人追赠为一品贞烈夫人。

左右僚属顿时齐声庆贺,说什么"同平章军国大事"就是当朝宰相啦。于是个个争先,人人趋附。杜宝一边向大家致谢,一边谦虚地说道:

"诸公年富力强,封侯有望。像我杜宝,垂老之年回朝而去,是不值得称道的。"

且不说杜宝与僚属之间相互赞美,彼此宴饮。那柳梦梅此刻已是饥饿难当,困乏异常,也不论什么礼数了,直向大堂上闯去,门子阻拦,两人难免纠缠在一起。喧闹之声传进大堂,安抚使大人发话道:

"军门外,是何人敢在此喧嚷?"

"是那个自称老爷女婿的,说他饿的发慌,前来冲席,咱们阻挡都遭他打了!"

杜宝闻言大怒:"可恶。本院早有禁约,何处寒酸游棍,敢来此胡闹!"也不听僚属劝止,吩咐中军官立即将他拿下,暂时监禁在

meanwhile and escort him to Lin'an for interrogation when he returned to the court. Thus, Liu Mengmei was maligned by his father-in-law when he tried to carry out a mission for his wife.

此,待他返朝时押至临安再审问发落。以此,女婿柳梦梅奉妻子之命前来探望岳丈,却被乃翁杜宝令人捉下狱去。

CHAPTER FOURTEEN

Family Reunion

While the banquet to celebrate peace was taking place in Huai'an, the capital city, Lin'an, was also in a jubilant mood. The emperor was overwhelmed with joy and the nobles of the court were extremely busy preparing the celebratory ceremony.

One morning, Chen Zuiliang, a subordinate of Pacification Commissioner Du Bao of Huaiyang and a former teacher in Nan'an, followed the minister of the Bureau of Military Affairs to the court to dedicate the letter of surrender from Li Quan. It happened that on the same day Miao Shunbin, the chief examiner of the imperial examination, went to the court as well. Miao wanted to ask the emperor to name the Number One Scholar so that the examination result could be released. The two ministers greeted each other, the palace drum was heard and a palace eunuch called, "Ministers who have a report, approach please."

Miao Shunbin knew that the suppression of Li Quan was a priority, so he asked the minister of the Bureau of Military Affairs to report first. The old minister accepted it as a gesture of goodwill and approached to kneel before the emperor, asking Chen Zuiliang to prostrate himself behind him. He reported loudly, "The minister in charge of national military affairs humbly reports. Congratulations, Your Majesty! Due to your imposing power, the bandits led by Li Quan in the Huaiyang area have surrendered and the Kin in the north dare not act rashly. Now, this is Chen Zuiliang from Nan'an. He was sent by Pacification Commissioner Du Bao to submit Li Quan's letter of surrender."

The palace eunuch announced the emperor's order. "Ask Chen Zuiliang to report in detail how Du Bao called on Li Quan to surrender."

Obeying the instruction Chen Zuiliang hastened to take a few steps towards the emperor. He gave a full account of how Du Bao had devised a trap to induce Li Quan to capitulate and told how when the Kin knew that Li Quan had surrendered they dared not to raise an army to invade

第十四章
全家团员

　　杜宝在淮安大开太平宴之际，京师临安也是一片欢腾，喜煞当今皇上，忙煞朝中显贵。

　　此日凌晨，主管全国军务的枢密院大臣，引领着淮扬安抚使杜宝的帐下，原南安府生员陈最良前来朝中献降表；前时廷试主考大臣苗舜宾也上朝来，请求圣上钦点状元好放榜。两位大臣招呼已过，内廷鼓响，即有内监呼道：

　　"奏事官员上前。"

　　平定李全乃头等大事，苗舜宾自然明白，便推枢密大臣先行上奏。老枢密也不推辞，上前跪下，招呼陈最良跪在身后，叩头拜见圣上，朗声高奏：

　　"掌管天下兵马知枢密院事臣谨奏：恭贺吾主，圣德天威。淮寇李全来降，北边金兵不敢妄动。现有淮扬安抚使杜宝，敬遣南安府学生员陈最良奏事，带有李全降表进呈。"

　　内监传达圣上旨意：

　　"杜宝招安李全一事，就差生员陈最良详奏！"

　　陈最良闻招，更趋前几步，将杜宝安抚使如何设计，招降李全；金人闻知李全投降，也不敢再进兵南下等等，一五一十地奏知主上。皇上听了他的奏对，叫内监让他去午门外听旨。

the south. After listening to report, the emperor ordered Chen Zuiliang to wait outside for further instructions.

Then Miao Shunbin approached to report that the imperial examination had ended long ago and so had the marking of the examination papers. Because of the rebellion in Huaiyang, the publication of results had been delayed. Now that Li Quan had surrendered and with the country peaceful again and the people happy, it was the best time to release the results and not let the candidates wait any longer. The emperor ordered them to wait outside too.

After the minister of the Bureau of Military Affairs and Miao Shunbin walked out of the palace, they began talking to each other. Miao Shunbin said, "The examination result ought to be released now. Those poor scholars have been waiting far too long." The old minister thought that the selection of talent was a matter of importance too. However, he looked down on Chen Zuiliang who had submitted the letter of surrender and said, "It seems far too easy for that scholar to obtain a position just for bringing a letter of surrender."

Before long the palace eunuch came out to announce the imperial orders. "I am very happy to hear that Li Quan's gangsters were suppressed and the Kin enemy is afraid to move south. This is all to Du Bao's credit. I have already issued a decree ordering him to take up an official position in the capital. As Chen Zuiliang brought me the good news, I designate him the Memorial Processor at the Palace Gate and grant him official robes and hats." As for the imperial examination, the emperor named Liu Mengmei as the Number One Scholar and ordered him to attend the banquet held for successful new candidates.

Ecstatic with such a change in fortune Chen Zuiliang flew to the eunuch, took the robe and hat and in no time at all had changed out of his scholar's apparel. The old minister and Miao Shunbin had to congratulate him albeit in a perfunctory way. "Congratulations! Tomorrow we will count on you to publish the examination result!"

Chen Zuiliang had no time to reply and asked again and again, "Your Excellency, where does the Number One Scholar Liu Mengmei come from?"

"He is from the south of the Mount Meiling. As a matter of fact, the young man had a most unusual experience."

As their audience at the court had finished, the old minister felt like a chat and asked Miao Shunbin to tell him about it.

212

苗舜宾见状，便接着趋前奏闻：廷试早已完毕，试卷也已阅完，只怕淮扬骚乱，久未放榜。今李全已降，四海升平，人人欢畅，不宜让应试士子空盼望，天开文运，宜早日放榜。

内监也传旨："午门外候旨。"

老枢密与苗舜宾这两个文武大臣便向殿外走去，出了殿门，两人交谈起来，苗舜宾说道："现今也该放榜了，那些寒儒，等得太久了。"

老枢密也认为选拔人才重要，不过对淮扬来进表的陈最良又不大看重，不无讥讽地说道：

"只是这个陈秀才，凭着辛苦，进呈平贼表就谋得一官半职，未免也太快了点儿。"

不一会儿，内监已出殿宣旨：

"朕闻李全贼平，金兵回避。甚喜，甚喜。此乃杜宝大功也。杜宝前已有旨，令其回京供职。陈最良有奔走口舌之才，可充黄门奏事官，赐其冠带。"至于殿试，也有旨意：状元柳梦梅，令其赴杏花苑去吃琼林宴。

陈最良自然是喜从天降，立刻就从内监手中接过皇上赐给的衣冠，换下那一套秀才打扮，俨然一个内廷官员了。老枢密、苗舜宾也只能向他打哈哈，说道："恭喜，恭喜。明日便要借重新黄门官儿唱榜了。"

陈最良不暇作答，只是问苗舜宾："苗大人，状元柳梦梅不知是何处人？"

"岭南人——说来此生的遭际还有些奇异。"

此刻反正退朝，老枢密心情颇好，有兴趣闲谈，便问道："有什么奇异之事？可说来听听。"

"说起这个秀才，倒也走运。考试那天，我试卷都看完了，正准

"That scholar is really lucky. On the examination day, just as I had finished going over the papers and was about to report to the emperor, there was a man wailing outside the hall pleading to take the examination. It was him. He explained why he missed the examination; he had traveled from the south of Mount Meiling to the capital with his wife. I pitied him and submitted his paper as a supplement. Who would have expected that His Majesty would name him as the Number One Scholar? Isn't that something unusual?"

The old minister nodded and agreed.

Chen Zuiliang thought to himself, "The Number One Scholar must be Liu Mengmei the grave-digger. How did he come to have a wife? Yes, perhaps he married Nun Shi." However, Chen Zuiliang said nothing about this and thought that now Liu Mengmei had become the Number One Scholar, the young man would surely enjoy bright prospects in the official hierarchy. Why not use the opportunity and claim a tie with him? He turned to the two ministers and said, "To tell you the truth, the new Number One Scholar, Liu Mengmei, is my friend."

"Oh, that also earns congratulations!" The two ministers made a few casual remarks and left separately.

The court picked out 200 to 300 outstanding scholars as the metropolitan graduates from each imperial examination. The candidates selected would be given a banquet by the emperor and were expected to compose a poem in the Apricot Garden. The best candidate was called the "Number One Scholar"and was paraded through the streets on horseback. It was a spectacular event and the scholars looked forward to it day and night. But this year was most unusual. All the metropolitan graduates attended the banquet except for the Number One Scholar, Liu Mengmei. None of the ministers in the court knew where he was. How could the banquet begin without the presentation of the Number One Scholar? The official in charge of the ceremony sent out two lieutenants to look for Liu Mengmei.

The lieutenants carried a board that read, "Liu Mengmei, named the Number One Scholar by the emperor, comes from the south of Mount Meiling. Age 27, medium height with fair complexion." They looked for him everywhere — boulevards, alleys, entertainment houses, even brothels — but just could not find him. After talking it over, they thought that if they failed to find him, they could replace him with someone else. But this was not possible because the Number One Scholar was expected to

备进呈皇上,这个当口,门外有人放声大哭,要求补考。正是这个秀才,他自陈因携带家小从岭南迁来京师,因此误了考期。我怜他辛苦,就将他的考卷放在备遗中进呈,想不到圣上恰恰点他为状元,这可不是奇事?"

"啊呀,原来如此!"老枢密也觉得此事不同一般。

陈最良私下想到:这肯定就是那个掘坟的柳梦梅了!他哪有家小?是了,是了,大概是和石道姑做了亲,成了一家人了。不过,他心中想的这些话,都未说出口,倒是想柳梦梅既然中了状元,此后前途不可量,何不趁此攀结,便回过头来对两位大臣说:"不瞒两位老先生,这柳梦梅也与晚生有交谊。"

"这更值得庆贺了。"两老敷衍着,各自散朝而去。

朝廷开科取士,每次都要选拔二、三百名优秀的考生,称为"天子门生",也就是进士。考中进士的照例要由皇上赏赐琼林宴,还要在杏苑题诗。第一名进士称状元,还要骑马游街,好不兴头。也是天下读书人日夜企求的事儿。这次有点儿怪,新进士纷纷前去赴席,唯独状元公柳梦梅久久未见影踪,朝中大臣也无人知道这个状元公。第一名不到,宴席怎能开始!主事官只得吩咐军校出去找柳状元。

军校拿着牌子,上面写着:"钦点状元岭南柳梦梅,年二十七岁,身中材,面白色",到处吆喝,各地寻觅,大街小巷,秦楼楚院,就是找不到这个柳状元。两个军校商量,真正寻不到,找个人去顶替也好;商量商量又觉此法不妥,状元可要题诗,不是随便找个什么人就能替代的。无可奈何,只得又去十字街头大声叫唤,但一直无人应声而来。

正在此时,街那头有个驼子,一脚高一脚低地蹒跚而来。听见军校叫喊"柳梦梅",他以为柳公子就在附近,便急急赶来,一个不

compose a poem and his place could not be filled by someone without talent. They had no choice but to return to the street and call his name. Nobody answered.

Just then a hunchback came hobbling along the street and heard a voice calling "Liu Mengmei." He thought that Master Liu was nearby and dashed to where the sound came from. He went so fast that he bumped into the lieutenants and fell down still calling "Liu Mengmei."

The lieutenants, annoyed by their failure to find Liu Mengmei, were furious at being bumped into by a hunchback and angrily rebuked him. "Oh, this is wonderful! We call Liu Mengmei and you call Liu Mengmei too. There must be a connection. Come with us, we'd like to talk to you."

The hunchback was none other than the grandson of Hunchback Guo who used to take care of trees for the Lius. He had traveled from the south of Mount Meiling to Nan'an where he was told that Master Liu had fled to Lin'an after robbing a tomb. That is why he was in Lin'an. When he heard from the lieutenants that Liu Mengmei had won the title of Number One Scholar and that they were looking for him so that he could attend the banquet, the grandson of Hunchback Guo was overjoyed. He said, "Officer, as he has won first place, you will surely find him somewhere. Don't worry!"

The lieutenants thought that this was quite reasonable and said, "All right! We won't do anything this time. Come with us to look for your master!"

How could the lieutenants, who were looking for Liu Mengmei everywhere in the streets, ever know that the man they sought was in jail?

After Du Bao returned to the capital, he assumed the post of joint manager of Important National Affairs, which was equal to the prime minister. When he first took up office, there were dinners that he could not avoid and procedures for the transition. It was not until he had settled into office that he remembered the impostor who claimed to be his son-in-law. As he was free that day, Du Bao decided to cross-examine him and sent an usher to bring the prisoner from jail.

When the usher arrived, the jailor was extorting money from Liu Mengmei. He was disappointed to find that Liu Mengmei was as poor as a church mouse and found no money or valuables in his bundle. The jailor, though took a fancy to the scroll. He thought that it was a portrait of the Avalokitesvara and intended taking it home to place in a shrine.

稳,便与军校相撞,跌倒在地,口中兀自叫"柳梦梅"不停。

军校寻人不着,已是十分恼火,平白又被驼子冲撞,勃然大怒,大声斥责:

"好呀,我们找柳梦梅,你也叫柳梦梅,必有缘故,先拿你去衙门中讲话!"

这驼子不是别人,正是替柳家种树的郭驼孙,他从岭南找到南安,在南安听说柳公子掘了坟逃走临安,所以又赶来临安。当他从军校口中得知他们找柳公子,是因为柳公子中了状元,要寻他去吃琼林宴,喜出望外,笑道:"长官,原来如此。他既然中了状元,还怕没处去寻!"

两个军校想来此话也不无道理,便说:"好罢,暂且饶了你,与我们一同去找你家的柳公子吧。"

正当军校大街小巷寻找状元郎时,他们哪曾想到柳梦梅如今正关在大牢里哩。

杜宝回京升任平章后,位同宰相,履任之初,自有一番交接、应酬,各种事务处置停当后,才想起在淮安捉住的那个假冒女婿的人来。今日稍有空闲,正好将他提出审讯,就派了府中祗候去牢中提人。

祗候来到大牢,牢头禁子正在敲诈柳梦梅的财物。其实柳梦梅穷得叮当响,身无分文,包袱里也没有值钱的衣物,只有一条破被单。他们捡来捡去,只看中画轴儿。他们以为这是轴观音像,既然没有贵重物品,这幅观音大士像也可取回去供养。偏偏柳梦梅就是死活不许,他想到:待杜宝提审之时,取出这幅画儿来,自然会相认。

正当他牢牢护住画轴、禁子拼命抢夺之际,祗候来提人了。牢

However, no matter how hard he tried, Liu Mengmei just would not let it go. He thought that when he was interrogated, he would produce the picture so that Du Bao would recognize it.

The usher arrived to fetch the prisoner just as the jailor was trying to wrest the scroll from him as he held it tightly in his arms. Seeing the usher, the jailor dared not misbehave and when Liu Mengmei said that the jailor had tried to rob him, the usher commanded the jailor to return the item to Liu Mengmei. The jailor obeyed immediately.

Liu Mengmei held Du Liniang's portrait in his hand as he followed the usher to Du Bao's mansion. Du Bao was already sitting high up in the hall with two rows of court officials standing at either side. As Liu Mengmei was escorted into the hall, the officials all cried out but Liu Mengmei ignored them and strode into the hall with a dignity that surprised Du Bao. He asked, "Who on earth are you? You broke the law, how dare you not kneel down before me?"

Liu Mengmei was not intimidated by the question and answered indignantly, "I am Liu Mengmei from the south of the Mount Meiling and the son-in-law of Your Excellency."

Liu Mengmei's insistence on maintaining this relationship enraged Du Bao. "My daughter died three years ago. When she was alive she was not betrothed to anyone. How can you be a son-in-law? It is not only ridiculous, it is abhorrent! Throw him into jail!"

"Don't anyone dare touch me!" Liu Mengmei shouted indignantly.

"I don't have a son-in-law like you. You are just an idler and a deceiver, out for money!"

"I, your son-in-law, am both knowledgeable and talented. I can make a fortune by myself. Why should I seek financial help from you?"

Du Bao was almost speechless with rage. He shouted angrily, "How dare you answer back! There must be bogus stamps and letters. Search his bundle so that we may catch the thief with his takings!" The usher opened the bundle and found only a girl's portrait. Nevertheless, when Du Bao recognized the girl in the portrait as none other than his own daughter, he became angrier and believed he was the grave robber. He ordered the court officials to torture Liu Mengmei to extract a confession.

Under the circumstances, Liu Mengmei had to relate the whole story: how he picked up the scroll; how Du Liniang's ghost asked him to open the coffin and how he helped her return to life. Du Bao had never heard such an odd story and was convinced that Liu Mengmei was a ghost. He

头禁子见了平章府的干办人员，不觉矮了三分。当柳梦梅诉说禁子抢劫之事时，祗候喝令归还原物，禁子敢不从命？

柳梦梅捧了杜丽娘的画像，跟随祗候来到平章府。只见杜宝已高坐在公堂之上，两旁衙众见祗候押了柳梦梅上来，齐声吆喝。柳梦梅由他们吆喝，昂然走上大堂。杜宝不禁对他的气概感到意外：

"你究竟是什么人？犯了法，在相府堂前还不下跪！"

杜宝的斥问并未吓倒柳梦梅，他理直气壮地回答：

"生员岭南柳梦梅，是老大人女婿。"

好一个柳梦梅，自始至终认定不改口，杜宝不由得不恼怒：

"呀呀呀，我女儿已亡过三年。她生前，不要说不曾请媒人说亲，就连指腹为婚的事儿也未曾有过。哪里跑出个女婿？真是可笑，可恨！祗候们替我拿下！"

"谁敢拿！"柳梦梅不禁也有些愤愤了。

"我哪有你这个女婿？你不过是一个游棍，前来打秋风骗些钱用！"

"你这个女婿，有才有学，自可立求富贵，何须向你面前打秋风？"

杜宝被他气得开不得口，恼怒地喝道：

"还敢强嘴！搜他包袱，定有假刻的印章书信，贼赃一齐拿获！"

祗候打开包袱，并没有什么印章，只见到女孩儿的画像。杜宝看到女儿画像，更是火冒三丈，认定他就是劫坟贼，吩咐左右用刑逼供。

柳梦梅不得不说出拾画经过，以及杜丽娘亡魂如何托他开棺起尸，助她还阳等等事情。杜宝闻所未闻，更认定他必也是鬼，叫

ordered him to be hung up and beaten with a peach tree's twig specially used to beat ghosts.

While Liu Mengmei was being beaten and crying out at the injustice, the lieutenants and the grandson of Hunchback Guo came by searching for Number One Scholar and were still shouting, "Where is the Number One Scholar Liu Mengmei?"

Liu Mengmei heard his name called and answered loudly. The grandson of Hunchback Guo said, "Alas, that sounds like my master's voice inside!" They forced their way into the hall. The grandson of Hunchback Guo recognized Liu Mengmei straight away and cried, "Alas, the man hanging there is none other than my young master!"

Liu Mengmei saw the intruders and cried for help. Without a thought for his limp legs the grandson of Hunchback Guo rushed forward and lifted his crutch to hit Du Bao. There was pandemonium with the two parties bickering at each other. The lieutenants claimed that Liu Mengmei was Number One Scholar of the imperial examination while Du Bao insisted he was either a thief or a ghost. Each party stuck to its own view and neither would give way.

The chief examiner Miao Shunbin, who had been told where Liu Mengmei was, arrived holding in the robes and footwear that the emperor granted to Number One Scholar. Although he explained what had happened, Du Bao just would not believe him but Miao Shunbin carried an imperial order and just took Liu Mengmei away. Du Bao had no say in the matter. He did not know what to do and asked Chen Zuiliang to explain the whole thing again. Afterwards he still insisted stubbornly that he should report to the emperor that Liu Mengmei was a grave robber and could not be called Number One Scholar.

Liu Mengmei paraded through the streets and later heard that his father-in-law had appealed to the emperor. So he submitted a memorandum to vindicate himself. The emperor knew from what Liu Mengmei said that Du Liniang was still alive and at once sent an official to summon her. Du Liniang, Madam Du, Chunxiang and Nun Shi learned that Liu Mengmei had become Number One Scholar. Of course, everyone was extremely happy and, when they learned that they had been summoned by the emperor, they took great care of their toilet, dressed in a hurry and followed the official to court.

Outside the palace Du Bao and Liu Mengmei waited to be summoned. Liu Mengmei smiled at Du Bao and called him "respected

人吊起来用打鬼的桃树枝条拷打。

正当他们一边拷打，一边叫屈之际，军校和郭驼孙一路寻找新状元而来,高呼:

"状元柳梦梅在哪里?"

柳梦梅听到喊声,大声答应着,喧闹之声传出衙外。郭驼孙一听:

"啊呀,里面像是我家公子的声音哩。"

一众闯上大堂来。郭驼孙一眼便认出柳梦梅,大声叫道:

"啊呀,那吊起的正是我家公子!"

柳梦梅见到来人,大叫救命。郭驼孙也不顾自己腿脚不灵,拼命向前,举起拐杖就向杜宝打去。大堂上顿时大乱,一伙人闹得不可开交,军校说柳梦梅是新科状元,杜宝认定他是贼是鬼,各据一词,互不相让。

这时,主考苗大人已得知确信,捧了御赐的状元衣冠前来。虽经苗大人说明真情,但杜宝硬是不承认。苗大人是奉了旨的,不管杜宝认不认帐,自行带走了新状元。

杜宝无可奈何,就把陈最良请出来问个究竟。听了陈最良的说明,他仍然顽固地要上本给皇上,说柳梦梅是掘坟之贼,不可选他为状元。

柳状元游街之后,得知老丈人上本告他,他也上本辩白。皇上从状元公处知道杜丽娘尚在人间,急急派员前来钱塘江下榻处召见。

杜丽娘、杜夫人、春香、石道姑一众到此时,方才知道柳梦梅中了状元,高兴异常。听说皇上召见,大家匆匆梳洗一番,随来员上朝去了。

且说杜宝与柳梦梅正呆在午门前等候召见。柳梦梅笑吟吟地

father-in-law." However, Du Bao did not consider himself a father to Liu Mengmei and sternly denounced him as a "criminal". Liu Mengmei replied in a relaxed way, "Why am I the criminal when, on the contrary, you are the criminal."

"I gave meritorious service by repulsing Li Quan. What charges can you accuse me of?" Du Bao had been goaded into fury.

"Well, isn't it funny? You can conceal it from the emperor but not from the whole nation. You have not suppressed Li Quan, you have suppressed only half of Li Quan." Liu Mengmei teased him intentionally.

Du Bao was puzzled. "What do you mean by half of Li Quan?"

"Well, you only induced Li Quan's wife to retreat. How can she be the complete Li Quan?" Du Bao's face turned purple and he became incoherent with rage.

Just then the emperor convened the court and Chen Zuiliang arrived with Madam Du and Du Liniang. Du Bao saw the two women and could not help crying out, "Ghost!"

During the audience with the emperor Du Bao still refused to accept that they were people and the emperor sent someone to bring a mirror to test them. Du Liniang's image appeared in the mirror and, when she was asked to stand under a tree, her shadow could be clearly seen. As a result they decided that Du Liniang was indeed human. However, Du Bao stuck to his own ideas and refused to admit it. After he had heard each side's account, the emperor agreed that it was a most unusual event and said that they deserved congratulations. He ordered every family member to recognize one another and they all obeyed except for the son-in-law and the father-in-law.

The imperial order came just when they were laughing, crying, bickering, and arguing, so they stopped quarreling and knelt down to receive it. The order read: "I have heard the unusual story of the Du family. Now I grant the family a reunion; promote the Joint Manager of Important National Affairs, Du Bao, one grade higher; confer on Du Bao's wife the title, Lady of Huaiyin City; appoint Number One Scholar, Liu Mengmei, to Chancellor of the Imperial Academy, and confer to Liu Mengmei's wife the title, Lady of Yanghe County. I order the Chief Ceremonial Minister Han Zicai to send them to their mansion."

Listening to the imperial order Liu Mengmei lifted his head and saw that the official messenger was his old friend Han Zicai. The two greeted each other and spoke of their experiences since they had parted. Han Zicai

招呼"老丈人"，杜宝却不认这个佳婿，当即斥责他是"罪人"。柳梦梅不急不忙地反驳道："小生有何罪？你老倒是罪人！"

"我有平李全大功，当得何罪？"杜宝气恼万分。

"唉哟，说来好笑人。你瞒得朝廷瞒不住天下。你哪曾平得个李全，你只平了个'李半'。"柳梦梅故意激逗他。

杜宝老大不解："怎只平个'李半'？"

"你不过哄得娘娘退兵，怎哄得全！"几句话把杜宝气得面孔姜紫，说不出辩白的话儿来。

正好皇上已坐朝问事，陈最良、杜夫人携着杜丽娘也先后来到。杜宝见到母女二人直呼"见鬼"。

他们一齐被传至殿上，杜宝抵死不认。圣上乃命人取来照胆镜验证，杜丽娘有形；又在花阴下察看，杜丽娘有影，委系人身，并不是鬼。但杜宝依然固执己见，不肯相认。皇上听了各方陈诉，认为事虽稀奇，但确系真情；就认可这桩喜事，命他们全家相认。女婿、丈母相认，夫妇相认；只是丈人、女婿彼此之间却不愿相认。

正当他们全家有喜有恼、又争又吵之际，忽传圣旨到，众人方才住口，齐齐跪下听宣：

"据奏奇异，敕赐团圆。平章杜宝，进阶一品。妻甄氏，封淮阴郡夫人。状元柳梦梅，赐翰林院学士。妻杜丽娘，封阳和县君。就着鸿胪官韩子才送归宅院。"

柳梦梅听完圣旨，抬起头来，捧旨而来的正是故友韩子才。两人又重新见过礼，互诉别后情况。原来韩子才沾先人韩愈的余光，被本府保送进京考试，现官鸿胪。柳梦梅见当年岭南故友，一一相会于京师，大为称异。

自然，最为高兴的乃是杜丽娘，她想：幸亏有柳相公救活了自

had benefited from his association with his ancestor, Han Yu, and had been sponsored by his local government to take the imperial examination. Now he held the post of Chief Ceremonial Minister. Liu Mengmei could not help marveling at the way that the old friends from the south of Mount Meiling had all met in the capital one after another.

Of course, the happiest person was Du Liniang. She thought that she was so lucky to have been brought back to life by Liu Mengmei. And all of this was due to her love for Liu Mengmei — among all the ghosts, who could be more devoted than her? No one could have had an ending as perfect as hers.

己，这也是自己钟情于他所致。天下做鬼的哪有像自己这样多情的啊，自然也就不能像自己一样有如此美好的结局。

图书在版编目（CIP）数据

牡丹亭：英汉对照 /（明）汤显祖著；陈美林改编.
－北京：新世界出版社，1999.1
ISBN 7－80005－433－0

Ⅰ.牡 … Ⅱ.①汤 … ②陈 … Ⅲ.戏剧－中国－明代
－英语－对照读物，英、汉 Ⅳ.H319.4:I
中国版本图书馆 CIP 数据核字(98)第 34344 号

牡 丹 亭

原　　著：汤显祖(明)
改　　编：陈美林
翻　　译：匡佩华　曹珊
责任编辑：张民捷
版式设计：李　辉
出版发行：新世界出版社
社　　址：北京阜成门外百万庄路 24 号　　邮政编码：100037
电　　话：0086－10－68994118
传　　真：0086－10－68326679
电子邮件：nwpcn@public.bta.net.cn
经　　销：新华书店　外文书店
印　　刷：北京顺义振华印刷厂印刷
开　　本：850×1168(毫米)　1/32　　字数：160 千
印　　张：7.625
印　　数：5001－9000 册
版　　次：1999 年 4 月(英、汉)第 1 版　2001 年 5 月北京第 2 次印刷
书　　号：ISBN 7－80005－433－0 /I·023
定　　价：22.00 元